BY L.V. DITCHKUS

Crimes of the Sasquatch: Book I of The Sasquatch Series

SOON TO COME

Legacy of the Sasquatch: Book III of The Sasquatch Series

Mission
of the
Sasquatch

Book II of The Sasquatch Series

Mission

of the

Sasquatch

Book II of The Sasquatch Series

L.V. Ditchkus

Pinon Press
Colorado

To Tina

Chapter 1

SALIDA, COLORADO—OCTOBER 4

Soldier, mercenary, or murderer—who would decide what I am? Blood stained my hands. I could not see it or smell the metallic tang, but it was there. I killed them the same as if I had strangled their throats and ripped apart their limbs. Flexing my fingers, I speculated whether anyone might uncover my connection to these atrocities. Convinced the goal justified my actions, I knelt and wiped my palms across the prickly pine-needle covered earth.

I looked toward the sky and watched the light fade. A crisp evening breeze tugged my hair. I smiled. The locals knew nothing of wind. The horrific gusts I had survived would leave these fragile forests leafless, collapsing stout trunks into unrecognizable shapes and buildings to sticks.

Time to return to camp, my base for the last several months. Before setting out, I turned in each direction to distinguish warning sounds. No abrasive scrape of hiker thighs, bicycle chain clink, or dog tag jingle. Alone. I stepped onto the trail and followed the root and rock-riddled path toward my temporary home.

Autumn's long shadows fell across the path, hardened by the lack of summer's afternoon rain showers. Dried twigs, leaves, and withered flowers littered the undergrowth—memories of blossoms that would not reemerge for months.

Wildflowers muted the tedium of the dull green and brown forests, but

I recognized these delicate specimens needed rain to flourish. I hated summer's erratic lightning with strafing hailstones. Once, I had watched a tree explode into flames when struck with a sizzling bolt. The subsequent hail fragmented the trunk into splinters and forced me to duck for cover.

At precisely two-thirds of the way to camp, I stumbled when a rodent crossed the trail to scurry into its burrow with reckless abandon. I issued a curse, which no one heard. Scanning the trees, I spotted an owl. Its eyes pierced the enveloping darkness and targeted the mouse like a sharpshooter's laser. *She'll get him,* I thought. Served him right for being out of his hole at that time of day.

Two ravines and a short bushwhack brought me to the campsite. I inventoried my bivouac and discovered nothing amiss. My precious comforts remained untouched. Stashed pine boughs and mosses sufficed for a soft bed. I nestled under the low branches of oak and pressed my back into the spiny stems. Scant autumn leaves provided minimal shelter against potential intruders and plummeting temperatures.

What would they do to me when I got back home? Maybe they were right to deem me unsuitable for this mission. Others had succeeded in similar assignments. They had their orders, stuck to the task, and got out. Maybe they were simple-minded and not distracted by the foreign environment or the sacrifices needed to survive.

They benefited from weeks of training, not merely survival skills about what to eat and how to create shelter but psychological counseling to ease the transition into and out of harsh foreign surroundings. Professionals, well versed in similar missions, helped operatives organize objectives, minimize risks, and develop strategies to meet goals. I had no such training, and it showed.

My nerve and instinct guided me, sometimes resulting in success and other times abject failure. The others stole my opportunity, but my success would prompt absolution. No, not merely forgiveness but veneration. My superiors were wrong to reject my application. I planned to stay on track and accomplish the job.

My transmissions produced positive results and ultimately drew my target near. Alas, four months earlier, he had abandoned the area. Who could predict his erratic behavior? I knew he would return, but my patience wore thinner with each passing day. I forced myself to focus on my objective and get back on track. He would come back, alone and vulnerable.

Sounds of the night replaced daylight chatter. Snakes slithered across last season's leaves and stirred a warning to intended prey. Infernal crickets blasted the silence with bold chirps. Who could live in this primitive place filled with vermin?

I pressed the flesh of my forearm between a thumb and index finger. If the filth and noise were not bad enough, the lack of food had eroded my body into a shell of its former self. My bony hips pressed into the dirt, a daily reminder of starvation. Dizzying at first, the gnawing sensation had become commonplace. Other operatives resorted to stealing from homes or waste sites. I toyed with foraging near populations but abandoned those plans when nearly detected. Getting caught would be disastrous and bring the mission to an immediate end. I vowed never again to take such risks. Lesson learned.

The lack of interaction with others haunted me, and loneliness cramped my psyche. I heard only meaningless noise where the voices of colleagues and friends should be. Instead of strategic communications, I listened to animals creep through the forest. I tolerated bird songs. Their lyrical calls were generally pleasing, except for the harsh scolding of a jay. I could do with less of that.

I wanted to be finished and go home. Settling my head into the crook of my arm, I forced regrets of my horrific deeds into a place where they need not be reassessed.

Chapter 2

CHICAGO, ILLINOIS—OCTOBER 4
DYLAN COX

Dylan Cox stared at the envelope. He flipped it over to look at the back and then to the front. The ecru heavyweight stationery showed the return address of the church on the upper left corner. Someone with impeccable penmanship had scripted Dylan's name and address in the center. Torn between opening it and shoving it into a stack of letters and fliers from yesterday's mail, he tapped the long edge on the table.

Tom Morrow, Dylan's roommate, best friend, and business partner in his detective agency, walked into the dining room. He pulled a Chippendale ball and claw chair away from the matching antique table and sat. Dylan saw nervous empathy on Tom's clean-shaven face.

Tom leaned back in the chair. He extracted a cloth covered hair-band from his wrist and gathered his ropey dreds at the base of his neck and secured them. He crossed muscular arms over his loose-fitting T-shirt. It advertised a marathon from a decade long past, and the printing was nearly invisible from hundreds of washings.

"What are you going to do?" Tom asked.

Dylan shifted his gaze from the letter to his friend. He hunched his lanky frame forward and leaned over the envelope like a bird protecting its nest. "Not sure. I want to know, but the timing's not right. I've got a lot on my mind. Maybe I'll focus on work."

"The last couple of months have been hard for you. Jen's death was a shock."

Dylan straightened. "We were just getting to know each other. I can't believe she's gone."

He'd met Jen Rickard, a wilderness-savvy woman, while he worked a case in Salida, Colorado, a small mountain town harboring a burgeoning artist community. Nate Stewart, Dylan's manipulative cousin, lured him to Salida—ostensibly to help find Trip, his missing six-year-old son. Nate appreciated the attention and wanted to keep the boy's investigation open, but finding the boy was not his goal.

Dylan's investigation was distracted by the town's believer community that decided Trip's abductor was a mythical, elusive Sasquatch. Dylan absolved the imaginary beast from any wrongdoing as he uncovered facts that explained the abduction and other crimes. Recent sightings of the creature and oversized footprints were rationalized when Dylan watched news reporters pay off an actor who, Dylan assumed, had donned a costume to act as a Bigfoot proxy. Four murderous attacks, two on humans, one on a steer, and one on a herd of mountain goats, were the work of earthly predators, likely a bear and a mountain lion.

Alone at her mountain cabin, Jen was one of the human victims. Dylan's guilt over being absent that fateful night consumed him. He returned to Chicago in a vacant haze that had not lifted.

Inertia propelled him to work each day. He drew no satisfaction from completing cases. Even before his trip to Colorado, he felt disenchanted with his work, mostly surveillance for suspicious spouses. But these jobs paid the bills and, somehow, Tom kept working his magic to come up with more leads. The dull employment kept Dylan busy and distracted from his loss and the role he had played.

Tom leaned across the table. "You need to stop beating yourself up for not being at the cabin that night. It wasn't your fault."

"Saying it doesn't make it true." Dylan held the envelope aloft. "As if losing Jen wasn't enough, then Nate blindsided me with news about my being adopted. Great timing. Why didn't he tell me before my parents were killed?"

Tom shrugged. "You assume he knew about it back then. You were both in college a decade ago. Maybe your aunt and uncle told Nate more recently."

"Nate doesn't blurt out his verbal daggers on an ad hoc basis. He keeps them locked away until the precise moment he wants to traumatize his victim. The tipping point happened when we uncovered the lie about his wife's reported suicide. He felt his power slipping. He needed to neutralize my advantage by bayonetting my heritage."

"It surprised me, too. You and your dad looked alike. Same brown wavy hair and green eyes." Tom paused to smile. "Of course, he was at least six inches shorter than you. Couldn't have been much over five-nine."

Dylan sighed. "No matter what this letter says, they will always be my parents."

"Do you think we shouldn't look for your birth mother?"

"Undecided." Dylan paused. "I'm grateful for your search through all my folks' crap in the attic."

After Dylan returned to Chicago in June, Tom scoured boxes of letters and documents stored in the top story of the Cox family home. The turn of the century Greystone house had been their residence since Dylan's parents' deaths. The furniture and other household goods remained virtually where his parents placed them during the thirty years they had lived there. After Tom searched the attic for weeks, he found a folder with adoption correspondence between Dylan's folks and their local church.

Incredulous that evidence of his birth history had been lying undisturbed above his head for twenty-nine years, Dylan wanted to know more but had no energy to follow up with the church. So Tom agreed to make the initial contact.

A phone call led to directions about how to issue a formal written request for information about Dylan's adoption. Tom had submitted, and Dylan held the church's response.

Dylan wondered if the letter would divulge facts to make him feel differently about his past. Two loving people raised him. But where did he come from, and who gave him away?

Tom offered, "Want to put it aside for a couple of days? You don't need to make your decision right now."

"Maybe not a bad idea." Dylan stared at the envelope, drawn by the allure of revelations but afraid his past might not be as he had long believed.

Firmly on the fence about what to do, he rose and tossed the letter on the table. Dylan walked to the window and stared outside. He fingered the button on the collar of his Oxford shirt.

Maple leaves had turned from summer green to brilliant crimson. It seemed early for fall colors. Across the street, a neighbor raked them into piles and stuffed them into stiff brown paper sacks. Seven full bags stood in a line along the curb. *Probably only half-finished,* he mused.

"I hope they don't blow this direction," Dylan said.

Tom stood and pulled a chair next to the window. He straddled the seat backward and draped his arms across the back, resting his chin on his hands. "I'll take the leaf blower out at midnight and shoot them back on their property."

Dylan smiled, picturing Tom in the middle of the night playing commando. "Is the midnight concept designed to keep your identity a secret? That blower can wake the dead. I'm not sure you'll be able to remain anonymous."

Tom reached up to give Dylan's shoulder a shove. "Got me there. But I don't mind raking. It's better than being cooped up in the house all day. Though there's plenty to do inside, too. Your folks kept up with maintenance as best they could, but stuff always needs attention."

Dylan appreciated Tom's dedication to keeping the house clean and in order. Their separation of duties allowed Dylan to focus on cases while Tom handled household responsibilities.

While he searched the attic, Tom had gone through decades of Christmas cards and postcards from all over the globe. He searched everything, from tax returns to bank statements summarizing the Coxes' financial status for their entire lives.

Tom's approach differed from what Dylan would have done, likely tearing open each box and shoving them aside after he had rifled through the contents.

Dylan returned to the table. He picked up the envelope and waved it toward Tom. "You're invested in this, too. You must be interested in their response."

"I'll wait until you're ready."

"Enough procrastination." Dylan tore open the flap. He drew out a letter, which matched the envelope's fine quality paper. At the top of the single sheet, thermographed lettering identified the church. The same precise handwriting on the envelope had drafted the letter.

"Well?" Tom asked.

Dylan finished reading and looked up. "Doesn't say much. The adoption took place locally, but the infant came from a sister church in Oregon." He returned to the letter.

"The infant?"

Tom's sarcastic tone forced Dylan to raise his eyes. He smiled. "Okay. They're talking about me. I'm from Oregon."

Tom crossed the dining room and passed through the archway into the living room. He returned with an ancient leather-bound atlas. "Does it say where in Oregon?"

"It's called Groverton." Dylan grinned and held up his battered cell phone. "But are you living in this decade? How about we look up the town on my phone?"

Tom scoffed. "The screen's too small. I won't be able to see what part of the state the town's in or how the location relates to the other states. Sorry, I need to see this the old-fashioned way."

Tom laid the massive book on the table and opened it to a two-page spread of Oregon. He scanned the map and ran fingers over the highways and rivers, looking for the town. Dylan raised an eyebrow. He decided to short cut the process and enlisted the phone's help.

Once he uncovered what part of the state to search, they found it in Oregon's northwest quadrant. The town sat between the National Forest and a small parcel of land under the jurisdiction of the Bureau of Indian Affairs.

Tom's index finger covered the town. He turned to Dylan. "Did they say anything to give you a hint about your birth parents?" Tom did not serve as a detective in their two-person agency. Still, his inquisitive nature had, at times, assisted Dylan to see events from a new perspective or to detect the hint of a yet uncovered motivation.

"Nope. They gave the name of the church in Oregon and suggested I contact them for more information."

"Think it's worth a call? Or I could write to them?"

Dylan stared at the letter, willing it to give him the next step. He weighed responsibilities to the business against wanting details about the past. Dylan considered the advantages of face-to-face engagement with the clergy in Groverton.

Meticulously, he returned the letter into the envelope. "I think this deserves a personal touch. I'll wrap up the case I'm working on and leave in the next day or so."

Dylan slid it into a leather messenger bag. "I'll drive through Colorado on my way out west. I owe someone a favor, and I can take care of it on the same trip."

Chapter 3

SALIDA, COLORADO—OCTOBER 8

A wave of familiarity hit Dylan as he parked the rental car next to the chain-link fence in front of Augie's trailer, which sat a few blocks from Salida's historic downtown. The single-wide, white paneled structure stood at the front of a weed-dotted lot. Lime green trim evoked the Cold War era of birthing baby boomers. A tiny windowless garage with wood rot in need of a coat of paint sat adjacent to the trailer.

Dylan shut off the engine and silenced blasting tunes that left a hum in his ears. Music helped to propel minutes into hours over the arduous sixteen-hour drive from Chicago to the tiny mountain town of Salida. Classic rock was the perfect antidote for the tedium of endless cornfields and wind turbines in Nebraska and northeastern Colorado.

In June, Dylan had grown to appreciate the little metropolis with barely over 5,000 inhabitants. Situated in a valley at the base of five mountains towering over 14,000 feet in elevation, the town lay at 7,000 feet above sea level. The altitude had slowed his daily running routine to a proverbial crawl.

Dylan left the car and stretched. He passed through the creaky gate and walked up the path to Augie's front door. Dead grass and spiky weeds bordered the walk.

In the summer, the late spring rains had spread budding glory to the mountainsides. Flowers in every imaginable color had peppered a blanket of pale green grasses.

Fall turned Salida to monochromatic hues of parched brown. Thankfully, the aspen trees were in full fall plumage and brought a slash of brilliant yellow to the landscape. Their leaves quaked in the cold, dry October wind and diminished the dreary impact of short days and coming winter months.

Augie's burgundy sedan sat at the curb, and Dylan figured he was home. Dylan knocked. The door opened. It took a few moments for the slender middle-aged man to register who stood on his front stoop.

Several days prior, Dylan had sent Augie a letter about his intended visit and plans to drive to Oregon. But how long did it take for a letter to travel from Chicago to Salida? Since Augie had no phone, Dylan could hardly send last-minute updates.

Dylan held his breath as Augie's expression shifted from impassive to thoughtful consideration and finally to pure delight. He stepped over the threshold to embrace Dylan and stiffly leaned the side of his face against Dylan's shoulder.

Augie pulled Dylan into his modest home, a residence inherited from an aunt who had cared for him until her death. Her lessons in basic cooking, cleaning, and home repair prepared the introverted man to manage for himself. The trailer remained decorated in his aunt's style with a plaid sofa, bulky oak shelves, laminate dinette, and leather recliner.

Grinning, Augie sat in the recliner, as if waiting for Dylan to elaborate on the plans he'd outlined in the letter. Dylan settled on the sofa and leaned forward, elbows on knees and hands clasped in front.

"Want to go with me to Oregon?" Dylan asked but knew full well Augie would give the world to accompany him. They planned to see Nate's wife, Destiny. Nate had goaded her to leave town earlier in the year, but unbeknownst to him, she returned to take their son with her. They all benefitted from the new living arrangements.

Augie squeezed the arms of the chair and tapped his heels on the floor. The recliner shuddered from the ferocity of the movement. "Yeah. When do we leave?"

"I have a few things to do in Salida before we go. So I think we could leave in two days. Do you need to talk to your boss about taking a vacation?"

Augie worked a couple of nights a week as a watchman at an abandoned mine site near the town of Leadville, Colorado. The place was more of a historical tourist attraction than a hoard of precious minerals, and Augie's job consisted of watching television in a shed and walking hourly rounds to look for vagrants or other trespassers. The work, combined with cash he earned helping to set up and take down events around town, provided sufficient income for his simple needs. Dylan knew that Augie took great pride in his independence.

"I talked to him when I got your letter. I can leave anytime. Kyle will do my work while I'm gone."

Dylan did not know about Kyle but felt relieved the time off would not jeopardize Augie's job. Dylan stood and wandered to an oak bookshelf sprinkled with delicate ceramic figurines. He assumed Augie spent endless hours dusting his aunt's treasures. The place looked immaculate. As Dylan picked up a Bo Peep, he heard Augie's sharp gasp. The man remained motionless while Dylan turned the piece to examine the details. When he returned Bo to her original position, Dylan took care to replicate the placement. Augie exhaled and relaxed his shoulders.

"Sheriff Austin told me Jen left her cabin to you in her will," said Dylan.

Augie's eyes fell to the worn beige carpet. "I don't know why she did it. I hate the cabin."

Dylan nodded. "She probably didn't expect you to move there but thought you could sell it and use the money."

"I have money."

"Never hurts to have more."

Augie looked at Dylan. "It hurt to lose Jen."

Dylan crossed the room to kneel before Augie's chair and placed a palm over his friend's hand. "Her death was painful for both of us. She left her cabin to you because she loved you and wanted you to not worry about money."

Augie nodded as Dylan continued, "Have you been there?" Dylan's question hung in the air, unanswered.

Dylan patted Augie's hand. "I'd like to stay at the cabin for a couple of nights before we leave. It's your place now. Would it be okay with you if I slept there?"

Augie met Dylan's gaze. He choked out a whispered response. "It's Jen's home. It's a bad place. I don't want to go there."

"I understand." Dylan sighed. He hoped a revised request might receive a different answer. "I know animals killed Jen outside of the cabin, but would you mind if I spent a couple of nights?"

Augie's face contorted. "You can't. What if they come back?"

"That's unlikely. Sheriff Austin told me there'd been no evidence of large animal attacks on Church Mountain since the summer. Maybe hunting season pushed the mountain lions and bears into remote areas." Augie looked skeptical. "There's plenty of rabbits and other small animals up there. Predators look for easy food. They wouldn't want to mess with me." Uncertain if he was offering something he could not deliver, he added, "I promise to be careful and not wander the property in the dark."

"Can't you stay in a hotel?"

"Not on my budget." Dylan smiled. "Besides, while Jen's place brings only bad memories for you, she and I spent a lot of time up there. I want to go and rekindle some of those memories."

"I can give you money for a hotel."

"I appreciate the offer, but I *want* to stay at the cabin. I'm not afraid. Please, let me spend time thinking of Jen."

Slowly, Augie nodded. "Be safe. I can't lose you, too."

"I'll be vigilant." He knew the cabin had sat unoccupied for several months and asked, "Are the water and electricity still turned on up there?"

"Kate said it was *wasteful* to leave it on."

It sounds like a word Kate would use, thought Dylan. Kate taught elementary school, and Dylan had met her in June. Once the deputies discovered Jen's will, which left all her possessions to Augie, the Sheriff enlisted Kate to help Augie. She sold Jen's Jeep and transferred accounts to Augie. But as far as Dylan knew, the cabin remained untouched since last summer's attack.

Dylan believed will-makers were people with children or those passing middle age. Jen fit neither of these categories. According to the Sheriff, Jen signed her will shortly after Augie's aunt had died. Dylan figured Jen had been impressed with his aunt's pre-planning. She may have realized

Augie needed additional financial security and decided to provide for him in case she would not be around to remain his advocate.

Before Dylan left for the cabin, he and Augie discussed details about the trip. As Augie's wardrobe consisted of mostly jeans and T-shirts, packing would be uncomplicated. "Do you have a suitcase?" Dylan asked.

Augie shrugged. "Nope."

"No worries. I'll pick up an extra duffle at a resale shop in town before I come by to help you pack."

Dylan pulled out his phone to show Augie their route. They stared at the screen while Dylan dragged a finger to move the digital map from Colorado through Utah, Idaho, and Oregon, Augie asked, "Don't you have a paper map?"

Dylan smirked. "You and Tom would get along great."

Augie cocked his head but said nothing in response.

As afternoon shadows grew long, fatigue from the drive forced Dylan to yawn. He needed rest and bid Augie goodnight.

Dylan stepped from the trailer and paused to look at the sky beyond the peaks. He watched it fade from brilliant blue with streaks of pink clouds to gunmetal gray. The temperature noticeably plummeted.

Dylan decided to make a quick stop at the grocery for bottled water and dinner. It would be full-on dark when he arrived at the cabin.

Chapter 4

The dirt road grew rutted as Dylan passed the point where upmarket homes ended, replaced by scattered ordinary houses and ramshackle cabins. He slowed the car to focus the beams on the wash-boarded sections, careful not to hit any potholes.

After he turned left at a junction, the road climbed to traverse a hillside. Tall pine trees formed a canopy over the road and blocked any ambient light from stars or the sliver of the moon. Dylan pulled into the hardpacked drive, and a dark outline of the cabin loomed in front of him. He steered next to the porch, as close to the door as possible.

Dylan stepped outside, instantly chilled. He rubbed his hands across his sleeves and stared at the cabin. Above the lattice of pine boughs sheltering the sturdy log dwelling, Dylan spotted the distant peaks. Their veins of early season snow glowed iridescent in reflected starlight.

He recalled his first visit to Jen's home. In June, an uncanny feeling of déjà vu had overwhelmed him as the place had appeared in a waking dream a week before he came to Colorado. That vision turned out to be the tipping point for Dylan's decision to help Nate find his missing son. *Funny how the mind can trick us to make decisions.*

Dylan recalled evenings tucked into the wilderness with Jen. They shared meals, drank brandy in front of the fire, and made love under a mountain of quilts. Pleasant times fought for equal time with his last memories of this place when he discovered her shredded body in the backyard.

He was grateful for the light spilling from the open car door and snatched supplies from the backseat. Dylan left on the interior and headlights while he transferred gear to the porch. Augie's key slid smoothly and opened the deadbolt. Dylan stepped inside to click on a flashlight.

The place smelled of dust and neglect. Dylan passed the beam over the walls and furniture. Except for the refrigerator, standing open and exposing empty shelves, everything looked as he remembered.

Dylan toured the cabin with the front door wide open. He surveyed the great room, including living, dining, and kitchen areas. The bedroom, bathroom, and tiny mudroom at the back of the cabin were equally undisturbed. He ran the flashlight beam over the rows of Jen's backpacks that hung on brass hooks in the mudroom. They looked as if they were waiting for Jen to make her selection and take them out for a hike. Never again.

Relieved no one had moved into the abandoned cabin, Dylan retrieved the groceries from the porch. To save his flashlight batteries, he lit candles and placed them around the living room. He recalled their scents from evenings spent with Jen.

Once he'd managed to coax a fire in the hearth, the room seemed lit enough to turn off the flashlight and eat rotisserie chicken and deli-prepared salad. Paper plates and plastic forks, inconsistent with his views about preserving the ecology, would suffice here in a pinch. He did not have the luxury of washing dishes. The gallon jug of water would be enough for cleaning his teeth and face but not much more.

After he cleared dinner, Dylan searched the cabinets for Jen's brandy stash. He pulled a cut crystal glass from a cupboard and poured himself a drink. As he sat in front of the fire, Dylan recalled Jen and the events of the summer.

In the short time they knew each other, Dylan fell in love with Jen. She was the personification of energy, and Dylan barely kept up with her despite his addiction to running and fitness. Her passion for life and the wilderness opened a new world for him. As she scaled mountains and spotted wildlife, Jen gained nourishment from the power of sunlight and mountain air.

Before Jen, Dylan dated a few women, most for an evening or two and a couple for as much as a few months. He found the opposite sex perplexing. They weren't direct, and he never knew how to respond to them. If Dylan attempted to be kind or supportive, they accused him of being patronizing. When he gave them space to work out issues on their own, they faulted him for indifference.

Upfront and independent, Jen understood everything related to the mountains. However, she deferred to others when their experience or knowledge exceeded hers. Jen never felt threatened by people or her surroundings. Most importantly, when they were together, she made Dylan feel valued and at peace.

Their whirlwind romance lasted only a week, but the passion felt real, at least to him. He hoped Destiny might know whether Jen had played Dylan to keep him close and unsuspecting or whether she returned his feelings.

Destiny and Trip now lived in a rural community not far from the church with information about his birth parents. In June, Dylan had promised Augie they would visit Destiny. Now, Dylan hoped this venture out west would serve three purposes. He could fulfill his commitment to Augie about the trip, learn the truth about Jen's affection, and uncover the particulars of his birth.

Vapor popped and hissed from a burning log. Dylan left the loveseat to crouch before the hearth and stabbed the fire with an iron poker. The flames mesmerized him as embers lifted from the coals and drifted up the chimney.

Wham! Dylan tensed and looked at the front of the house. What was that? His heart pounded as he stared at the curtainless window. Anyone outside could see him, but darkness camouflaged them.

He tiptoed to the door and laid an ear near the jamb. Dylan listened. He cracked open the door and slowly allowed the meager cabin light to spill into the yard. Dylan poked his head beyond the frame to look at the porch under the window.

A cluster of rags lay on the decking. Dylan crept outside to inch toward the bundle. He held his breath and reached out a tentative finger.

Suddenly, Dylan jerked backward. Not rags, but a raven beat its wings in a frenzy before taking three drunken hops and flying into the black night. Dylan straightened and stared after the bird.

Must have hit the window and knocked itself out. Dylan eyed the bird's flight path.

Dylan released a long sigh and stepped back inside the cabin. He shut and bolted the door. As he leaned with his back against the door, his heartbeats returned to their natural rhythm.

"Lucky bird," Dylan said with a shake of his head. He wished he could move on as quickly.

Dylan picked up the glass from the coffee table and downed the remaining brandy. After he refilled the drink, Dylan kicked off his shoes and nestled into the loveseat. He left behind the thought of oddly behaving birds.

Nate's revelation about his adoption still stung. Why had his parents never told him? Maybe they were embarrassed about their inability to conceive a child. Perhaps they thought Dylan might think less of their relationship as a family.

Dylan knew adopted children. Most were aware of their histories. For example, Jen told Dylan about her adoptive parents' childless marriage. Her birth mother had passed through Salida and left Jen behind. Jen understood that her parents had jumped at the opportunity to give undying love to this abandoned baby girl. They also trusted Jen to know about her ancestry.

Maybe his folks intended to tell him the full story when he was older. How could they predict the car accident that cut short their lives? The collision robbed them of the opportunity to share. Dylan pondered the mystery until he fell into a restless sleep curled on the cushions.

Chapter 5

OCTOBER 9
KALEV

I knew he would return. It was only a matter of time. My patience had paid off.

Boards protested with each step as I crept across the porch to peek inside. I worried he might catch me. Leaning, ever so slowly, I shifted in front of the window. While the moon was far from full, its meager light cast my shadow into the room.

The interior looked similar. But the fireplace glowed red, and I saw the target sitting before it. When my breath fogged the window, I gently swiped the glass to regain the view.

He shifted under the blankets, and I froze. He rolled to his other side and yanked the covers up to his chin. Had he heard me, or was he adjusting to be more comfortable? I remained motionless.

My eyes shifted between the target and my shadow. Would he rise to investigate? I could retreat to the forest in an instant, but a miscalculated board creak might frighten him. I watched until the fire died and left the room in darkness.

I stayed up the rest of the night to watch in case the target emerged. I alternated between pacing the perimeter and climbing a stout pine to maintain a visual reconnaissance of the area. The plan was back on track.

After the moon set, a porcupine lumbered across the yard, oblivious to my eagerness.

Shortly after dawn, the target opened the front door to stand on the porch. He wore tight clothes that covered nearly all of his body. Only his face, with its stubbly beard, was exposed to the air. He rubbed together his gloved hands and moved to the steps and stretched. I hid in the trees across the yard to watch his every move.

The target started a slow jog along the driveway. He turned left at the intersection and away from the town. The road meandered up a mountain and switchback to a summit with a gentle grade. He would pass a few homes along the route. Did he have an objective?

While too soon to approach him, I tracked him and kept trees and bushes between myself and the road. In a few barren spots, I moved ahead or stayed behind with stealth to be sure he did not spot me. I knew this route, every tree and turn, from my months of preparation.

He ran faster than others I had seen on the trails. But not as quickly as some, and certainly not as fast as me. I heard his labored breathing when the road steepened and smiled when he leaned forward to push himself to reach the level grade.

After the third switchback, the target paused at the edge of the road. I held onto a tree and leaned through a patch of scrub oak bushes to gain a better view and watch him from above.

He placed hands on his hips and shook his head to stare at a can laying on the ground. It was an ordinary can, not exceptionally large or oddly shaped. Why would he bother to stop and stare at it? Over the summer, I had watched dozens of individuals toss them from vehicles.

In a swift movement, the target set the can on end and smashed it with his heel. Then he picked it up and tucked it into his jacket pocket.

I marveled at his deed. If everyone took such care of the environment, there would be less discarded waste.

Chapter 6

DYLAN COX

A branch rustled from atop the berm above the road. Dylan scanned the slope as pebbles skittered through the mat of grass and desiccated leaves. He braced an arm across his forehead to block the low-angle sun rays and strained to see what had caused the mini rockslide.

Dylan called out. He expected a response from a hiker or a loose dog on a trail above him. There was no further sound or movement, just a nagging feeling of being watched.

Jen had told him about mountain lions that lived in these hills. They attacked with speed and stealth. Her stories had spoken of unwary joggers who fell prey, typically in a secluded canyon or near a rock face where a cat could attack from above. This area seemed too open. Unable to shake the feeling, he decided to go back to the cabin. He retreated slowly and glanced back now and then to see if anything followed.

His downhill pace brought him to Jen's place considerably faster than his speed on the way up. Dylan stood on the porch to face the driveway and take deep breaths. Nothing had come from behind. Once inside, he loaded toiletries and fresh clothes into a small duffle for his planned excursions.

Dylan glanced back at the cabin before he opened the car door and tossed in his gear. *All the doors and windows are locked, and I'll only be away for a few hours.*

Dylan drove into town and parked in a lot adjacent to Salida's municipal hot springs pool. Better to run in a less remote area.

From the lot, Dylan jogged through town and uphill to the top of Tenderfoot Hill. He kept his focus on the big white 'S' embellished on the side of the little peak facing the Arkansas River. The prominent letter honored the municipality of Salida. Dylan figured his roundtrip distance at less than three miles, but the gain topped out at over 600 feet, plenty for his first day back.

As expected, his trip up Tenderfoot included several breaks to walk rather than run. However, his goal was to complete the excursion without stopping. Mission accomplished.

As he re-entered the parking lot, Dylan raised both hands into the air and stamped a victory dance. After he grabbed his duffle from the backseat, Dylan approached the Salida aquatic center, an immense open-concept structure with three steaming pools.

The air inside felt like a hot and humid day in Chicago in the middle of August. Vapor condensed on Dylan's skin the minute he entered the building. It was billed as the largest indoor hot springs facility in North America, and Dylan expected the sting of chlorine in his eyes and nose. He smelled nothing except a faint scent of mildew from moisture-saturated wood. For a couple of dollars, he took a shower and a good, long soak in the pools.

Clean and refreshed, Dylan drove to his favorite coffee shop, Café Dawn. He ate a bowl of heated granola laced with dried fruits and hearty nuts. Between bites, Dylan sipped a latte from a magenta ceramic mug. He held his drink in both hands and rolled it to transfer heat to his fingers. Dylan blew across the surface of the beverage to destroy the leaf pattern created by the barista in the frothed milk. He smiled as he set down his cup.

Dylan recalled the place was originally a gas station in the early 1900s. The converted building housed the café and the adjacent barbershop. Groups of seniors, their faces peppered with age spots and wrinkles from too much laughter or sun or both, clustered at worn linoleum-topped tables on mismatched chairs to catch up on daily events. Other tables hosted millennials in front of laptop computers, all in their own world. They typed or stared at the screens and fingered Bluetooth mice. Some of these solo patrons probably made this place their office. Dylan envied their work setting.

Dylan sat at a table in the front of the shop, next to the window. In June, he'd always taken his breakfast outside on the rickety deck. The day's chilly fall temperature chased him indoors. Through the window, Dylan noticed a seated, die-hard, outdoorsy couple bundled in brightly colored, puffy down jackets. *Heartier than me,* he concluded.

"Dylan? Is that you?" Dylan looked up from his breakfast and recognized Officer Merle Hodges. "I didn't realize you were back in town." Without waiting for an invitation, Merle snatched off his sunglasses and tossed them on the table. He dropped into the seat opposite Dylan and rested his meaty forearms on the table.

"Have you come back to continue your search for Trip Stewart?" he asked.

Dylan mustered a look of concern. "I'm working on another case. This time, I'm looking for a missing parent." Merle cocked his head. "I think you folks have the Stewart investigation under control. You don't need me involved in the mix."

Merle nodded. "The case is still inactive. The Sheriff's convinced that animals took Trip. It'll be a sad day when someone finds his body."

Dylan mimicked Merle's stoic nod but knew a body would never be recovered, as Trip was alive and starting a new life with his mother, Destiny, in Oregon. "What's new in Salida since June?" Dylan asked.

Merle swiped a hand across his salt-and-pepper crew cut. "Same routine as always. The force has a presence at June's Arkansas River rafting festival and the Art Walk. Those take more resources than the craft brewers' rendezvous in July or the fiber festival in September. There's a bunch more, like mountain bike races and music festivals, but those are the biggies that keep us busy."

"Sounds like I missed a lot of action in the past four months."

Merle smiled. "The events were well attended, but what warms my heart is the number of volunteers who come out to support the schedule.

Salida's sense of community is what makes us special."

"I recognized that when I visited last summer. I heard *your* commitment to volunteerism is legendary."

Merle leaned back as if distancing himself from the compliment. "I try to contribute when I can, but I'm only one of the hundreds who give time and resources. Thankfully, the weather's been great this summer—not too hot and not much rain, but enough to keep the ground moist. Fire risk was low."

"Hadn't thought about fires. Is it a problem?"

"Can be. A year ago, nearly 9,000 acres burned less than two miles from town. They brought in about a thousand firefighters and doused the forest with water and chemicals from helicopters. Thankfully, we only lost two homes." Merle nodded for emphasis. "The blaze started with a lightning strike. Low snowpack and a dry summer created perfect conditions for an immediately out-of-control blaze. It took firefighters months to get it fully contained. Wasn't completely out until winter."

"That's a lot of devastation. Chicago's had its share of catastrophic fires but not for many years." Dylan sipped his coffee. "Any news on Salida's Bigfoot?" Dylan knew that Merle, a committed believer, assumed one of the giant beasts had taken up residence near Salida.

Merle frowned and shook his head. "The hunt for the Sasquatch has slowed. There haven't been any more sightings since you were here in June."

"I noticed some news vans since I've been in town. Are they still here in search of Bigfoot, or are they after another story?"

"No. This piece is still attracting national attention, but without sightings or other new evidence like footprints, they're losing interest."

"Not surprising." Dylan considered whether to share his doubts about the June sighting. "I know someone reported they saw the creature in June, but I'm not convinced the report was legit."

Merle sighed and gave Dylan a look to suggest he'd had this discussion one too many times. "Why do you say that?"

"Just a hunch." Dylan left it at that. "So tell me. Why are you a staunch believer? Have you ever seen one?"

"Unfortunately, I have not. But sightings happen all over the United States." Merle straightened. "Actually, all over the world. There's a substantial network of believers, including dedicated amateurs as well as respected academic researchers. Some researchers have even sacrificed their careers at major universities because they stood by their views."

"I'm not suggesting the concept of a Bigfoot, Sasquatch, or Yeti isn't intriguing. It certainly captures the imagination. But where's the proof?"

"There's been sightings, many from credible witnesses. Nonbelievers spot them and become believers. These people were simply doing routine activities, like driving cars or walking near their homes. The sightings changed their lives." Merle's voice grew passionate. "The *hard* evidence is in the footprints, hair, and scat left behind." He slapped the table. "This bipedal animal does exist."

"Bipedal, as in walks-on-two-feet?"

"Sure."

"Let's talk about the evidence. Since I've been back in Chicago, I did some Bigfoot research."

Merle smiled. "I'm impressed."

Dylan returned his grin. He knew his research involved less than an hour of chat rooms and videos. "I read opposing views about whether the footprints were real or faked. After analysis, the hair and feces samples were either identified as a regular woodland animal, like a bear, or as *inconclusive primate*. It seems like the evidence, when viewed on a case-by-case basis, is circumstantial."

"But when viewed as a whole, the proof is overwhelming. Characteristics of the scat and hair samples are common to both humans and non-human mammals. How do you reconcile that without concluding a human-*like* animal really does exist in the wilderness?"

"Yeah, but I'm used to concrete evidence. For example, my background is in linguistics. The history of languages is traceable. Human decisions validate the evolution of words. First, the language is colloquially modified orally. Then the change is codified through respected sources, like religious texts or lists of words and their meanings."

"Like a dictionary?"

"Exactly. The ability to track how something came to be and how it continues to evolve makes sense to me. The Sasquatch theory is disjointed. It's loosely tied threads of conversations and hearsay. I don't see the precision."

Merle scoffed. "Not sure I agree with your assessment on languages or any other anthropological study. Think about how many theories about civilizations have changed as more information became available."

"I'm not following."

"Let me give you an example. Think about all the theories about how to translate the hieroglyphic language before they discovered the Rosetta Stone. That inscribed rock included a single proclamation in three languages. Two were already well understood, but the other was hieroglyphics. Before the Rosetta Stone, linguists struggled to understand hieroglyphics. The Stone gave researchers the information they needed to do accurate translations."

Dylan countered, "While theories and translations have evolved, the evidence of languages can be seen in texts or heard, in the case of verbal tongues. If these animals have been around as long as humans have existed, then why haven't we ever come across a body? In modern times, why hasn't someone hit one with their car? It doesn't make sense."

"People believe in lots of things they can't see. We believed in molecules and viruses long before we invented microscopes to view them. We know the moon affects our tides, but there is nothing visual to support the theory. At the dawn of every discovery, some people have faith before it can be proven. For now, I guess Sasquatch falls in that category."

Dylan offered a sincere smile. "We may have to agree to disagree. I respect your view, but I can't say I share your opinion."

"There may come a time when you change your mind. If you plan to stick around for a while, consider attending the Sasquatch believer conference here in Salida. It's on the weekend of November 18th. We have a full schedule of events planned with guest speakers from all over the U.S."

"Like a longer version of the meeting I went to in June?"

Merle nodded. "Yes, but with workshops and scholars who've made the study of Sasquatch their life's work."

"I suspect I'll be back in Chicago by November, but I'll keep the date in mind."

Dylan straightened in his chair and looked out the window. A petite woman with a mass of flaming red hair crossed the street and approached the café. With each step, her curls and bosom bounded in unpredictable directions. She wore a skintight sheath of a dress that failed to constrain her voluptuous curves. Dylan nodded toward her. "I'd wondered if Cynthia was still around."

Merle shook his head and issued a tsk before he retrieved his sunglasses. Maybe Merle thought his sunglasses would render him invisible.

Freelance writer Cynthia Waters had come to Salida from back East to follow the Bigfoot story in June. Had she been in town since Dylan last saw her?

Merle leaned toward Dylan and whispered, "She's a real pain in my ass."

As Cynthia approached their table, Dylan gave her an off-hand wave. He hoped she would not bother to stop.

Cynthia beelined to Dylan's chair. She stopped several inches closer than his comfort zone. "Dylan, love, I didn't think I'd have the privilege of your company again. You left in quite a hurry last summer. What brings you back to town?" She asked with a thick New York accent.

He scooted back and crossed his arms across his chest to suggest she stay in her own space. "Just passing through and visiting friends."

"Where are you headed after Salida?"

"Not sure yet. I feel the need for a road trip. What about you? Still after the big story on Bigfoot?"

Before she responded, Cynthia glanced at Merle as he tilted backward and hooked his thumbs into his leather duty belt. She said, "I've had a few articles published since I've been here." She braced a hand on her hip and pointed a red lacquered nail toward Merle. "Officer Hodges has read them. Right, Merle?"

Merle eyed Cynthia over the top of his sunglasses. "I don't know who you conned into talking with you, but I'm certain they were misquoted or misinformed."

Cynthia's eyes narrowed. Her lips curled into a sly smile. "I can't divulge my sources, but I'm confident they were knowledgeable and candid." Cynthia retracted her finger and smoothed her dress into place. "I'm here to pick up drinks. I'll let you boys catch up."

As if she'd removed their tongues, both men stared at her in silence.

She ordered, paid, and headed to the exit with her coffees. The moment the door swung shut, Dylan asked, "I can see there's no love lost between you two. What did she do to piss you off?"

Merle shrugged. "I know she wants to write sensational stories. Those are the ones that sell. But twisting the words of honest people to make them look foolish is wrong. Any chance you saw her articles?"

Dylan shook his head.

"Cynthia wrote a series about how Salida is capitalizing on the Sasquatch story. She claimed the townspeople fit into two categories—those who profit from defrauding the public and those who are too dumb to know better. The most brutal rant received national distribution."

Merle sighed and glanced at his black rubber watch. "Most of the folks around here wouldn't speak to her after the article came out. She named names. Her so-called profiteers included the mayor, hoteliers, and restaurateurs. She characterized the Sheriff and Police Offices as incompetent yokels. Sheriff Austin took her comments with a grain of salt, but my son Erle and I can't forgive her for how she described us. Everyone should be entitled to maintain their beliefs without public ridicule. In her view, believers are complete freaks."

He tsked again and nodded toward the window. "You might be interested to know she's taken up with your cousin Nate."

Chapter 7

KATE MEYERS

As late afternoon shadows fell, Kate walked into the restaurant with calm authority. She turned fifty in the summertime but was pleased her face bore no apparent signs of aging. In her youth, she'd detested the spray of freckles across her nose and cheeks. Grateful they had not morphed into blotchy patches of dark skin linked with advanced years, Kate still felt her visibility diminishing.

The door shut behind her, and patrons glanced up from their meals. In years past, men's attention would linger far longer than their female counterparts. Recently, she barely caught a notice.

Kate ran a hand through the front of her wispy blonde hair and pushed aside the shortest layers from her forehead. She categorized Dylan as geographically undesirable, but he might be tempted to move to Salida for the *right* prospect. After all, he fell for Jen Rickard last time he came to Colorado. While attractive in an athletic sort of way, Jen was not a woman of substance or higher education.

She glanced toward the four booths against the far wall and the dozen tables in the center section. Most customers sat at the massive L-shaped bar to take advantage of two-for-one beers and half-price appetizers.

Kate spotted Dylan in a booth. He concentrated on a small notebook and flipped the pages as if searching for an elusive piece of information. *Not as modern as I expected,* she concluded as she had pictured him tapping on a cell phone with his thumbs. He seemed thinner than she remembered but was still familiar with his dress shirt sleeves rolled midway between wrist and elbow and his wavy chestnut hair overdue for a cut.

"Is that your little black book?" She kidded and slid into the booth to face him.

Dylan rose slightly. "Kate. Good to see you."

She folded a black knitted poncho and pushed it to the end of the bench. Kate leaned forward across the blemished table. "I hear you're taking my new BFF on a road trip?"

Dylan's brows furrowed. "BFF?"

"Where have you been? Best Friends Forever—a popular concept with my first-graders."

Dylan chuckled. "Maybe I should start hanging out with more children."

"Not if you don't have to," Kate scoffed. She loved teaching youngsters but wanted the next ten years to pass quickly. Early retirement was within reach, and Kate longed to stop raising other people's offspring. While she enjoyed her students' fresh perspectives on the world, Kate found it challenging to keep them engaged for an entire day. Thankfully, her class had no demon spawn this year. She could not say the same for some of her colleagues' classes.

The waitress approached, and Kate ordered an iced tea and a grilled chicken salad. Dylan turned to the server and made eye contact after a glance at her name tag. "Susan, how's your day so far?"

She returned his smile. "Second shift for today, but fine. I appreciate the work. Thank you for asking. Can I take your order?"

"You may. This is my lucky day. I see you have walleye on the menu. Believe it or not, it's my favorite type of fish. When I was a kid, my family took fishing vacations to northern Minnesota. We'd stay at a rustic lodge, and a fishing guide brought us out at the crack of dawn or maybe even earlier. All I needed to do was cast a lure into the lake, and I'd get a strike. It was a feeding frenzy. I'll bet it's not like that anymore."

Susan tapped her pen on the order pad as Dylan continued. "At any rate, we ate dinner at the lodge each night. That's where I was introduced to walleye. To this day, it's my absolute favorite."

The waitress scratched her temple with the back of her pen. "We're out. Sorry for any inconvenience. Can I recommend the salmon?"

Dylan's shoulders slumped. "It's a poor substitute."

"Did your folks buy you hamburgers? They're great here."

He smiled. "Sold. Give me a barbeque cheeseburger with bacon."

Kate addressed the waitress. "My friend is on a health food diet."

"Bacon should be on everyone's diet," Dylan added as Susan left the table.

Kate reached across the table to place her hand over Dylan's. She knew from his call he'd spent the night at Jen's place, but the visit must have affected him. "How did your night at the cabin go?"

Dylan took a long breath before he responded. "Probably needs to be aired out a bit, but nobody has broken in or taken up residence."

"Well, that's good to know, but I'm thinking about you. Was it tough for you to stay there without Jen?"

"Yeah. I'm still hurting. It brought back intense memories of last summer. I felt close to her."

"Like you sensed her there?"

"Sounds weird to say it out loud, but yes. Jen was such a part of the place. Maybe her spirit stayed there to protect me."

"Protect you from what?"

Dylan smiled. "Great question. I guess from my dark thoughts."

Kate nodded. "I understand."

Dylan slid his hand from under hers and fidgeted with the cardboard coaster advertising a local brewer. "What are your plans for the place? Augie certainly isn't interested in moving out there."

Kate thought for a moment before she responded. "I'm reluctant to put it up for sale right away. The stigma of Jen's death is still fresh in everyone's mind around here. I'm afraid it could affect the property value, which would be bad for Augie."

"Hadn't considered that, but you're right. I assume your mission is to try to get the best price to safeguard Augie's inheritance."

"Exactly what I had in mind. Listing the property next May might let memories of the attack fade a bit. Older mountain properties, like Jen's cabin, sell well in the spring and summer months when out-of-towners are in Salida to hike and mountain bike. They come here to play and end up buying their piece of paradise. The cabin would be a great second home for Denverites or people from farther away. If the buyer didn't have a personal connection with Jen, of course."

Kate wanted to change the line of discussion. So she circled back to Dylan's imminent trip with Augie. "I'm serious," Kate chided good-naturedly. "Why are you taking Augie on a trip?"

From working with Augie over the past few months, Kate understood his disabilities prevented him from complete independence, but he took pride in living on his own. Augie inherited the trailer home from his aunt and could keep it clean and maintained. Paying bills were not a problem as notification came in the mail. One-off tasks, such as transferring Jen's assets into his name or setting up his investments, challenged Augie. As long as he felt comfortable with their arrangement, she would continue to help him in any way she could.

Over the past months, she and Augie had developed a friendship built on trust and mutual respect. She felt obligated to protect Augie from anyone who may not have his best interests at heart. Dylan seemed harmless, but she wanted to be clear on his motive for taking Augie out of town.

Dylan ignored her question and asked if her life had settled down since last June when she witnessed a Bigfoot, or something that looked like a Bigfoot, in her yard. She put both hands over her face and exhaled deeply. "I wish I'd never reported that incident."

While they ate dinner, she gave Dylan an update about how her days had progressed since early summer. "The harassing mob of reporters isn't camped out in my front yard anymore. Finally, I can run errands and start the school year without their distraction."

"I've seen less news presence, but Merle Hodges says they're still around in search of Sasquatch."

"You've seen Merle?" she asked. *So he called on Merle before me?*

"We crossed paths at Café Dawn."

She straightened, pleased Dylan called *her* to get together and Merle's meeting was happenstance. "He'd know the score on the Bigfoot front," she said before she stabbed a piece of grilled chicken and stuffed it in her mouth.

For the rest of the meal, Dylan listened, and Kate rambled about the good yields in her vegetable and herb gardens and her first-graders. When they finished, Dylan leaned forward and took her hand in both of his. The gesture triggered a flutter in her chest.

"Kate, I know you believe you saw a real Bigfoot last summer, but I think it may have been a hoax."

Saddened he had not moved toward a more intimate topic, Kate reflected on the night she spotted the beast. As time passed, the sighting grew foggy. A huge hairy man had stood in her garden and drank the nectar from her hummingbird feeder. How *could* it have been true? "What do you know?"

"A day or two after your sighting, I caught Cynthia Waters with an actor who dresses up like Sasquatch for business promotions."

"Why was Cynthia with him?"

"She hired him to pose with her for photos to accompany her Bigfoot articles. This man stood over seven feet tall. If I planned to hire someone to play Bigfoot, he would have been first on my list. I didn't see his costume, but if you saw Cynthia's articles, you might know whether it seemed convincing."

"I saw her photos. He looked like what you'd expect for a Bigfoot—ape-like. My guy seemed more athletic and not so hairy in the face." She paused to smile. "Thanks for trying to give me a way out."

"Out of what?"

"I don't want to be lumped in with the league of Sasquatch sighters."

As they paid the bill, Kate realized Dylan had still not answered her question about the trip with Augie. "I'm not giving up. Why are you going away with Augie?"

"I have some business out west and thought Augie could use a change in scenery."

"He doesn't seem a likely holiday companion for you." Kate's eyes narrowed as she challenged Dylan.

"My relationship with Jen, however brief, felt intense. I loved her. Augie knew her a lot longer than I did. He's suffered a great loss. This trip will give us a breather from normal routines to do some healing."

Kate scrutinized his expression. Was he hiding something? Perhaps her teacher-skepticism was working overtime. Or maybe her cynicism stemmed from disappointment over Jen catching Dylan's attention. He seemed reluctant to go further than friendship with Kate. No matter. She convinced herself to let it go.

Chapter 8

DYLAN COX

fter dinner, Dylan gave Kate a brotherly hug goodbye and left town for Jen's cabin. When he pulled into the driveway, he followed the same routine as the previous evening and left the car lights on while he opened the front door.

Dylan looked inside to see if everything looked as he had left it. Satisfied, he returned to the car, shut off the lights, and locked the doors. When he stepped back onto the porch, he glanced around the yard.

Maybe he should rein in his suspicions. Well, Dylan did pledge caution to Augie.

Dylan lit candles and made a fire. Flickering light danced on the walls and strobed across the paintings and rugs on the otherwise stark logs. After he poured a brandy, he circled the room to admire Jen's artwork. *Guess it's Augie's artwork now,* figured Dylan with a shrug

Each canvas included either a bird or a small animal, such as a chipmunk or a prairie dog. Colorful woodland blossoms circled the creatures. He recalled the plants' names from hikes with Jen: wild iris, phlox, and crocus. Other flowers were unfamiliar, and Dylan assumed they might bloom in the later summer months after he had returned to Chicago.

Dylan settled on the loveseat and pulled a thick wool blanket over his legs. The fire had thrust some initial heat into the room, but it would take a while before the air warmed to a comfortable temperature. He took stock of the little woodpile and decided his stash would not last through the evening. Dylan set down his drink and picked up the canvas log sling and a headlamp before heading outside.

Once on the porch, Dylan noticed the inconsequential light cast on the yard from the cabin windows. The tallest trees mostly obscured the rising moon. The lack of moonlight allowed the stars to shine brightly and dot the black velvet background with millions of minute points of light. Dylan looked up at the heavens and spotted one particularly brilliant star in the western sky. It peeked between the canopy of pine boughs. Could it be a planet? Maybe Jen had a star chart among her field guides.

Without his coat, the cold night air prompted a shiver that shook his body. The woodpile lay along the side wall, so he abandoned stargazing to get to his task.

As he passed the window struck by the bird on the previous evening, he paused to pluck an ebony feather standing upright between the floorboards. Dylan swiped it across the glass pane. What would cause a bird to crash into the window? Maybe it had been attracted to the light.

He had heard of birds striking buildings when they saw through to the other side or when they flew into a structure clad with mirrored glass. Nighttime collisions might be rare. Dylan dropped the feather and watched it pendulum on subtle wind currents until it landed in the yard beyond the porch.

Dylan rounded the corner to the side yard. Inky darkness closed in. He switched on his headlamp to wash the ground with light. Dylan approached the woodpile and knelt to smooth the sling on the ground. Three at a time, he transferred logs from the pile.

As he laid the last bunch on the sling, a creaking sound echoed from the forest. Dylan grabbed a stout stick to serve as a weapon and turned to stare into the woods. He strained to understand what could have made the sound. Gentle breezes moved the trees like ocean waves creeping across a sandy beach.

Dylan stood and smacked the limb against his palm. He hoped the sound might be perceived as aggression and frighten off an intruder. Dylan stepped toward the back of the house to peek around the corner.

His heart pounded as he directed the lamp's beam through the blackness. Both the back door and fringes of the yard stood silent. Nothing moved. He returned to the woodpile and stooped to heft the sling. As he straightened, the creak sounded again. Shrill and rasping—something otherworldly. Was it headed his way?

He spun to face the trees and frantically slashed the light across the bushes, desperate to find the source. "Enough," Dylan called to the trees. He did not expect a response and was grateful when none came.

Dylan recalled Jen's attack. A mountain lion and a bear came at her in the dark. Could they be back? The Sheriff had told Dylan no one had spotted cats or bears in the area for months. He focused the beam at the edge of the yard to search for any sign of movement or reflective eyes. Nothing.

"Who are you?" he yelled.

Dylan inhaled deep breaths until he came to terms with his paranoia. A smile curled the corner of his lips, and he released a single chortle.

"Hey Bigfoot, quit hiding. I promise not to hurt you."

He yanked the straps higher on his shoulder and walked to the front porch with commanding strides.

As he approached the door, flashing shapes floated into his vision—the typical precursor to one of his migraine headaches. Black and white forms swirled in front of his eyes to block out the world.

He dropped his load. Logs scattered across the porch. Dylan reached for the wicker chairs that he knew sat on the porch last summer. His hand flailed in space. Kate must have cleared the porch furniture. He had not noticed the change before.

"Some detective I am," he scoffed and stepped down to sit on the stairs. Dylan rested his head between his hands and massaged his temples.

Astonishingly, the flashes slowed and started to clear. The massage must have helped this time. Dylan's migraines always had a consistent progression, from the loss of vision to a throbbing pain at the temples, and finally a dull headache radiating from the base of his neck through his forehead.

Last summer, migraines plagued him each night at the cabin. Jen assumed the altitude triggered them, but he had no hint of one last night, and this one was fading. What was different? He refused to believe Jen's absence cured his headaches. Time of year? Perhaps the brandy? He drank brandy on both nights. He smiled, not an unpleasant antidote.

Dylan stayed on the porch and rubbed his temples, the dread of a stalker all but forgotten. The flashes continued to fade. He wanted to get back to the warmth of the fire and stood to collect the escaped logs back into the canvas. Before going inside, he glanced over his shoulder toward the forest.

He straightened and puzzled over what he saw. Instead of the yard and his parked car, all he saw was a still image, like a photograph blocking his view. The vision was of a familiar house's back porch in the gently eroding light of day. A woman, frozen in time, stood outside and held the backdoor open. She had wispy blonde hair and wore loose-fitting, gauzy clothes. Dylan strained to focus his vision on the place miles away from the cabin. He couldn't be sure, but he thought the woman was Kate Meyers. Her mouth gaped open in a scream. Terror filled her eyes.

What did Kate see?

Chapter 9

OCTOBER 10

Despite the truncated headache and sleeping in a curled, fetal position on the loveseat, Dylan rested well and woke when morning light streamed through the windows. The vision had not interrupted his ability to sleep, as he decided the combination of brandy and a migraine must have generated a waking dream. Since he saw Kate at dinner and they discussed her Bigfoot sighting, the subject of the vision seemed no great surprise.

Dylan collected his belongings into the suitcase and threw remnants of food into a trash bag. He didn't want to leave any incentive for rodents to move into the cabin. Kate would have his head.

After he packed the car, Dylan returned to lock the cabin. He stopped short as he neared the door. Scratch marks marred the door frame. Were they there before and not apparent in the darkness? Surely he would have noticed them the previous morning. He examined the front windows and ran a finger down the frame. It bore the same marks. Dylan turned to scan the forest beyond the parking area as if the trees could tell him who had left the marks.

As he stared, feet apart and hands on hips, last night's creak sounded again. Dylan stormed past the car and into the side yard. Once again, the friction of chafing surfaces mocked him from the dense stand of trees.

The light of day made the culprit easy to spot. A dead snag leaned against a neighboring pine. When the wind blew with sufficient enthusiasm, the chafing bark protested with an eerie grind. Dylan shook his head. He returned to lock the cabin and drove to town.

Augie sat on the wrought-iron steps next to two brown paper bags. Dylan figured he would have sat there for hours, patiently waiting—irrespective of what time Dylan showed up.

After Dylan retrieved the newly purchased duffle from the backseat, the pair transferred Augie's clean T-shirts, jeans, and underwear from the sacks.

As he folded the empty bags, Dylan asked, "Did you pack your toothbrush, shampoo, deodorant, and shaving gear?" Augie gave him a wide-eyed stare. "You can go inside and get them, or we can buy new stuff once we're on the road. Your choice."

Augie gave an immediate response. "I like mine."

"Good point. If you're only comfortable with certain brands, you might want to take what you'll need from the house."

Augie nodded and returned shortly. He held another brown sack with toiletries. After Dylan transferred the latest items into the duffle, he took his cabin trash and Augie's empty bags to the bins at the side of the trailer.

As Dylan stuffed everything into a can, Augie came from behind and moved the paper bags into a separate container. "Recycles," Augie said.

"Of course, sorry about that," said Dylan sheepishly.

Augie settled into his seat and buckled up as if vacations were a regular occurrence. Without a glance toward Dylan, Augie placed his hands on his blue jean-clad thighs and stared out the front window. Dylan smiled and started the car.

On the way out of town, Dylan stopped at Café Dawn for a latte and hot chocolate for the road. He walked out of the shop with their drinks and paused to look down First Street toward his cousin's art gallery.

When Nate bought the building, he completely remodeled the façade. In contrast to the historic red-brick buildings along the block, brushed aluminum and floor-to-ceiling windows clad the gallery. *Just as out of place as my worthless cousin*, thought Dylan as he crossed to the car.

As he tapped Augie's window to pass him the drinks, Dylan heard a familiar voice from across the street. "Hey, Dylan. Is that you?" Dylan turned to face the gallery. Nate stood at the front door and held it open with one hand. He beckoned with the other. "I heard you were in town. Come on in. I've got news for you."

Terrific, not an encounter he'd been looking forward to. Part of Dylan wanted to return the wave and escape in the car. The other felt an incomprehensible need for Nate's approval. *What about Nate keeps pulling me in?*

Augie slipped the drinks into the cup holders in the console. When Dylan made no move to walk around to the driver's side, Augie followed Dylan's gaze toward Nate at the front of the gallery. He said, "You have time. Family is important."

Dylan smiled. He admired Augie's ability to see beyond Nate's shortcomings. "Last time I saw Nate, I destroyed one of his paintings. Maybe he wants to give me a bill for the repair."

Augie smiled. "If you broke something, you should fix it."

"As usual, you're right. I'll try to make this short." Dylan strolled across the street and gave his cousin a less than enthusiastic wave.

Nate held the door open until Dylan stepped inside. As he shut and locked the door, Nate motioned behind a counter toward a seating area with a polished round conference table and six chairs upholstered in rich chocolate-colored leather.

As Dylan walked to the table, he noticed a new display of Nate's work. Several abstract pieces hung along the walls, suspended from wires attached to the ceiling. They were lit from above by accent lamps to highlight the textures of the paint.

When Nate was into painting landscapes, Dylan thought his art looked primitive, flat, and obvious. During the past year, Nate changed his technique. His new work drew attention. Dylan hated to admit it, but he liked the change and figured Nate might be able to sell some of the more recent pieces.

A few tags indicated *Sold* rather than a price. Suspicious of Nate's success, Dylan doubted whether the Sold cards were real. Nate could be using them as a marketing technique. People might buy one if they thought the paintings were in short supply.

Nate's coffee maker coughed its final stage. Nate selected a cup from a pyramid of mugs stacked next to the machine. He added healthy amounts of sugar and creamer, filled it with coffee, and placed it on a leather coaster on the conference table. Nate instructed Dylan to help himself before he sat in the chair with the best view of the street and the peaks beyond.

Dylan took a cup, thought about Augie waiting in the car, and pushed it back into the stack. He took a seat across from Nate.

Dylan realized his cousin looked unchanged since the summer. Still in mobster attire, Nate wore a uniform of tan dress slacks and a black silk shirt with a raised floral pattern. The open shirt exposed Nate's hairless chest and clunky gold necklace. Dylan found Nate's signature look a bit high-fashion for a town known for outdoor recreations and ranches.

Nate leaned forward. "While it's great to see you, cuz, I'm curious why you're in town. I figured you wouldn't be back here after you failed miserably to find Trip."

Dylan straightened, angry with himself for coming to the gallery and allowing his cousin to push his buttons. Nate dispensed magnetism and brutality in equal measure, and Dylan lacked the skills to deflect either.

"Yeah well, I ran out of leads, and the Sheriff's Office seemed to have a good handle on the case."

"If the Sheriff's men would listen to me and keep searching where they last saw Trip, I'm sure they would find clues about where he went. Or at least, they'd find his body."

"Last summer, you were convinced he was still alive."

"The Sheriff believes animals killed him."

Dylan raised a brow. "Have you decided he might be right?"

Nate exhaled the long, slow breath of a beaten man. Had Nate sprouted feelings for his son over the last months? "I can't believe he's gone," Nate said.

Bewildered at Nate's apparent new-found parental instincts, Dylan recalled Nate's antics from June. With the flexibility to pursue any available female, his cousin basked in attention and played the life of an unencumbered bachelor. Dylan said, "I thought you'd started to move on with your life."

"Move on? You're talking about my son."

Dylan raised his hands in surrender. "Sorry, I didn't mean to imply anything."

"My life without Trip is hollow. I will live each day in a fog until I can find out what happened to him."

Nate's compassion seemed genuine. Maybe Nate had finally started to understand the value of his family. He leaned toward Nate. Before Dylan could stop himself, he asked, "Have you thought about hiring another detective?"

Nate raised his gaze from the cup to look at Dylan. Moisture glistened in his eyes. His brow creased with concern. He ran a manicured nail around the rim of his coffee mug. "Do you think that would help?"

Torn between defending Destiny's secret and budding empathy for his troubled cousin, Dylan speculated whether Trip's parents might forge a compromise about the boy's guardianship. Maybe he should suggest Nate communicate with Destiny and work something out.

Before Dylan offered information about Trip's whereabouts, Nate shook his head and sighed. "People must think I'm a horrific father."

There's the nugget. Nate was not concerned for Trip. Nate felt *judged* about his parenting prowess. This might be the first time Dylan had not fallen into his cousin's trap. Was he learning, or had Nate's cunning slipped?

Swiftly, Dylan switched to champion Destiny's side. He reached over to pat Nate's hand. "Everyone in town knows you've done everything you could to find him. The Sheriff's a good man. I'm sure he'll work hard to find Trip, but he needs more time."

Nate nodded and looked up, coldness returned to his eyes. "There'd need to be some changes, though." Nate regarded the ceiling, and Dylan imagined his cousin pondering alternatives. "Perhaps a military school would toughen him up, or my folks could take him for a couple of months. He'd like Chicago. There are lots of nerdy computer-addicted kids there." After a pause, Nate asked, "Where have you been staying?"

"Jen's cabin."

Nate blinked, and Dylan could almost hear his cousin trying to work out Dylan's angle. "Why are you staying there? Must be all closed up, right?"

"You're right. There's no electricity, but it's comfortable and a free place to stay."

"Seems like you'd want to stay closer to town." Nate's eyes narrowed. "You find anything worthwhile up there?"

"I'm sleeping there. I haven't been poking around."

Nate laughed and responded with authority. "Wouldn't hurt to do a little treasure hunting. The place has been in Jen's family for generations." With an eyebrow raised, Nate asked, "Do you think they stashed anything in the woods or the walls? I heard her father was a nonconformist and off-the-charts into the wilderness. Rumors around town said he did mercenary work in California before he moved back to Salida. It wouldn't surprise me if he hid money or gold near the cabin."

"I think you've got a romantic notion of Jen's father. She never led me to believe there'd be anything hidden up there." Dylan switched gears. "How about you? Were you able to dodge the bullet with the pregnant teenager? Casey is her name, right?"

"That was taken care of months ago." Nate scoffed with a dismissive wave.

"Did you have her killed?" Dylan responded, dead-panned.

Nate grinned. "I guess that would have solved the problem, too. But I didn't have to go so far. I convinced her father an abortion would be the best solution for everyone. He persuaded her to get herself taken care of at a Denver clinic. The locals were none the wiser."

"Was she okay with your solution?" Dylan worried that two highly influential men might have pressured her into something she did not want to do. When confronted with Nate and her father, Casey's opinion would get buried.

"I guess so. She did it, and it wasn't any concern of mine."

"You were the father, right?"

Nate shrugged. "Maybe. But it wasn't my problem. Anyway, without a baby, there'd be no paternity test. Casey was delusional if she believed I'd commit to her."

Dylan ineffectively submerged his sarcasm. "I guess things worked out well for you." He desperately wanted to switch the topic. "I've heard you and Cynthia Waters have hooked up."

Nate broke into a lusty grin. "Yep. She's incredibly hot. There's a lot to be said for young pussy like Casey. They've got tight bodies and will try anything. But I say, let'm age about ten or twenty years. Older women know what to do, and they're hungry for it. Cynthia's amazing." He paused to tilt his head. "Although she can be overly independent at times."

"I'll take that as a compliment." Cynthia, dressed in a silk robe and high heels, clacked through the open doorway that led to Nate's upstairs apartment. She moved behind Nate's chair and wrapped her arms around his neck. Her heavy breasts pressed seductively into the base of his neck as they nearly escaped from the flimsy robe.

"Good to see you again, Dylan." How had she managed to silence her stilettos to move down the stairs?

"Cynthia. You're looking as magnificent as ever. I congratulate you and Nate for finding each other. You make a wonderful couple."

"Somehow, I'm not feeling the love from you." She straightened. With both hands, she gathered her massive auburn ringlets behind her neck. As her elbows splayed out to the side, the robe opened wider. Fabric parted seductively across her breasts and stopped short of exposing nipples. Dylan figured she'd practiced the move upstairs. Cynthia leaned forward, and her robe went slack as she nipped at Nate's earlobe with porcelain white teeth.

Dylan tried to mask his disrespect for the man-eating Siren with an innocuous question about how well her latest article was received. Cynthia tapped a crimson fingernail against her chin and paused before she responded. "It was a huge success. There's been a flood of compliments about my style and reporting rigor. There may be a journalism award in my future."

She can't be thinking Pulitzer, reasoned Dylan. He recanted his assumption. Her bloated ego could have brought her to an assortment of remarkable conclusions. Dylan attempted to stifle Merle's opinion about how she infuriated the locals. "I haven't had a chance to read your article about Salida and the Sasquatch, but I've read some of your earlier investigative reporting. In my view, your work cuts through the chaff and gets to the truth."

Cynthia shifted her gaze from Nate to Dylan. Her eyes widened and focused solely on him, as her chest heaved with each breath. Despite his disdain, he felt his heartbeat quicken, drawn by her enchantment. "It's my best work so far. I have a copy if you'd like to read it."

Before he could respond, Cynthia moved to the counter. She placed a palm on the surface and leaned forward to explore the cabinet below. As Cynthia bent from the waist, her robe inched up her toned and tanned thighs. Right before Dylan could see whether or not she wore panties, she straightened, and the fabric fell back to a modest position.

She pulled a few stapled sheets from the top of a pile and returned the extras to the countertop. Cynthia scanned the top page and shimmied back to her post behind Nate. She brushed across his shoulder with a breast and reached around Nate to slide the papers across the conference table. Dylan thanked her and gave assurance he would read the article later. He folded the sheets into quarters and slipped them into the chest pocket of his jacket.

As she retracted her attention from Dylan, he felt her pull diminish. In a loud stage-whisper, she told Nate she would wait for him upstairs. Both Dylan and Nate watched her retreat. Her magnificently rounded bottom tugged her robe with each step.

Still focused on the doorway after she had disappeared to ascend the stairs, Nate adjusted the front of his slacks. "While this reunion has been fun, I'm gonna have to ask you to leave."

"No worries. Augie's in the car waiting for me anyway." As he left the gallery, Dylan felt relieved to leave the spider's den.

Chapter 10

JAMESVILLE, OREGON—OCTOBER 11

Dylan pulled the rental car to the curb in front of a craftsman-style bungalow. At nearly ten in the evening, the neighborhood glowed yellow from the row of street lights. Cars lined both curbs.

As Dylan stepped from the car, he stretched limbs cramped from the long drive. He sucked moisture-rich air into his lungs and felt a stark contrast from arid Salida. No one strolled the sidewalks except a lone woman across the street. Bundled in an oversized plaid jacket and wool hat, she tugged her hound's leash and urged him with, "Jackson, I haven't got all night. Do your business."

Dylan scanned the block of tidy houses and manicured lawns. A few homes had open curtains, and Dylan could see the evening news flashing on television sets. He turned toward Destiny's home. From the illumination of a porch light, Dylan could make out gray-green siding with tea green woodwork.

Augie stood next to the car with his limp wrists flapping like flags in a stiff breeze. Dylan assumed the motion revealed Augie's anticipation of a reunion with Destiny. To gain Augie's attention, Dylan tapped the roof and pointed at their duffels.

They walked along a flagstone path lined with neatly trimmed boxwood shrubs. Three concrete steps led to the porch, an inviting space with a teakwood table and hanging swing. Dylan suspected Destiny, a woman with secrets, would not spend much time on the porch.

A rectangular leaded glass window fit above eye level in the oak front door. A stained-glass holly wreath with a red bow nestled in the center of the window. The light spilled from inside the house and cast a red and green reflection on the porch.

Augie looked at Dylan as if asking whether to knock or press the bell. Dylan tipped his head toward the door. Augie extended a fist, but before his knuckles connected, Destiny flung open the door and greeted Augie with an immediate embrace.

She patted his back. "I can't believe you're finally here."

While Dylan had met her before, he had forgotten her height. She stood several inches taller than Augie, whose head fit comfortably on her angular shoulder. *She must be nearly six feet tall.*

He stood behind Augie and waited until his friend let go. When they parted, Dylan extended a hand to the beanpole of a woman. She ignored his offering and embraced him, too. Her layers of wool and fleece helped to soften the impact of her bony frame. Did genetics or stress keep her thin?

"I hear your heritage in your voice," said Dylan.

"I've worked hard to keep the *Down East* of North Carolina under control. It comes out like crazy when I'm back home, but usually I manage to stifle it when I'm away. I'm surprised you can hear it."

"It's subtle but still there. Sounds nice." Dylan paused to step back and give a nod toward his traveling companion. "I have Augie to thank for connecting us. Jen thought so much of you. I hope we can be friends."

She embraced him again. "I do, too. Thank you for bringing Augie to see us."

Destiny ushered them into her home and asked them to remove their shoes. Dylan placed his on a thick rubber mat that held boots and running shoes of both mother and son. Once they stowed their shoes, Destiny grabbed Augie's hands and held him at arm's length. She stared at his face. "You haven't changed at all. I've missed you."

Augie grinned in return. "Your hair is short."

She laughed and tucked an auburn strand behind her ear at the end of her narrow dark-framed glasses, fashionable several years past. Modern trends in eyewear might be out of her financial reach. No doubt, her move to Oregon had set her back.

Destiny likely started her pharmaceutical career from scratch to avoid contact between her current employer and the Salida drugstore. Except for Augie and Nate, everyone else in Salida believed Destiny was dead.

They passed through a dimly lit living room, decorated in mission style with pine vertical lines and worn leather. Probably rental stuff or maybe the place came furnished.

The group stepped through an archway and emerged into a kitchen. A scent like food from the Caribbean spice islands enveloped them. Dylan inhaled and attempted to place the fragrance—ginger, cinnamon, or nutmeg? A plate of cookies sat in the middle of a table.

The oval pedestal table could seat six, but four sturdy chairs clustered at one end to provide intimacy. Augie snatched a cookie from the platter and sniffed. His eyes closed. "Umm, gingersnaps," he said, before taking a bite.

Destiny smiled. "Still your favorite?"

Augie swallowed and nodded vigorously.

Dylan regarded a young boy leaning over a spiral notebook at the end of the table. "This must be Trip?"

Oblivious to the visitors, the youngster sat with his head tipped forward to expose wavy sandy-brown hair. Trip concentrated on entering repeated letters across a lined page. After he completed a row, Trip looked up at his mother. He waited, perhaps for instructions on how to respond to the invasion of their kitchen.

Destiny attempted to engage Trip. "Trip, do you remember Augie? And this is Dylan. He's Augie's buddy. Dylan and Jen were good friends."

Trip turned sable-brown eyes first toward Dylan and then Augie as if deciding whether to respond. He fixed on Dylan. "Hello." Trip ignored Augie and turned back to his school work. While the boy's jawline mirrored his mother's, Dylan recognized Nate's facial symmetry and wide-set eyes.

Destiny tilted her head. "Sweetie, Augie and Dylan have come from Colorado to see us. Why don't you take a break from your homework and talk with them?" She took a seat and pushed the plate of cookies in his direction. Her eyes twinkled with adoration toward her son. "I know it's late, but this is a special occasion. Would you like another cookie?"

Trip took one and stuffed it in his mouth to devour it. He shot a snarl at Augie and gathered the notebook and pencils into his arms before he left the room.

Destiny sighed and shook her head. "I'm truly sorry. He's usually a sweetheart." She stared at the doorway.

Augie reached for another cookie. "He hates me."

Destiny moved around the table to kneel next to Augie. She placed a hand on his leg. "Don't say that. He doesn't hate you."

"He's mad at me for what happened in the woods."

"Augie, what are you talking about?" Dylan asked.

"I had a flat tire. We were late. Trip got scared in the woods."

Augie referred to his role in delivering Trip to Destiny on the day her son disappeared from Salida. Dylan had heard the story from Augie before but had not anticipated Trip's reaction.

As directed, Trip had connected with Augie on a dirt road above the farm hosting a school event. The short drive between their rendezvous point to the Continental Divide Welcome Center, where Destiny waited to take Trip to Oregon, evolved into several hours of wrestling with a jack and a spare tire during an unrelenting downpour.

Destiny turned to Dylan. "It wasn't Augie's fault. Anyone can get a flat, especially on those washboard roads above highway 291. They finally made it to our meeting point, and that's all that matters. I'm afraid Trip had a hard time with the delay. When he got to my car, he was hysterical. He figured if they were late, I might leave. Then he'd have to go back to live with his dad. Trip has difficulty with changes in routines or plans."

She looked at Augie. "He'll get over it eventually. Give him time." Augie nodded. "Tell me about your trip. Did you stop to see some interesting sites?"

Augie responded with, "I slept a lot." He pursed his lips and glanced at the ceiling before he added, "We stopped for hamburgers and milkshakes."

Dylan smiled, pleased that Augie's description did not focus on the boredom of their arduous, two day, nineteen-hour drive. Quiet during their journey, Augie seemed to appreciate Dylan's selection of classic rock music. Aerosmith's "Sweet Emotion" and Van Halen's "Everybody Wants Some" had Augie tapping his thigh and nodding his head in time to the beat.

About an hour before Dylan had planned to stop for the night, he had noticed accommodations with brand names were limited. Family run establishments were the rule, and those were many miles apart. One marquee caught his eye as it bragged of an exceptionally clean hot tub and color TV. What other types of TV were there?

Long after anticipated, Dylan pulled into the lot of an antiquated motel in Idaho with clean bedding and questionable carpets. Taped to the bathroom mirror, a laminated sign instructed occupants to avoid cleaning game in the room. Neither Dylan nor Augie had removed their shoes, except for right before they lifted them from the floor into bed.

That night, Dylan dreamt of Jen's cabin. He typically did not remember dreams, but he remembered this one. There were no people to give context to a story or predicament. Yet the solitude of the familiar place felt welcoming.

Without characters or a storyline, the cabin appeared like a photo frozen in time. Stately pines stood motionless above the roofline, without a flicker of a breeze. Above the trees, he saw the tips of far off mountain peaks, streaked with snow and glowing pink.

When he had awoken, he imagined having visited the place. His nose had tickled from the familiar smell of the decayed aspen leaves. Dylan decided not to mention the dream to Destiny.

Most of the other stops had been for gas, bio-breaks, or food. Dylan turned to Destiny. "I'm afraid we had burgers in the car for nearly every meal. They're cheap and fast. We didn't take time to enjoy the journey, as we were both anxious to get here. Maybe we can spend time looking around on the way back. It depends on how long we're here and when Augie needs to be back at work."

"How long do you hope to stay?"

Dylan shrugged. "Probably a couple of nights, if that's okay with you. Thanks for hosting us."

"It's our pleasure." Destiny gave a seemingly sincere nod. "I need to work tomorrow and the next day, but I might be able to take some time off while you're here."

"We don't want to put you out. I'll bet the cost of living is high here. Since we're not staying at a hotel, maybe we can give you something for your hospitality?"

"There's no need for that. The hospital pays pharmacy techs a decent wage. Now that they've seen how much I know, they give me plenty of hours."

"How long before you're a regular pharmacist again?"

"While I'm hiding out here with Trip, I'll stay a tech. There are fewer license requirements and no paper trail back to my work in Salida." She smiled. "What prompted you to bring Augie out?"

"Partially to fulfill my promise to him." Dylan paused to nod in Augie's direction. "Last summer, I told him I would take him to see you and Trip. But there's another reason. I want to visit a church that played a part in my adoption. It's not far from here, in Groverton."

"Yeah, Groverton's about an hour south." Destiny looked out of the window, presumably in the direction of the town. "What did your parents tell you about the adoption?"

"Nothing at all. They were killed in a car accident a few years ago. I didn't know I was adopted until Nate broke the news to me last summer when I visited Salida."

Destiny sighed. "I'll bet it tickled him to be the one to tell you."

"He might have suspected, but I didn't let on I hadn't known."

"Probably a good thing. No need to boost Nate's ego."

Dylan glanced at the doorway where Trip had made his exit. He hoped the boy had not heard the remark about his father.

Destiny caught his glance and changed the subject. "I've heard adoption agencies can be reluctant to divulge information about birth parents. What's your plan for dealing with the church?"

Dylan conjured a boyish grin. "I'm going to charm the information out of them. How could they resist telling me what I want to know?"

Chapter 11

GROVERTON, OREGON—OCTOBER 12
JOANN WHITED

More comfortable in suits by Chanel than Liz Claiborne, Joann Whited tended to a young couple huddled in the white plastic chairs positioned in front of her desk.

The husband clenched and unclenched his hands. Water dripped from the ends of the wife's dishwater blonde hair and ran down the sleeve of her polyester shirt before it puddled on the floor.

Joann handed each of them a hot cup of coffee and placed sugar and creamer packets on the desk within reach. They held the mugs in both hands to absorb the heat. Joann hoped their shivering would soon cease.

"My husband, James, made a pear tart this morning. It's still warm. Can I cut you a piece?" Joann asked as she smoothed the sides of her navy wool suit. They looked at each other as if wanting the other to agree first. Without waiting for a response, Joann moved with grace to the sideboard to slice the pastry.

The couple cut into their pieces with plastic forks. Joann tucked one side of her trendy brunette bob, colored and highlighted to hide any hint of gray, behind her ear. "I don't think you just stopped by for a piece of my tart. How may I help you?"

The young man cleared his throat, glanced at his wife and then at Joann. "We're from north of Portland and are headed to Eugene. I haven't had much work in the past few months. We heard there's a lot of jobs in construction around Eugene. They're remodeling old homes and building new ones in the suburbs. I'm good with my hands."

"Sounds like a suitable plan. How did you end up in Groverton?"

He sighed.

When his shoulder dropped, his wife straightened and chimed in. "The car started to sputter and rock. Then it stalled, and we couldn't get it started. The guy at the station said it would take a few hundred bucks to repair it. We don't have that kind of money. He suggested we come here and talk with you."

Joann smiled. "It's a perfect suggestion. You're in the right place. Let me see what I can do." She opened the middle desk drawer and removed a binder filled with plastic sheets stuffed with business cards. She slipped on her tortoiseshell readers to scan the cards. "Are you willing to pick fruit for cash? There's a small orchard not far from here. They could take you on short-term."

He said, "We'd do anything to pay for the repairs and get us on our way. Long hours, physical work, no problem." Their heads nodded in unison. Joann picked up the phone and called the farmer, who agreed to give them work.

"Does he have a barn or someplace for us to stay?" The wife asked before Joann concluded the call.

Joann held up a polished, manicured finger and nodded. She had a better idea and finished with the farmer.

She sandwiched the phone between her ear and shoulder and held down the switch hook before making the next call. "I know a gal who might have some room for you. She's a couple of blocks from the Griffith Orchard."

The couple agreed, and Joann arranged for them to stay in the bunk room behind Emily's Day Spa. Emily wouldn't expect them to pay, but Joann suggested they give her a little something before leaving town.

As they bundled up in rain jackets and prepared to reenter the dreary October chill, Joann reminded them of the time for Sunday service, if they had time to worship before moving on to Eugene.

She watched them walk away from the church toward the repair shop to pick up what they would need while in town. Joann loved to help people, and her job in the church office allowed her to feed her passion every day.

Joann settled into her desk chair to enter upcoming events into the electronic church calendar. She heard the buzzer that sounded when the front door opened. Joann stepped outside of her office into the atrium and looked to see who had arrived.

Dylan stood in the center of the vaulted room and looked up at the arched ceiling as he jiggled his umbrella over a gray rug. Joann approached and admired his neatly pressed beige slacks and button-down shirt. At slightly over five feet tall, Joann had to tilt back her head to look him in the eyes, which were startlingly green like new leaves in the spring.

Over one shoulder, he carried a messenger bag made of brushed leather with tarnished brass buckles. She had heard the term *murse* for man-purse and pondered whether he knew the expression.

"You can leave your umbrella in one of the stands by the door," she suggested.

Dylan glanced down at the dark spot growing near his feet. "Sorry about the mess."

"No worries. The rug will dry. Not the first time it's been wet. How may I help you?"

As he deposited the umbrella into a white plastic stand, Dylan looked her over. "Great suit."

She lowered her eyes, and a slight smile curled the edge of her lips. "Not from this season's collection, but my mother raised me to shop with a discerning eye and only buy quality. I'm invincible at the resale stores."

"Classic. It'll last a lifetime." Dylan paused as if thinking about what to say next.

Joann stepped forward to touch his arm. "What brings you here today?"

"My mother is lost, and I hope you can help me find her." Dylan's grin radiated warmth and sincerity. Joann immediately knew that she wanted to help him. She invited him into her office and offered coffee and a piece of the tart.

"No sweets for me," Dylan said as he patted his stomach.

Joann figured he was too fit to worry about his weight but poured two cups of coffee and handed one to Dylan. She rounded the desk and sat facing him.

As Dylan described his journey from Chicago to Salida to Groverton, Joann marveled that Dylan lived in Chicago, a place she had heard of but never seen.

She imagined architectural river tours, shopping the Magnificent Mile, deep-dish pizza, and the din of millions of people creating the city's own heartbeat. Joann believed Chicago would never rest. How different from the sleepy nights in Groverton when both the residents and the town went to bed shortly after the last rays of sun disappeared in the western sky. Not better or worse, just different.

"I have a letter from your sister church in Chicago." Dylan pulled an envelope from his bag and handed it to her.

She scanned the letter and laid it on the desk in front of her. The name seemed familiar. As Joann smoothed the paper with both hands, she looked at Dylan and visually traced his jawline, eye shape, and nose. How might he have looked as a baby?

Joann pointed at the signature. "I know Reverend Lutz from your congregation in Chicago. He visited our church about a year ago."

Dylan gave her a sheepish smile. "He's the minister at my parents' church. They died several years ago, and I haven't attended in a while."

"No worries. There's always time to go back into your congregation."

Dylan nodded in agreement. "I'll keep that in mind." He leaned forward and placed a hand on the front edge of her desk.

She noticed his clean and trimmed nails, a stark juxtaposition to the earthy couple she helped earlier. He continued. "The reason I'm here is to find out more about my birth parents."

"Well, I'm not sure I can help you with that." Joann took a sip of coffee. "You'll need to talk with Reverend Erwin. He's in his office but busy with this week's sermon." Joann lowered her voice to a whisper as if sheltering the Reverend. "He doesn't like to be interrupted when he's at work." Joann knew he imposed a strict *do not disturb rule.*

Dylan slumped, eyes filled with despair. "My parents were probably waiting for the right time to tell me, but they died in a car crash. I know they'd want me to hear about my past. I've come a long way. Couldn't you see if the Reverend might see me? I won't take much of his time."

Torn between protecting her boss's inspiration time and assisting the polite young man, Joann stood to place her half-filled cup on the sideboard.

She looked at him and then the letter, the sole thread of connection to his heritage. Perhaps these circumstances deserved some flexibility. "I could see if he's available to talk with you for a few minutes."

Dylan jumped to his feet. "That'd be super. You'd really be helping me out."

Joann smiled and stood. "I'll check to see if he can spare some time."

Chapter 12

DYLAN COX

Left alone in the office, Dylan stood and paced, too anxious to sit. Perched on the austere white desk, a brass plate identified the church's office manager as Joann Whited. He paused next to the desk chair and admired her blotter's flaming red border around the image of Van Gogh's Starry Night complete with an indigo night sky, spinning clouds, and a dandelion-colored crescent moon. The bold blotter seemed consistent with the sporadically displayed artworks that changed the room's ambiance from pious to boisterous.

Dylan strolled around the office and stopped in front of each piece. Whether a painting, tapestry, or mosaic, each abstract object exposed bold slashes of primary colors, sparingly enhanced with orange, green, and purple secondary hues.

Joann's return with Reverend Erwin interrupted Dylan's close inspection of a painted plaster masterpiece.

Nearly as tall as Dylan, the balding Reverend Erwin took command of the room without a word. He even looked like a minister in dark gray slacks and a starched open-collar shirt. The man dwarfed petite Joann, who walked submissively behind him.

Dylan accepted Erwin's firm handshake and knew the man shook a lot of hands on any given day, undoubtedly a necessary part of his profession.

"Welcome," said the Reverend in a soothing deep-bass. Dylan smiled, convinced everyone with that type of voice should be a minister.

"I'd like to take you to my office, but I'm afraid it's an explosion of books and papers right now. I'm in the middle of research for Sunday's service. Would you mind if we talked in the sanctuary?" Dylan nodded.

The Reverend steered Dylan through the atrium and into the church. The sanctuary's arched ceiling, paneled with varnished knotty pine planks, stood at least twenty feet high in the center. The side walls matched the white theme of Joann's office, with occasional breaks for stunning stained-glass windows with religious narratives.

The nave held two pine lecterns, one more substantial on a raised platform with paneled sides and the other austere with a simple angled top supported by four light wood vertical posts. The lecterns were separated by at least forty feet of pale gray carpet, broken in the center with a white altar adorned with two polished silver vases overflowing with lilies and brilliant red carnations.

Based on the splash of color, Dylan assumed Joann had chosen the flowers. Above the altar hung a massive brass cross, radiantly backlit to give the ambiance of sunshine, which emphasized the symbol's importance in the sanctuary and to the parishioners.

Erwin motioned to a pew at the front, and Dylan took a seat. The Reverend sat next to him. He first paused to face the cross, then angled his body toward Dylan. As Erwin ever so slightly leaned forward, he asked, "How may I help you?"

"First, I'd like to thank you for taking time away from your work to talk with me. What's the topic of your sermon on Sunday?"

The Reverend smiled and slid an arm on the back of the pew. "Facing giants," he said.

"That's a big topic."

Erwin laughed. "You're right, even more because of the times. Whether real or imagined, we face barriers that feel insurmountable—financial pressure, a lunatic boss, uncaring spouse, out-of-control children. Our fear of failing to overcome these giants paralyzes us."

Dylan nodded. "I've been there."

"We all have."

"What guidance do you plan to give?"

"Suppress your fear and face your demons because God will have your back."

"Do you ever feel like you're alone when facing your giants?"

"Sometimes, but my faith helps me through those times."

Dylan nodded. He handed the letter to the Reverend Erwin and filled in the background about his adoptive parents and the quest to find information about his birth parents.

The Reverend listened quietly. He looked from Dylan to the letter. After a moment of thoughtful reflection, he responded. "I'd like to help you, but I'm not sure I can give you any information."

Surprised and disappointed at the finality of Erwin's response, Dylan forced a steady cordial tone. "Why's that?"

Erwin's demeanor never wavered. "Birth records are kept confidential. We don't divulge information unless the parents want to contact the child."

"Is there a way for me to initiate the contact? For instance, could you tell them I'd like to meet?"

The Reverend paused, evidently pondering Dylan's request. "That's not really how it's done here. We've found many birth parents have a different life than the one they had when they decided to give up their child. Unsolicited contact can be traumatic for the birth parent. We try to avoid that type of stress by not initiating the engagement. We feel this policy helps new parents who are considering offering their children for adoption. It puts them at ease to know they retain control over whether or when they're contacted."

"Not so nice for the child who wants to understand his past," Dylan countered.

"I agree with you, but it sounds like you had a rich and rewarding life with your adoptive parents. We hope you can find peace in recalling the meaningful memories of your life, not what birth records might tell you."

Dylan speculated about a child's right to know. "I feel like finding out more about my past is one of my giants. Do you ever tell worshipers to give up the battle?"

"No. Scripture tells us to persevere."

"Any idea on another avenue to look for clues?"

The Reverend's smile radiated devout grace. "If you are meant to find the answer, you will."

Dylan sensed a dead end with the clergyman. He decided there must be another source or lead, but how could he uncover more? He needed to pick up his bag and talk with Joann. Dylan thanked Reverend Erwin and volunteered to walk himself out.

The Reverend rose from the pew. "Thank you for stopping by. I hear my research calling me because I must finish Sunday's sermon today. I'll be out for the next few days."

Before he could stop, Dylan responded with sarcasm. "Spreading the word or feeding the poor?"

Erwin's stoic reply told Dylan he understood the disappointment. "Some of both. A forest fire south of here left several families homeless. I'm going there to help clear debris and meet with people sheltering at the high school."

The Reverend gave Dylan a nod and crossed the sanctuary to exit through a door behind the large lectern. Dylan imagined Erwin's office with piles of authoritative texts concealed behind the door.

After a few moments of reflection, Dylan stood and walked the carpeted aisle toward the back of the sanctuary. At the atrium, he turned to Joann's office and poked his head through the doorway. She looked up from her computer screen and smiled. "I hope the Reverend was able to help you."

"Not quite, but I'm still committed to my search. You've been a great help. Thank you, Ms. Whited."

She stood to shake his extended hand. "Please, call me Joann. Are you sure I can't tempt you with a piece of my husband's tart?"

"No, but thank you." As Dylan shouldered his bag, he asked, "What does your husband do? Besides baking, that is."

With great zeal, Joann pulled a stack of fliers from the corner of the credenza and handed one to Dylan. "He's always been an avid hunter, but lately he's become interested in hunting with cameras rather than a gun."

Dylan took the leaflet as Joann proudly explained how she helped James with the design. The flier announced the annual autumn Sasquatch search party scheduled for October 14. Anyone interested should meet at the front of the church at 7:00 in the evening. For a minimal fee, the event included a discussion about the most recent sightings and several hours in the forest for a chance to view the elusive beast. After the activities, everyone was invited to the church's community room to swap stories over hot beverages and snacks.

"Is this party open to everyone?" asked Dylan.

"Of course. Depending on the weather, there are usually about 20 to 30 people. It's a regular event for most folks, but there are always a few recruits or those who hear about it over the radio. This year, James set up a website for The Groverton Believers Society." Joann tapped the stack of announcements. "There could be a bigger crowd with the extra publicity."

Dylan smiled. "If I come, I'll be sure to get here early to reserve a spot."

Joann's eyes twinkled. "It would be wonderful if you would join in. It's an evening with lots of excitement and mysterious energy."

"Has there ever been an actual sighting?"

Joann scoffed. "No, and I suspect there won't be one this year either, but it's fun to think about the possibility." Joann straightened the fliers with a quick tap along the long edge and returned them to the credenza.

"Thanks." Dylan gestured toward a painting. "I wanted to ask you where you came across this incredible artwork."

Joann glanced around the room with pride in her smile. "I've picked up most of them at art fairs nearby." She pointed toward an oil painting that looked like a deconstructed skyscraper with crimson girders and cobalt rebar snaking up from the wreckage. "This artist is from Portland, but I bought her painting at Groverton's Art Walk weekend last July."

"What about this one?" Dylan pointed to the piece that had captivated him earlier. A collection of textures and colors swirled and intertwined. Shiny brass wires undulated around tubes and ribbons of emerald green and neon orange. At the center sat an amoeba-shaped plaster dome with ragged edges and a tiny raised point in the center.

Joann blushed and lowered her eyes. "I did it," she responded softly as she handed Dylan the leather bag he'd left in her office.

"It's hypnotizing. Does the dome in the center symbolize something? I feel like the whole piece is a tribute to that element."

Dylan saw Joann's blush deepen. He watched her wrestle with divulging the meaning of her artwork. Did it symbolize something too personal to share? She stepped toward Dylan and whispered, "Don't tell Reverend Erwin, but it's a plaster cast of my breast."

Chapter 13

JAMESVILLE, OREGON

By the time Dylan pulled to the curb at Destiny's home, darkness had fallen. The lights from inside the house spilled across the porch from behind sheers. Destiny had given Dylan a key so he could let himself into the house without disturbing anyone. He opened the door to a pastoral sight.

Destiny sat in the middle of the sofa with Augie and Trip on opposite sides. All three stared at a movie playing on a television hanging above the ornate fireplace. Built-in bookcases of quarter-sawn oak framed each side of the hearth. Behind the leaded glass doors, Dylan saw volumes of hardbacked tomes, some literary classics but most about chemistry and drugs, undoubtedly to keep Destiny's pharmacy training up to date. Dylan entered the room and walked to a bookcase to examine one of the framed photos of Destiny and Trip.

Destiny tapped the remote to pause the movie, and Trip groaned. She admonished her son. "You've seen this film a dozen times. I've stopped it for a second." Then she asked Dylan, "How did everything go at the church?"

"Some good and some bad. I can tell you more about it after the movie's over." Dylan set the photo back in place and glanced at the other frames. The pictures were all recently taken as none included Trip as an infant or toddler. Dylan knew Nate forced Destiny to leave Salida in a hurry, probably without time to take memorabilia. He recalled seeing boxes of Trip's toys and family photos tucked away in one of Nate's closets. He was sad that souvenirs of Trip's past were under Nate's control rather than with Destiny, as she would no doubt treasure their sentimental value.

Destiny tapped her watch. "The movie should finish in about twenty minutes. If Augie and Dylan pitch in, dinner can be ready about twenty past that."

"I can help." Dylan settled into one of the leather side chairs. He inhaled deeply to detect any menu revealing scents. His mouth watered as he registered roasting poultry.

Dylan recognized the child appropriate monster movie. By the end, all except one of the mean, scary characters would decide to become friendly monsters. On the verge of being banished, the final holdout would change his mind and opt to join the good guys. Dylan appreciated the message and questioned why real life never seemed to emulate the cartoon. In his line of work, Dylan saw many evil people with opportunities to change. Usually, bad characters stayed bad.

Destiny shut off the television, turned to Trip, and said, "Upstairs to work on your homework until I call you for dinner." Trip nodded and retreated.

A keen delegator, Destiny offered a vegetable peeler and carrots to Augie. Dylan received a teakwood cutting board, paring knife, and a pile of pre-washed salad fixings. Destiny basted the oven roasted chicken.

"So what happened at the church?" she asked.

After Dylan ripped up mixed greens into bite-size pieces, he stabbed a knife into a vine ripened tomato. "They may have information but aren't willing to give it to me unless my birth parents initiate the request."

Destiny closed the oven door and rested her hands on her hips. She asked, "Can't the church contact them to see if they want to meet you?"

"Nope. It's all on the parents, and they haven't indicated an interest."

After she retrieved a bowl of cream cheese frosting from the fridge, Destiny troweled the topping on a naked carrot cake. She said, "Well, that kind of sucks. There could be a million reasons for them not to initiate contact. What if they don't realize meeting is an option? What if they're out of the picture or assume you are?"

Dylan looked up from the board, his knife poised above an English cucumber. "Meaning dead?"

"I wasn't going to say it, but yes."

"Reverend Erwin didn't seem to think that mattered." Dylan sliced the cucumber into rough cut pieces. "His assistant, Joann Whited, didn't help much but wanted to feed me fresh pear tart. She's quite a character. I'm not sure if she always colors between the lines."

"What does that mean?" asked Augie as he placed the carrot peeler in the sink.

Softening, Dylan smiled. He transferred Augie's carrots onto the board for slicing. Destiny filled a pot with water and set it on the stove to boil. Dylan said, "I suspect she genuinely wants to help but is bound by the protocol implemented by Reverend Erwin."

"What does that have to do with coloring?" Augie pressed.

"Oh, that. I meant Joann doesn't always follow the rules. She lets her sense of right and wrong dictate her decisions."

"Joann sounds nice. Sometimes nice people can be helpful. Especially if they do the right thing instead of what the rules say," Augie offered.

Dylan considered the significance of Augie's statement as he scraped the sliced carrots into the pot. "You know, Augie, you're right. She *is* a nice person." Joann probably had access to all the church's records. He needed to talk with her without Reverend Erwin hovering nearby. If Erwin planned to be away from the church with missionary work for a couple of days, the morning would be the perfect time to revisit the church.

Destiny interrupted his thoughts. "I know a pharmacist who works a couple of days a week at Groverton's grocery store pharmacy. Would you like me to call him and see what I can find out about the church secretary?"

Dylan agreed. After all, Reverend Erwin encouraged him to persevere against his giant.

Chapter 14

SALIDA, COLORADO
NATE STEWART

Nate slipped the sleeves of a camel sport coat over his black silk shirt. Maybe a bit warm for a crowded room, but the jacket was new, and he wanted everyone to assume he was a big player at the event. Once a month, the Steamplant hosted a charity night called Salida Soup. Each attendee paid a modest cash contribution and brought food for a potluck.

During dinner, three community members gave five-minute pitches for projects to benefit the local area. At the end of the event, donors voted for the venture they deemed most worthy. The project with the most votes took the entire pot. Nate liked the idea of winner takes all.

Officer Merle Hodges insisted Nate attend on this particular night because Merle and his son Erle were making a pitch for funds. As lead members of Salida's Sasquatch believer group, the men hoped to take home the prize.

As Nate walked toward the event center, he heard the river. He crossed into the green space separating the Steamplant from the rocky shore. While he watched the tumbling current, Nate formulated a plan.

Once satisfied with an approach, he meandered back to the Steamplant by weaving through the display of iron yard art at the front of the building.

Nate stepped inside the lobby. He paid the required donation and picked up three proposal fliers. Nate was flipping through the leaflets when someone slugged his shoulder. He turned to see Merle Hodges still dressed in his Salida Police uniform.

Merle said, "Stiff competition for us tonight."

"You trying to intimidate voters with your get-up?" Nate gave him a once over.

Merle looked down the front of his snug navy shirt and placed his hands on soft hips slightly above his jam-packed duty belt. He said, "Nah. I just got off work. Are you sure the uniform could draw more votes?"

Nate delivered a sarcastic grin and held up his hands in surrender. "You've got mine, Officer."

"Very funny. I don't want anyone to assume I'm using my uniform to influence voters."

"I think you're safe. With all the charity work you do, no one's going to accuse you of using your uniform to sway the vote. It's not like anyone here doesn't already know you're a cop."

"Good point." Merle glanced at the crowd. "Have you seen Erle? He walked over from the Courthouse. I need to catch up with him before the presentations start."

"I just got here and haven't seen him."

Merle grabbed Nate by the lapels and drew him close. A hint of a smile ticked at the corner of Merle's lips. "Remember to ignore the roller derby gals' presentation. If you can't handle it, close your eyes."

Nate pulled back and laughed. "I heard *MillyTant* and *SuperMax* are doing their presentation in full gear. Should be provocative. Can't wait to see them climb up to the stage on their skates. Why are they asking for money? New fishnets?"

Merle scoffed. "The team wants to host an outreach training day for the high school girls."

"I'd vote for that presentation if they let me come to watch. I'd even volunteer to be their videographer."

Merle scanned the vicinity as if looking to see if anyone could overhear their conversation. "When did you become such a pervert?"

Nate threw back his head and laughed. Merle continued. "I'm not joking about needing your vote. I know you won't vote for the senior swimming scholarships, but the roller derby girls are a risk."

"Don't be so paranoid. Women never get in the way of what I want. I'm here to support your cause." Nate's definitiveness appeared to calm

Merle. He patted Nate on the arm and headed off to look for his son.

After he dropped his potluck contribution, a regifted box of Girl Scout cookies, at the food line, Nate wandered toward the bar. He paused short of the line to tap the shoulder of Mayor Rhodes, a gnome of a man with an iridescent silver combover and a patch of facial hair hiding his double chin. "David Rhodes, do you have an interest in this event, or are you out campaigning?" Nate asked.

The mayor turned away from his interrupted conversation and gave a cold stare. After he recognized Nate, the mayor broke into a sincere grin. Nate guessed the warm reception stemmed from recently offering to host a 'Reelect Rhodes' gala at the gallery. As a local business owner, Nate understood the power of keeping politicians happy.

"Out pressing the flesh at a great cause," the mayor said as he pumped Nate's hand. "I didn't see your name on the presenter's list. Are you supporting someone specific?"

"They're all deserving, but I'm here to root for the Hodges."

"The Bigfoot presentation?"

Nate nodded. "Merle told me they could use some micro-funding to offset last-minute expenses for the Sasquatch conference next month."

"It surprised me that they came here. I thought the organizers finalized plans a long time ago."

"You're right about the basics. But at the last minute, a big shot researcher from Texas offered to host one of the workshops. He'll only come if the organizers agreed to pick up his travel expenses. There are still a few tickets available, and this speaker could be the draw they need to fill the conference."

Mayor Rhodes rubbed his white goatee. "A full conference would increase room rentals and restaurant sales. Merchants wouldn't mind more foot traffic in November. The shoulder season between hiking and skiing could use any boost—especially the weekend before Thanksgiving. That's one of our lowest sales tax revenue weeks."

Nate nodded. "I hope you'll vote for their presentation."

"They face tough competition from the Senior Swimmers and the Salida Rollers. But, I'll keep an open mind."

The mayor turned to leave, but Nate grabbed his arm. "One more thing. You grew up in Salida. Did you know Jen Rickard's father?"

"Robert Rickard? There's a blast from the past. He's been dead for at least five years." The mayor raised his eyes toward the ceiling, apparently to think. "If I recall correctly, he was quite a character, a real woodsy-type, and opposed to any development in the county." He met Nate's gaze and added, "Shame what happened to his daughter last summer."

Nate hung his head in mock melancholy. "Yeah. Jen and Trip were close. It'll crush him to find out about her attack."

"How's the investigation into Trip's disappearance coming along?"

"No major developments, but I can't vouch for the abilities of our law enforcement community."

The mayor stepped back, hands raised in defense. "Sorry, Nate. I'll have to disagree with you on that one. The police, sheriff, and forest service departments are spread thin, but they get the job done. Great outreach programs, too."

Nate backpedaled, "You're right. But I'm frustrated there's been no progress on finding Trip. He's been gone for five months now." Nate paused, then continued. "But back to Robert Rickard—what can you tell me about him?"

"What's your interest?"

Nate took a breath to spin the story he'd formulated on the walk to the Steamplant. "Jen had some of Trip's stuff up at her cabin, mainly clothes and books. I don't want his belongings to end up in an estate sale or the trash." Rhodes nodded in understanding as Nate continued. "I've thought about going out there to find them, but I'm worried. If her dad was a nut case, he might have boobytrapped the place."

Mayor Rhodes cocked his head, eyes narrowed. Nate hoped Rhodes would shed more light on Rickard's frame of mind. "Never thought of him as a vigilante. Maybe an environmentalist or preservationist."

"Sounds like he didn't trust the government to take care of the land. Do you think he had faith in other establishments?"

"Like what, for instance?"

"Oh, I don't know. Churches, schools, banks—stuff like that."

"I never saw Rickard at *our* church, but he could have belonged to one of two dozen others in town. Jen wasn't home-schooled. So he must have been okay with public schools. Based on his politics, maybe Rickard would be the type to bury a box of cash in the yard. But he certainly didn't amass a fortune working construction." He gave Nate a brisk nod. "If you're concerned about going to the cabin alone, you should take Sheriff Austin with you."

"Great idea. I'll think about it." Nate knew he would never make the call. Valuables hidden at Jen's cabin could go a long way to settle her debt. She owed him big time.

The lights flickered to call donors into the presentation hall. As Nate followed the crowd, he glanced at the front door right when Cynthia entered. She clung to the arm of the very married owner of the *Salida Sentinel.*

Chapter 15

JAMESVILLE, OREGON—OCTOBER 13
DYLAN COX

Dylan wanted to get an early start driving back to Groverton. He woke before dawn, but Destiny beat him to the kitchen. The smell of freshly brewed coffee filled the air, and Dylan poured himself a cup while Destiny prepared breakfast.

Placemats of natural fibers and pristine white china sat on the table. Next to Trip's spot lay a blue plastic box divided into compartments. A transparent lid snapped over the top. Dylan could see a hearty half sandwich in the largest section. The others held celery sticks, trail mix, and a slice of last night's carrot cake. Must be Trip's lunch.

Dylan recalled his own Fievel lunchbox from the second grade, decorated with a brave cartoon mouse who wore a huge floppy hat and Cossack costume. The Fievel stories repeated the same theme. Early on, the young mouse became separated from his parents. As the tale progressed, the mouse faced nearly insurmountable obstacles but finally reconnected with his folks.

Dylan chuckled as he recalled how his mother had lovingly packed his lunch into a box portraying the story of a boy and his missing family. He ran a finger across the top of Trip's lunchbox and considered whether the irony ever crossed his mother's mind.

"What?" Destiny asked as she drew the container away from Dylan and slipped it into Trip's backpack.

Dylan shrugged. "I was thinking about why my parents kept my adoption a secret. It baffles me."

"Try not to think badly of them. I'd like to believe parents do the best they can based under the circumstances at the time. It's easy to second-guess someone's motives with hindsight, but you'll never really know the truth about why they decided to do what they did. Try to give them the benefit of the doubt."

"I'll try to cut them some slack on why they didn't tell me, but I still want to know who my real parents are."

"Fair enough." She sunk a serving spoon into a tub of yogurt and set it on the table. "Augie mentioned you stayed at Jen's cabin while you were in Salida. How did that go for you?"

"Being close to where the attack took place was tough, but the cabin made me feel near her." He added cream to his coffee from a pitcher shaped like a tiny cow. "I had a couple of weird experiences at the cabin. I went for a run one morning and could swear something followed me along the road. The other time happened at night when I heard strange sounds while gathering firewood."

Destiny raised an eyebrow as she opened the juice and filled the glasses. "Any ideas?"

"Absolutely. I have an overactive imagination." Dylan smiled. "It's hard not to think whatever took Jen is still near the cabin, but I'm sure it's long gone." Dylan sighed. "A part of me feels like I could have saved her if I'd been there that night."

"Don't blame yourself. Animals are unpredictable." Destiny turned toward Dylan as the pain of loss creased her face. "You know Jen cared a lot about you."

"She didn't keep me close to track my investigation into Trip's disappearance?" Dylan stared at her eyes to assess any reaction.

Destiny smiled and wiped her brow. "Well, watching you may have been her initial motivation, but she fessed up to me that she'd fallen for you. Something about all of your boyish charm and wit." Her grin widened as she added, "Personally, I don't see it. But she always had a strange taste in men."

Dylan returned her smile as he appreciated her gibe. "Thanks for letting me know she cared. It means a lot to me. We didn't have time to talk about where our relationship was headed. Before her, I never dated a woman who could speak to me in a way I understood. She seemed upfront and honest. When I discovered she'd kept the circumstances of Trip's disappearance from me, it made me think the entire relationship might have been a sham."

"I know she returned your feelings. It tore her up to lie about Trip's whereabouts. The night of her attack, she asked me to let you in on the real story. At the time, I told her not to tell you. I was afraid you'd tell Nate, and he would come here to claim Trip."

Dylan nodded in understanding. "If I were in your shoes, I wouldn't have trusted a stranger with that information either, particularly someone related to Nate."

"Since you were adopted, you aren't Nate's blood relative."

Dylan smiled. "Well, that's a silver lining for me." He sipped his coffee. "When did you start distrusting Nate?"

"Right after we moved to Salida, I became friends with a guy from the Sheriff's office. He'd stop in the pharmacy nearly every day to talk with me. One day, he asked if I'd meet him for coffee after my shift. I felt sure Nate would object, but the officer seemed harmless. So I agreed to meet him at Café Dawn. I got there, and he already had a table outside, far from the other customers. When I joined him, he seemed nervous. It made me think I'd made a mistake to meet him." Destiny paused, deep in thought.

"Did he come on to you?"

She gave Dylan a dismissive wave. "Not at all. The officer told me a few times a week he drives around to all the teenagers' parking spots to break up the action. He wouldn't knock on their windows, but he'd pull up behind them and shine his spotlight into their cars until they'd move on."

Dylan sighed and shook his head. "Don't tell me. He did this to Nate's car?"

Destiny placed her hands on her cheeks in embarrassment. "Yeah. The officer told me he was lighting up Nate's car a couple times a week. He wanted me to know."

"What did you do? Did you confront Nate?"

"I tried to, but it didn't work out well. That evening, I started by saying I met an officer for coffee. That's as far as I got because Nate went off on me. He accused me of being attracted to the cop. My meeting was a date and a precursor to an affair. He threw a plate at me.”

“He hit you?”

Destiny smirked. “No. He knew how to throw things in my general direction for maximum effect. It smashed against a cabinet next to my head. I found china splinters for months afterward. I never got up the courage to bring it up again.”

She hesitated and poured herself a cup of coffee. “I didn’t like the circumstances of how Nate forced me to leave Salida, but I’m lucky to have escaped him.” Destiny glanced toward the hallway leading to the stairs. “Trip’s lucky to be away from him, too.”

Dylan nodded in agreement. “You’re right. Things would have only gotten worse. Nate’s only interested in himself and what others can do for him. He doesn’t have much time for thinking about a six-year-old.”

“Seven.”

“When?”

“June fifth.”

Dylan raised an eyebrow. “That’s when I arrived in Salida. Nate and I had dinner. He didn’t mention Trip’s birthday.”

“You’d think it should be foremost on his mind. But, I’m not sure he’d remember it even if Trip lived with him.”

Destiny turned to the pot of hot cereal and absentmindedly ladled out spoonfuls of oatmeal into bowls. “I nearly forgot to tell you something. After you went to bed, I heard back from my colleague in Groverton. He knows Joann Whited and her husband. Did you know he believes in Bigfoot?”

Dylan chuckled. “Joann told me he’s organizing a Bigfoot search tomorrow night near Groverton. I assumed all the Sasquatch groupies were back in Colorado.” He thought about the event. Perhaps he might be able to work this angle with James to gain Joann’s assistance.

Destiny rested her palm on the counter next to the stove and stared off into space. She smiled. “I saw advertisements for meetings in Salida. Frankly, I never really paid much attention to it.”

“Some people in Salida blamed Bigfoot for Trip’s disappearance.”

“Yes, Jen mentioned it. While I thought it was silly, I appreciated the diversion to sidetrack an investigation or cover any clues I had left behind."

"Not everyone believed Bigfoot was a legitimate suspect. Despite that, you covered your tracks well. I don't think it's crossed Nate's mind that Trip might be here." Dylan looked past the archway and toward Trip's upstairs room to confirm the youngster was not within earshot. Still, he lowered his voice to finish the thought. "Finding Trip is not Nate's highest priority."

Destiny gazed downward, either in shame for herself or disgust at Nate. Too distraught about the situation to confirm, Dylan spoke gently and hoped to comfort her. "We all know Trip's better off with you. Nate only thinks about himself. That's no environment for a child."

"In my heart, I know you're right, but I'm guilty about the lies and secrecy. I feel like we're on the run and won't be able to live in peace." She looked at Dylan with tension in her doe-like eyes. "Do you think he'll come looking for us?"

Dylan considered her question carefully, as he did not want to jump to an immediate conclusion. He had worked cases where an alienated parent abducted his or her children. In Dylan's experience, the noncustodial parent rationalized kidnapping the child by citing a threat of abuse by the other parent. Trip's circumstances were typical.

"I can't imagine he'd come to confront you. He enjoys the attention of being a celebrity in Salida. Sorry if I'm telling you more than you want to know, but he revels in being a single man."

"I figured as much and hope it satisfies his need for power and praise. But I worry he'll look for us if he gets bored or if the fame wears off."

"I believe Nate's primary reason to hire me was to keep the pressure on the Sheriff's office. Sheriff Austin had stopped searching for Trip because the evidence pointed toward a predator, like a mountain lion. When they called off the search, folks in Salida went back to their routines. Nate felt his spotlight fade and invited me to rejuvenate public interest. Did you know he tracks how often his name appears in the *Salida Sentinel*? Every reference elevates his mood."

Destiny sighed. "Somehow both predictable and sad."

"I'm certain he'll think of new ways to make himself the center of attention in Salida. He's got the gallery and studio to keep him busy, and that's when he's not chasing women. Hunting you down would be too much work."

"I hated to deceive everyone in Salida, but it seemed the best way to make a clean break."

"You should know that Sheriff Austin is aware you're alive and Trip's here. He moved the case to inactive after your folks told him about you and Nate colluding on your suicide story. The Sheriff has verified that an elementary school out here registered Nate Stewart III for first grade last May. As far as I know, Austin has told no one else."

Destiny leaned against the counter. Her lips drew into a firm line. "He'll keep my secret."

"That's my impression, too. But how are you so sure?"

Destiny turned to face Dylan but said nothing.

"Is he the officer who used to follow Nate and break up his parking dates?"

She nodded and moved forward to hug Dylan. "Thank you for coming here." Destiny broke the embrace, as Augie and Trip arrived in the kitchen.

Dylan turned to Augie. "Trip's in school and Destiny's at work today. Want to take a ride with me?"

"Yeah," Augie responded without questions about the destination or the purpose. For Augie, it seemed sufficient to be asked along. Dylan admired his easy-going friend.

Chapter 16

GROVERTON, OREGON
JOANN WHITED

Joann hauled the third file box of archived documents from the basement storage room and placed them on her shelf-paper protected credenza. She examined her hands. Thankfully, no broken nails.

Joann brushed the dust from the front of her designer wrap dress and paused to rub the exceptional fabric between her thumb and fingers. She smiled. Joann refused to become inattentive to fashion, a plague affecting other women her age.

After she wiped the dust-coated lid with a moist rag, Joann pulled the inventory from the box. She laid the sheet on top of the others and moved to her desk. She scanned each list. The cartons contained a mishmash of folders from a variety of dates and topics—annual picnic menus, board meeting agendas, Sunday morning greeter schedules, and financial information. How did the records get in such a state?

Joann recalled Reverend Erwin's dismay when he first saw the dozen overstuffed cabinets lining the wall outside of his office. He knew Joann's full schedule could not accommodate a significant file purge. So Erwin suggested she ask for volunteers from the congregation to organize the records for storage.

In response to Joann's plea in the weekly bulletin, three good-hearted homemakers came to the rescue. For a full week, Joann managed the well-meaning but inept crew who sought fresh baked goods and time away from the house. First, she hovered over their work but finally yielded to their erratic clerical skills.

"Sometimes, you get what you pay for," muttered Joann. She ran a finger methodically down the lists and paused at each entry that might be relevant to her search. Finally, Joann spotted the needed folders. She crossed to the boxes to read the file tabs and compare the names to the inventory. Joann expected errors and missing folders but sighed with satisfaction as each entry matched a file. She pulled two beige folders from the boxes and placed them on the corner of her desk.

Joann smiled. Her efficiency doubled on days Reverend Erwin went out. While she appreciated his requests and the increased activity around the church when he was in, his mission work gave her uninterrupted time to catch up on tasks she could not address when the Reverend had her at his beck and call.

After she had settled back into her desk chair, Joann opened the first folder and removed a paperclipped Polaroid snapshot of a newborn. She brought the photo close to her face and rubbed the image of the baby's cheek. "There you are. I knew I recognized your name."

Startled by the front door buzzer, Joann swept the papers and photo back into the folder. She slipped the files into the center desk drawer and left the office. As Joann approached the two men in the atrium, she extended a hand to the familiar visitor. "Dylan Cox. It's so nice to see you again."

"I'm surprised you remember my name. You must meet dozens of people every day." He shook her hand as she took stock of his attire. Dylan wore neatly pressed cotton slacks and a button-down shirt with an open collar. She preferred this type of apparel to the more typical jeans and T-shirts, but not everyone could afford to dress sharply.

Interestingly, when people in need rifled through the bins of clothing stored at the church, jeans and T-shirts were the first selected. Numerous pairs of dress slacks and collared shirts remained in the containers for years. Perhaps the poor liked a more relaxed appearance. Or maybe they wanted casual garments that did not need maintenance, like ironing or costly dry cleaning.

Dylan continued. "I hoped you'd be around today. I want to introduce you to my friend, Augie."

Augie turned with a start at the mention of his name. He looked at Dylan as if checking to be sure he should engage. Dylan nodded, and Augie offered a hand to Joann.

She gave him her friendliest smile and encircled his hand with both of hers to let him know she welcomed him. Ever so slightly, his arm jerked at her contact. *He doesn't like that.* Out of respect for his preferences, she would be careful to avoid touching him in the future.

She gave her attention to Dylan. He said, "I have a few more questions about my birth parents."

"Didn't Reverend Erwin give you the information you came for?" Joann's response reflected genuine distress, but she knew the policies and suspected the Reverend had not provided Dylan with any meaningful information.

"I'll be honest with you, Joann. He told me the church has a strict policy. Only birth parents can initiate contact with their forsaken children, and not the other way around."

She winced at the term *forsaken*. First abandoned by his parents and now the church. "I don't know if I can help at all, but please come in for a visit. I have some freshly baked cinnamon rolls in my office. James' pastries are unrivaled."

Dylan looked dejected but agreed to join her for rolls and a talk. Joann asked them to take a seat while she moved behind her desk to secure the center drawer with her thumbs.

She stepped to the coffee service and started to fill three cups. "I assume you both drink coffee?"

"Nope," Augie responded.

Joann placed a Styrofoam cup on her desk in front of Dylan. "What may I get for you, Augie? I have hot water and can make tea or mix you a cup of hot cocoa?"

Augie thought before he answered. "Cocoa, please."

"Coming right up."

She gave the hot chocolate to Augie and turned to collect cinnamon rolls. "I had a suspicion I'd see you again."

Dylan raised an eyebrow. "Why is that?"

"Sometimes, I sense these things. I didn't believe you'd concluded your business here." Joann handed each of them a paper plate topped with a bun oozing with the scent of cinnamon and covered with gooey icing. Dylan eagerly accepted one, but Augie looked tentative and turned the plate in several directions before he rested it on his thigh. Joann continued, "Tell me about your life in Chicago. It's exciting to hear about big cities. Do you go to shows? Have you lived there your whole life?"

He told her about living in his boyhood home, a typical Chicago Greystone, a short train ride from the skyscrapers and lakefront that characterize the iconic city. He enjoyed the city's offerings with a continual stream of free concerts, museum days, a zoo, and parks hosting cultural events.

"It's nice you still live in your family home. I recall you mentioned your parents have passed. I'm so sorry for your loss," Joann offered with a solemn expression. "Seems like they died young. You must miss them very much."

"They were great parents who always encouraged me in school and with sports. They provided for my education, gave me a beautiful home, and showed their love every day. I only recently found out I'm adopted. I wouldn't have guessed. They never treated me like I wasn't their own."

Dylan's description warmed Joann's heart. Family placement did not always work out so well. He and his parents were fortunate.

She turned to Augie and asked about where he was from and how he and Dylan had become friends. After a few one-word responses, she decided the art of polite conversation remained elusive for Augie and refrained from questioning him.

When Dylan turned the conversation to Joann, she shared that she had lived in Groverton for most of her life. She and James, her husband of forty-two years, met shortly after high school in Portland. He found work in the timber industry nearby, and they bought a newly built little house a few blocks from the church. Diligent about visiting new residents, the pastor introduced himself to the Whiteds and invited them to join.

"Our minister moved the congregation in ways I'd never seen before. Only a few months after we'd signed up, he convinced me to work for the church. At first, I signed on for a few hours each week to give me time to set up our new home." She paused. "Before I knew it, I was working full-time and enjoying every minute of it."

"Sounds like rewarding work. Do you and James have children?"

Her eyes lowered as she said, "God did not have a plan for giving us children. So I fill my days with the joy of helping others."

Without missing a beat, Dylan said, "James is a lucky man."

Joann blushed. "Oh, I don't know about that. I have my days. He's a good man, and we feel blessed with excellent health and a wonderful circle of friends. We couldn't ask for more." She smiled. "James retired two years ago. He'd like me to be around the house more, but I'm not ready to stop working."

Dylan nodded. "You'll know when you're ready. There'll come a day when someone walks in here with a problem. Instead of wanting to help, you'll think to yourself, 'I really don't care.' That will be the day you need to retire."

Joann laughed. "I doubt that day will ever come. It makes me feel good to help people in any way I can."

She set her coffee cup on the blotter and absentmindedly ran a stir stick around the circumference. Did she dare to help him? Joann raised her head. "Would you like to take Augie on a tour of the sanctuary?"

"Wouldn't you like to show us around?" Dylan asked.

"No, I should get back to work. But I have a map of the sanctuary and descriptions from the artist about the stained-glass windows." She pulled a folded brochure from a rubber-banded stack next to her inbox and handed it to Dylan. "The map's on the front side, and the window descriptions are on the back. Take time to appreciate each one. They're great works of art. Don't worry about your coats and bags. You can leave them here, and I'll watch them while you're looking around."

Joann stood to usher them toward the office door and into the sanctuary, confident in her plan to ease Dylan's distress.

Chapter 17

DYLAN COX

Dylan held the window plan in one hand and read the introduction as they entered the sanctuary. The church commissioned an award-winning glass painter from Santa Fe, New Mexico, to create fifteen windows. Each scene included stories based on the Apostles or the Holy Family, designed to educate and inspire.

As they stood before the first panel, Dylan read aloud the story of Peter. "This scene depicts Peter as he held his ailing mother-in-law. Jesus approaches from behind to come and heal her. Notice the sea scene in the background with men fishing, as this was Peter's vocation before he followed Jesus."

"That's Peter?" Augie pointed toward a man kneeling on the ground with crimson robes. Portrayed with an older woman in his arms, Peter glanced over his shoulder at the approaching Savior.

"What do you think?" Dylan expected a brief reply.

"I think Peter is sad she's sick, but he also has hope."

Surprised at Augie's interpretation, Dylan asked, "Why do you think so?"

Augie turned to Dylan. "You can see it in his eyes."

Dylan looked at the panel and attempted to see the emotions visible to Augie but failed. Maybe people who lacked mainstream skills were enhanced in other ways. Augie's sensitivity to facial expressions seemed extraordinary.

After they reviewed the remaining windows, Dylan and Augie walked toward the front and sat in the first pew. A faint hum from the lights provided the only sound in the room.

Dylan sat quietly, but Augie soon started to drum his heels on the floor and tap his thumb on a thigh. Dylan touched his friend's shirt pocket holding an MP3 player, a gift from one of Salida's librarians. Augie understood the hint. He turned it on and plugged in his earbuds. The familiar sounds calmed him immediately. Dylan could faintly hear Michael Jackson's *Thriller* playing as Augie nodded his head to the beat of the music.

Dylan imagined Joann as she worked in her office while the Reverend ministered to the needy. What might compel her to divulge information about his birth parents? If not her directly, maybe James could help. Would a relationship with her husband be enough to tempt her to bend protocol? Worth a shot, but he wouldn't be in the area long enough to develop a strong relationship. The Sasquatch event could be a start.

After a few songs, Augie started to fidget. Dylan rose to walk back to Joann's office. As they picked up their jackets, Dylan gave a final appeal. "I don't suppose there is any way you can look up any of the old documents about my birth?"

Joann's cheerful expression faded. "If Reverend Erwin authorized me to look it up, I'd be happy to do it. Unless he agrees, I can't. I'm so sorry."

"That's okay. I understand there are procedures. Hey, I'll see you tomorrow night, though. I look forward to meeting your husband." Dylan paused to smile, "And maybe a Bigfoot."

As they walked to the car, Augie asked about lunch. Dylan recalled the paper plate and untouched cinnamon roll Augie had discarded before they went into the sanctuary. *Must have looked a little too alien for Augie's tastes*, concluded Dylan. He realized the time and asked, "How 'bout a burger?"

Dylan pulled into the lot of the nearest Burgerville. He placed both hands on the wheel and sighed. Augie patiently sat as if waiting for Dylan to make a move before he opened the door. Destiny's passion for wholesome foods crossed his mind. Did his inclination toward convenience harm his health? What about setting a bad example for Augie?

Before he checked whether the place had healthy alternatives, Dylan slapped the steering wheel and restarted the car. "Let's find a local restaurant with a slower pace that might offer more options. Destiny would be proud of us, right?" He smiled and looked toward Augie.

Augie grinned and nodded. "Yeah."

Not far down the highway, they found a small family restaurant serving meals with ingredients identified as *locally sourced*. They found an empty table in the center row as a young waitress in black jeans and a navy T-shirt approached. The name of the restaurant was stenciled above her left breast in an arc of white letters. A plastic nametag was pinned to the other side of her chest. A mosaic of tattoos spilled down each arm to right above her wrists.

"May I take your order?" she asked. The black lacquer nail of her index finger tapped the screen of her electronic tablet positioned to input their order. Dylan tilted his head. Something seemed wrong. He expected the ebony-haired waitress to hold a lined pad of guest checks and a ballpoint pen—not a tablet.

In an attempt to break his depressed mood, Dylan toyed with the waitress. "Kayla, can you bring us lunch *and* some sunshine?"

She glanced over her shoulder and past the booths next to the window into the gloomy day. "You're not from around here. Are you?"

Dylan chuckled. "Pretty obvious, I guess. We're passing through."

After more good-natured banter about the dreary Oregon weather, they ordered lunch. Augie asked for a hamburger. *No changing his mind once he decides,* figured Dylan. Dylan opted for a spinach salad with hot bacon dressing. Not exactly health food, but perhaps the spinach would negate the ill effects of the bacon fat.

"Bacon should be its own food group," he said to Kayla.

"I know, right? My mom's a nurse, and she says the focus on fatty foods is overdone. Low cholesterol is actually worse than high cholesterol, but the pharmaceutical companies don't make a drug for low cholesterol, so there's no emphasis on that."

"Well then double down on the bacon bits," Dylan said, with a wave of his hand.

While they waited for their food, Dylan pulled open his bag to retrieve the letter from his folks' church. He glanced at Augie. "Why do I keep re-

reading the letter? It doesn't tell me anything new."

Augie smiled. "It's a piece of paper. It doesn't talk."

Dylan started to respond with a smart remark, but something in his bag distracted him. A yellowed document lay next to the letter from his parents' church. "This wasn't here before," he said.

Dylan pulled a frail, folded certificate from his bag. He held one corner to secure it to the tabletop and smoothed it with the side of his hand.

"I don't believe it." Dylan's eyes widened with surprise. Augie waited patiently for Dylan's explanation. "Joann must have slipped this in my bag while we were in the sanctuary." He paused to lean over the table and kiss the paper. "It's not a real birth certificate, but something like an intake document from when my birth parents brought me to the church."

Dylan looked up from the page. "It lists my real parents' names." Dylan scrutinized the certificate further. "Well, maybe it's their names. It only has one word on the lines where each name should be listed."

"What are their names?" asked Augie.

"*Hekewi* is listed for Mother and *Desyelni* for Father."

Augie scrunched his nose as if sensing a pungent odor. "Those are funny names."

Dylan smiled and nodded in agreement. "Yes, they are. Based on where we are, maybe they're Native American names." Dylan's mind raced. How could he find out more about his mysterious parents?

Shortly, Kayla returned with their food. When Augie received his burger, he promptly lifted the top and removed the pickles and lettuce. Augie laid the garnishes at the far end of his plate and compressed the bun with a palm before he lifted the squashed sandwich to take a bite.

As she watched Augie's ritual, Kayla said, "Ketchup and mustard are on the table. Do you need anything else?"

Before she could leave, Dylan slid the certificate to the edge of the table. He pointed at the lines identifying his parents. "Hang on a minute. Have you ever heard of names like this?"

She picked up the document and narrowed her eyes to scrutinize the text more closely. Kayla tucked an errant strand of coal-black hair behind her ear and asked, "What is this?"

"It's part of my birth record. It seems like the church listed my parents with only one name for each. Any ideas?"

She handed the paper back to Dylan with a shrug. "Not a clue. There are several reservations around here. Maybe your parents were Indians? I have Indian friends, but they all have typical first and last names." Kayla thought for a moment and added, "Someone told me once that certain tribes have regular names to use around us and different names to use when they are not around us."

"Us?" Dylan assumed the locals would have a more inclusive view of the area's Native American population.

Kayla backpedaled. "I only meant they use *mainstream* names in school or business, like a name for when they're away from the reservation. Within their own culture, they may have names that are more traditional for their tribe. I've heard one person can have a bunch of Indian names."

Dylan leaned forward with interest. "How so?"

"Some tribes give children new names as they grow older. Others call people by nicknames, which can change over the years. Look, I don't know if anything I've heard is true or if it's the same for all groups. It's what people have told me. You should find someone who knows what they're talking about."

Dylan told her he appreciated her insights. As they finished lunch in silence, Dylan explored potential options. Should he return to the church and ask Joann about the certificate? Would the county offices have information about the names or an actual birth certificate? If Hekewi and Desyelni were Native American names, then conventional records of these people might not exist.

He chewed the last forkful of bacon-coated spinach. Dylan looked at Augie. "Where to now?"

"You should find someone who knows your parents."

"Brilliant idea." Dylan pulled out his cell phone. He connected to the restaurant's internet service and searched for the closest college with a program in Native American studies.

"Bingo," he said with a nod toward the register by the door.

Chapter 18

EDBURY, OREGON

After they drove through an hour of drizzle, Dylan and Augie entered a campus dotted with a mixture of Gothic buildings, modern low-rise structures, and green space. Students, protected from the elements by Gore-Tex jackets and waterproof boots, crisscrossed the quads with backpacks inside rain covers in neon green and red.

They stopped for directions from a ruddy cheeked coed. Shortly after that, Dylan found a parking spot near the university's Ethnic Studies building.

The entrance to the steel and glass structure opened into a three-story lobby. The atrium housed several exhibits related to a variety of ethnic groups. High gloss posters rested on tables covered with textiles, fur, and plastic food. A colorful totem pole stood in one corner of the open space. Its enormity drew Dylan forward. The vertical cedar pole was stacked with animals and human-like figures painted in earthy shades of burgundy, forest, and jonquil. The pair glanced at exhibits on their way to stand before the pole.

"Well, that's impressive," Dylan's head tipped back to take in each multifaceted layer.

"Yeah," Augie uttered, as he mimicked Dylan's stance and gaze. As they admired the ancient artwork, a petite student with dark eyes framed by sculpted brows approached from the side of the display. Her prominent cheekbones and thick black braid made Dylan guess her heritage as American Indian.

The girl introduced herself as Sarah. She welcomed them to the exhibit, designed to showcase the nine federally recognized Native American tribes in Oregon.

"This is quite a display," Dylan said as he motioned toward the artifacts and presentation boards.

Sarah adjusted a pair of dark-framed glasses. "The students update the displays each year with new information and artifacts. We're quite proud of it."

"I can see why. We haven't looked at the whole exhibit, but from what we've seen, it covers a wide range of topics and history."

Sarah nodded. "Everything from the power structure of the tribes to what a typical person ate in a day."

"It must have taken years to research all of this information."

"It's an ongoing process. Thanks for recognizing our work."

She joined them to stroll around the exhibits and answer questions from Dylan about languages. He said, "My focus in college was Hebrew because I wanted to read ancient texts. But I also studied a couple of dialects in the Uto-Aztecan family."

"One of the largest linguistic families of Native American tongues." She smiled. "I'm impressed."

They completed the circuit, and Dylan said, "While these exhibits are interesting, we're not simply here to find out about the tribes of Oregon. We're on a personal heritage mission."

Sarah looked at Dylan and then Augie. "Are you connected with a tribe?"

"Not sure." Dylan dug for the certificate. "I was adopted, and this is the only information I have about my birth parents."

He opened the document and pointed to the names typed near the bottom. "What do you make of this? Do you know why they might only list one name for each person?"

Sarah leaned forward to review the entire certificate before she focused on the lines for parents. Her brows creased as she puzzled. "This doesn't seem right. I'm not sure they're names."

Maybe words would be a better clue to his heritage than names. He asked her to explain.

She straightened and flicked her braid behind a shoulder. "I'm not comfortable talking about this on my own. Let's go upstairs and find a professor to help us."

With the document still in her hand, Sarah ushered them across the lobby to a vestibule adjacent to the staircase, a stainless steel and glass affair with open risers and charcoal black stairs. As she passed the steps and approached an elevator, Dylan reached out to grab her by the arm. With a friendly smirk, he chided, "We're not walking up?"

"It only goes to the second floor. There are meeting rooms up there but no classrooms or offices. We need to take the elevator to the fourth floor."

Once inside the elevator, Sarah pulled a plastic ID from her pocket and waved it in front of an access control reader before she pushed the button.

Dylan asked, "Why all the security? Have there been threats?"

Sarah shook her head. "None I know of, but the students feel safer. Honestly, it's not going to stop a student with a psycho-grudge, but he'd need to remember to carry his ID for an attack."

She tapped the edge of Dylan's folded certificate against the palm of her hand as they rode in silence. At the fourth floor, they walked into a sea of gray cubicles. Fluorescent fixtures tracked into the distance and forced Dylan to squint after the subtle lights inside the elevator. Offices lined the perimeter, their interior walls punctured with windows to allow natural light to penetrate the common area. Sarah stopped at the open door of a large office with a grand city view.

Probably a professor with authority, Dylan concluded.

Behind an imposing desk covered with stacks of manuscripts and papers, a stocky woman sat with long gray hair pulled over one shoulder. While her clothing gave no hint of ethnicity, she wore turquoise earrings shaped like feathers and a heavy silver bracelet encrusted with crimson and ebony stones. Her nameplate bore the name Dr. Frances Breedlove, Director of Indigenous Nations Studies. When Sarah knocked on the door frame, the professor stood, smiled at the intrusion, and walked around the desk.

Sarah apologized for the lack of notice or appointment and introduced Dylan and Augie. Dr. Breedlove's warm greeting indicated her open door policy was just that. With a wave of her hand, she welcomed them into her office.

As they took seats in front of the professor's desk, Dylan glanced at the artwork in her office. Every wall held a painting or fabric work in traditional Indian American themes, from boldly patterned rugs to portraits of stoic chieftains.

Two pieces sat at the front of her cluttered desk. The first was a round shield about four inches in diameter perched between two jet-black poles. Beads, quillwork, and feathers decorated the shield. The other was a tiny pewter Starship Enterprise. Dylan smiled at the juxtaposition.

Sarah handed over the certificate and summarized Dylan's story. Dr. Breedlove examined the document. When she reached the bottom lines listing Dylan's parents, she snorted and broke into a wide grin.

"What's funny?" Dylan asked. He bristled, as he dreaded another dead end to his search.

The professor looked up and gazed at Dylan, her piercing gray eyes full of empathy. "I believe that was the intention. Sorry if this might disturb you, but these are not people's names."

"I respect your opinion, but why are you so sure?"

She rose and walked to a bookcase with neatly organized texts and notebooks. Without hesitation, she pulled a thick binder from the shelf and returned to the desk. Methodically, Dr. Breedlove flipped through plastic sleeves holding photos of wall paintings, totem poles, and statues. "This is the one," she announced.

The professor clicked open the binder and handed Dylan a color print of a painting on a wood panel. "The words are possibly phonetic representations of terms from one of Oregon's tribal nations."

Dylan took the page as she continued. "The word Hekewi, which is listed for your mother's name, when said out loud is their term for making a joke."

"A joke like a story to amuse people or more like a riddle?"

She tapped a finger to her chin. "Definitely not a riddle. There isn't a one-for-one translation, but similar to a person giving a wisecrack or being sarcastic."

"So less like 'Have you heard the one about' and more like 'When asked what's up? He said, the sky.'?"

Dr. Breedlove chuckled. "You've hit it on the head.

"Not sure I'm happy about someone who thought the information on my certificate is a laughing matter." He frowned. "What about Desyelni? Is that word related to this picture?"

"It is. The word Desyelni, which is identified for your father's name, isn't quite as straightforward as Hekewi."

She rose to round the desk and stood at Dylan's shoulder. "I believe it relates to the folk story in this painting. The tribe has a term that sounds like Desyelni. It's seldom used and has mythical origins."

Dr. Breedlove reached over Dylan's shoulder and pointed toward the image. "I can make a copy of this photo to take with you. I think the closest translation of Desyelni into English would be *foundling* or a *baby found in the woods*."

Chapter 19

SALIDA, COLORADO
NATE STEWART

Nate pulled up in front of Jen's cabin as late afternoon shadows darkened the dirt packed yard. *What a crap day.* When he and Cynthia were not arguing, he tried to paint but found no solace in his work. She had shown up at the Salida Soup without advance notice. What was she thinking?

Nate sat in the car and recalled Cynthia's grand entrance with the owner of the *Salida Sentinel.*

Nate had not cared about her being there because he figured she needed something for a story. She *never* did anything without wanting something in return. So Nate had ignored her and headed to the Steamplant's auditorium. When he looked around to see where she landed, Nate spotted her up front with Merle and Erle. He watched the back of her mass of auburn curls bounce up and down as she squirmed in her seat. Nate fumed.

At the end of Merle and Erle's five-minute appeal for funds, Cynthia had the nerve to explode out of her seat and burst into applause. She turned to the audience and called out, "While I'm not personally a Bigfoot believer, I believe in Salida. If Merle and Erle can draw a world-class speaker to next month's conference, they'll put Salida on the map for premier believer events. This symposium could evolve into an annual affair. Let's do what we can to support these guys!"

Cynthia stole the show. Despite Nate's ballot for the roller derby team, Merle and Erle won the most votes. When they announced the winner, Cynthia jumped up and down like a cheerleader at a tie game. In comparison, the roller derby presenters looked like homespun teenagers. They didn't have a chance.

Before the awards presentation, Nate stalked out alone. He paced the apartment and plotted how to react when Cynthia came home.

He had finished his second whiskey when he heard the alarm chirp to warn him the gallery door had opened. Full of adrenalin and herself for helping the guys take home the donated funds, she erupted into the room.

Nate ignored her and swirled the cubes in his drink as she rattled on. "These hayseeds are stupid as sheep. Did you see how they rallied behind the Bigfoot conference? Do they understand that notoriety for something idiotic is not the same as distinction for something meaningful?" She laughed as she stripped off her trench coat and flung it across the arm of a leather side chair.

"Hey, you look mopey. What's up with you?" Cynthia hiked her skintight dress up to her waist and straddled Nate. She left nothing between her and his slacks except a thin strip of black thong underwear.

Nate debated for a split second. Stand on principle or deal with Cynthia's transgression in the morning? Better to wait until later. He released his anger and frustration into her willing body.

Over coffee in the morning, Nate tried to work her. "I didn't know you planned to come to Salida Soup last night. Weren't you going to the movies to see a chick flick?"

Cynthia yawned and raised her arms above her head to fluff her curls and loosen her robe. "I saw the owner of the *Sentinel* on my way to the theater. He tried to give me a piece of his mind about the last article I wrote about Salida's fascination with Bigfoot. After a few minutes of newspaper banter, I had him eating out of my hand. He's a regular at the Soup, so I walked over with him."

"Want to tell me why you sat with Merle and Erle instead of me?"

Cynthia looked at Nate with apparent simulated wonder. "Baby, are *you* jealous?"

Nate scoffed. "Of course not. I just don't want them to get the idea you're available."

Cynthia cocked her head. "I never took you for the considerate type. Is this about them or you?"

"Actually, it's about you. It seemed like you led them on. It'd be a shame for the Hodges to label you a tease." That's when the fight started.

Destiny had been easy to manipulate. But Cynthia would have none of it. While she fell short of packing up her stuff, she had threatened to leave if he did not back off.

Nate grabbed the steering wheel and straightened. He would need to find a new strategy to get Cynthia in line. But first he would search Jen's cabin. Nate picked up his flashlight and stepped from the car.

Once on the porch, he rammed the butt end of the light into a window. Glass shattered and fell inside onto the coiled, living room rug. Nate reached through the pane and slid the latch to unlock the window. Once he'd gained access, he spent an hour rifling through drawers and cabinets.

Confident Jen's father had hidden treasure in the cabin, he rationalized why it belonged to him. He had paid for dozens of meals eaten by Jen and Trip when she babysat. Did she ever offer to pay her share? Not once. She even helped herself to drinks from his fridge and never contributed a single soft drink or juice box. Besides feeding her, he shelled out gas money for picking up Trip from school. He probably gave her way more than needed, but she never offered him change.

Now that she was dead, his generosity would remain unreciprocated. She owed him.

He figured the best way to break even was to find something of value at the cabin. After all, he had a right to recover what she owed.

Unsure of what to look for, he opened everything from coffee cans to the tops of aerosol cans. He tilted each painting from the wall and lifted the rugs to check for hidden compartments. Fanning the pages of Jen's collection of nature and guide books proved time-consuming and futile. He grew more frustrated with each book that hit the floor. No currency fluttered from the pages.

On all fours, Nate dug through her closet. He pushed aside an empty wicker laundry hamper and tossed out a stack of folded blankets before he felt a metal box at the back wall. Nate drew the flashlight from his waistband and shined the beam on a green metal ammo box sealed with a small dangling padlock. Nate grinned. *Score.*

He hefted the box to the front of the house. Nate wanted to take advantage of the scant late afternoon sunlight streaming through the windows. After he collected a mallet-shaped meat tenderizer from Jen's utensil crock, Nate pounded on the lock until it fractured.

The lid snapped open with a tug on the double flap. Folded legal documents lay on top. Nate lifted two sets of stapled papers from the box. He flipped through the cover sheets and decided they were copies of deeds, one for the cabin and another for property in California. He tossed them aside and tipped the remaining contents to the floor.

Nate tilted a scratched aluminum-cased lighter to make out an outline of Vietnam and the words "We the unwilling, led by the unqualified, to kill the unfortunate, die for the ungrateful." He scoffed and tossed the memento back into the box with a clang.

Other keepsakes followed the lighter. They included a dozen poker chips, a gold-colored pen engraved with the name Robert J. Rickard, three campaign buttons for the 1976 Carter-Mondale ticket, and a half dozen linked keychains with advertisements for local businesses that had closed decades earlier.

A narrow velvet box held some promise. Nate pried open the corner and found a steel link identification bracelet with the name *Bobby* and two rings—a class ring from Salida High School and a plain gold wedding band.

Nate tried on the rings, but both were several sizes too large for his slender fingers. He slipped the jewelry into the front pocket of his slacks before he closed the lid and took the box back to the closet.

That bitch must have been hiding something more valuable, thought Nate. Why else would Dylan stay here? Certainly not for nostalgia.

Nate moved to the mudroom at the back of the house. Jen's backpacks hung on hooks screwed into the wall. He lifted each pack until he found one with more weight than nylon and buckles. "Ah-ha."

After Nate unloaded and then reloaded a camp stove, first aid kit, Mylar blanket, and handfuls of other emergency equipment, he flung the pack back against the wall.

He looked toward the door. "Something must be buried outside."

A shovel stood in the corner. Nate grabbed it before he flipped the deadbolt to explore the grounds. He inspected the woodpile and poked the shovel around the foundation, but the dirt appeared undisturbed.

Nate rounded the building. Long shadows from the woods fell across the yard. A breeze rustled remnant leaves and rocked a snag against a neighboring tree.

Nate stepped forward and leaned on the shovel handle. He turned to look at the cabin and the surrounding landscape. Where next?

It's getting late. It'll be dark soon, and I'd hate to tempt another fit from Cynthia. Nate slapped a palm against the top of the handle.

Something caught Nate's eye. It moved in the trees beyond the parking area. Nate froze. His heart pounded. "Hey!" He called toward the edge of the yard. No response.

Unwilling to confirm whether the intruder was human or animal, Nate figured his best bet was to leave. But if he had left something in the house, the Sheriff might tie him to the break-in. Would they bother to dust for prints? Nah. They would probably assume teenagers broke in for a place to have a few beers.

A dark shape slipped between the trees. "Show yourself!" Nate called as he strained to see. Nothing moved except boughs pushed by the wind.

"I've had enough of this. I'm out of here." Nate slid his hand into his pocket to retrieve his car keys. He touched a couple of crumpled receipts. No keys.

Nate glanced at the cabin. They must be on the kitchen counter. He shook his head in frustration.

After he checked the perimeter for movement, Nate half ran and half stumbled toward the cabin. *Why did I lock the car?* He thought with desperation as he passed the parked BMW.

His heart raced as he sped toward the cabin. Nate's outstretched arms strained to reach the railing. He yanked himself onto the front porch and practically flew over the steps.

He heard pounding footfalls from behind but did not dare take time to look back. *I'm going to make it.*

As Nate reached for the door handle, a massive weight thudded on his back and hurtled him to the porch. Teeth pierced his calf.

Chapter 20

JAMESVILLE, OREGON
DESTINY STEWART, NÉE KUSIK

Augie and Dylan returned late in the evening. Destiny sat in the living room, cross-legged with a tablet computer on her lap. When they opened the door, Destiny removed her glasses and rubbed the fatigue from her eyes.

After Trip had gone to bed, she had spent the evening with pharmaceutical journals. Her head buzzed from memorizing which new drugs misbehaved when taken with old standbys.

Recent clinical cases touted breakthroughs for asthma, diabetes, and hypertension. New government regulations further restricted a pharmacist's ability to counsel customers about nonprescription drugs. Keeping up with changes felt like a third full-time job after being Trip's mom and her work as a pharmacy tech.

Good time for a break, Destiny concluded, as she greeted Augie and Dylan. She unfolded from the recliner and smoothed her gray sweatshirt over the top of the stretch pants.

"Are you hungry?" she asked. "When you missed dinner, I thought you'd be looking for food when you got back. I made up a couple of plates for the fridge. It won't take a minute to heat them. I hope you like meatloaf. It's ground turkey."

Dylan smiled. "Based on our not-very-health-conscious lunch, turkey is perfect. Thanks for thinking of us. We should have called to let you know we'd be late."

In the kitchen, Destiny retrieved two plates heaped with slices of meatloaf, mashed yams, and steamed broccoli. While Dylan poured himself a beer and a soft drink for Augie, Destiny heated their dinners in the microwave. Augie fetched silverware and set the table.

As the men started their meals, Destiny filled a glass with white wine from an open bottle in the fridge. She joined them and grasped the glass in both hands.

Destiny took a long sip and swallowed to clear her head of drug trials and chemical interactions. She successfully switched gears to pelt them with questions about what happened at the church and why they were gone all day.

Dylan put down his fork to retrieve his bag from where he had dropped it in the living room. He handed the intake certificate to Destiny. She scanned the document as she listened to Dylan talk about their tour of the sanctuary and Joann's covert gift.

Destiny turned to Augie. "You were right. Nice people can be helpful." Augie smiled at the compliment.

After Destiny heard about their excursion to the university, she asked, "What do you make of Hekewi meaning *a joke*?"

Dylan shrugged. "I suspect they felt that asking for legitimate names was a joke. Either they didn't know or didn't want the church to know."

Destiny nodded. "Makes sense. What do you think the professor meant by *foundling*?"

"Well, that's the million-dollar question." Dylan pushed food around the plate with his folk.

She noticed he had eaten very little of the heaping portion. "Can I make you something else?"

Dylan smiled at her offer but shook his head. "Dr. Breedlove didn't know much about the mythology surrounding the term, but she felt it came from an account orally handed down in a tribe of Oregon Indian Americans."

"Did she tell you the story?"

"She did. She also had a photo of a painting that illustrated the little-known myth." Dylan retrieved the copy of Dr. Breedlove's photo and handed it to Destiny.

Her brows furrowed as she puzzled at the photograph of a mystical folk painting on a disk, crosscut from a tree trunk. "Well? Don't keep me waiting. What do you make of this?"

Dylan turned to Augie. "Keep me honest, Augie. If I tell it wrong, let me know." Augie nodded in agreement.

Dylan told the story of a young Indian maiden. As the most beautiful girl in her tribe, she caught the eye of numerous young warriors who continually vied for her attention. They were keen to be her choice for a mate.

She enjoyed the boys' attentiveness but recognized she received considerably more attention than her friends. This saddened the maiden, as she believed the suitors' interest unwarranted. She did not want her friends to feel slighted.

One moonless autumn night, the maiden went into the forest to ask the stars for guidance about choosing a mate. She traveled slowly along the familiar track, being cautious not to trip over precarious roots or partially buried rocks. Comforted by the night sounds of the owl hoots and distant coyote howls, she continued deeper into the woods.

Upon entering a meadow, she could see the outline of two distant peaks against the speckled night sky. The taller mountain, veined with streaks of early season snow, glistened in the starlight. In the gap between the peaks, she spotted a cluster of stars known to her tribe as the Spirit Path.

A formidable Douglas fir stood at the edge of the meadow, thick at the bottom and nearly transparent in the top branches. The maiden knelt next to the tree to face the distant peaks, her head thrown back and arms wide.

She called to the Spirit Path and asked for guidance. But the stars were not the only ones listening. While she described her desire not to alienate friends and how she did not have a favorite among the horde of suitors, the sturdy tree took human form.

Enchanted by her ebony hair, smooth olive skin, and simple adornments, the man-tree sat before her and took her hands in his. Without fear or surprise, the maiden confided in the stranger.

Her humility and kindness captured his heart. He encouraged her to choose a mate who would give her the respect she deserved. He suggested she select someone steady and reliable, a mate who would always put her needs first.

She asked him how to find these traits, as most of her suitors demonstrated how well they played games or musical instruments. These activities impressed her, but she felt the boys competed with each other rather than showing they wanted to understand her.

He told the maiden she would know when the right boy approached her. She stayed with him all night. By the time she returned to the tribe, she had fallen deeply in love with her forest suitor and was heavy with his child.

Two days later, she bore a baby who did not look like the others in her tribe. The infant had pale skin and grew feverish. Soon after the boy's birth, the maiden returned to the woods to find her lover. As the forest opened into the meadow, she paused to stare at the ancient fir. How could she call upon the Spirit Path to awaken the tree?

The maiden approached. As she held her infant in the crook of her arm, she rubbed the tree's flat, soft needles between her fingers.

"Share your wisdom with me," she whispered. "You must help me to save our son." The tree did not respond. So the maiden curled with the boy on a bed of fragrant needles and slept.

As dusk fell, a tender hand caressed her shoulder. She awoke to see that the tree, once again, had taken human form. She offered him her sickly infant and asked if he knew how to make the child well. He comforted her and told her the illness resulted from the infant's parents existing between two different worlds.

He offered two ways to save her newborn son. Her lover could stay in the human world, but he would die at first light, never to return. Alternatively, she could mate with him and become a tree. Either choice would give the boy a chance to live in the human world.

She adored her tiny son and desperately wanted him to survive. If she chose to sacrifice her lover, guilt would taint her life forever, but becoming a tree would banish her from her family's world. Her affection for the infant and suitor took precedence, so she agreed to become a tree. Her lover placed the infant at her feet and wrapped his arms around the maiden.

When her parents came to look for their daughter the next morning, they found a healthy baby boy at the base of two stately firs. The trees came from separate roots, but their trunks entwined into a braid. The branches cradled over the child as if to protect the infant from harm.

The maiden's parents brought their grandchild home to the tribe and called him Desyelni.

Mesmerized by the tale, Destiny stared at the photo. "What an incredible story." She traced a finger across the bottom border of the print. On the crosscut disk, the artist had painted two inky black evergreens with interwoven trunks. A pale sliver of moon hung in a Buckingham blue sky and shone through the branches. Squirrels, two foxes, and a solitary hawk stood at attention on a grassy knoll and stared at the base of the connected trees. The animals were mesmerized by a small bundle of gray cloth held together with tanned leather straps. A tiny pink face poked from above the fabric and smiled with a toothless grin. His almond-shaped eyes glistened pale green.

Dylan shrugged and turned to Augie. "Did I leave anything out?"

"Yep. The end." Augie punctuated his response with a single nod.

"You're right. The tribe raised Desyelni to be a brave warrior. Ultimately, they chose him to become the tribe's chief, and they lived prosperously under his leadership. Sorry, Augie, I didn't think that part was the most important, but it does complete the story."

Destiny tapped the page and puzzled over the story. How could it relate to Dylan's history? "I take it Desyelni is their word for foundling because the tribe raised the maiden's child after they found him in the woods?"

Dylan shrugged. "That's how I understand it, too."

"Okay, so now tell me why someone put that name on your birth record?"

"Great question. Unfortunately, I don't have an answer yet, but I plan to find out."

Chapter 21

OCTOBER 14
DYLAN COX

Dylan woke alone in the guest room as Augie's neatly made twin bed was empty. After he glanced at his watch, Dylan discovered most of the morning had slipped away. *I must have needed the extra sleep.*

He stood to stretch and spotted the paperback biography he had brought from Chicago. With good intentions to read for relaxation before bed, he had not touched it except to place the book on the bed stand. Moisture in the air bowed the cover and curled the pages and forced the shape from rectangle to trapezoid. How many days in Salida's dry air would it take for the book to resume its original condition?

Dylan dug through his suitcase to look for jogging clothes. He missed running over the last two days when they scheduled themselves from dawn until time for bed. He needed a long run to relax his muscles and clear his head.

He found Augie downstairs in the living room watching a movie, the same cartoon film with monsters that played the night before last. Augie seemed mesmerized by the film. Dylan walked between him and the screen. He waved his arm to catch Augie's attention. Augie grabbed the remote and paused the action.

"I'm going for a run. Are you okay here on your own?"

"I'm fine," Augie said with a shrug.

Dylan turned toward the TV and asked, "Isn't that the same movie you watched with Destiny and Trip the other night?"

Augie looked at the screen and then back to Dylan. "Yeah."

"Why are you watching it again?"

"I liked it."

"Aren't there other movies in Destiny's collection you haven't seen?"

"I like this one." Augie looked back at the set and pushed the play button. Dylan assumed Augie probably preferred the familiar over the unknown and left the house for his run

Dylan started his workout with a brief calf stretch on the curb. As he jogged down the first block, his legs fell into a familiar rhythm and heartbeats accelerated. As his chest heaved, Dylan sucked the moist air into his lungs. He lost the sense of time or place and ran with his thoughts racing between the story of Desyelni, the intake certificate, and the upcoming Sasquatch search party.

How long had Joann worked at the church? If she was there when he was adopted, then she might have met his birth parents. At least, Joann may know who filled in the form. Even if she wasn't there, she might know people who were. Joann gave him the certificate—would she give him more? Could a budding friendship with her husband work in his favor?

A horn blasted as Dylan entered an intersection. He slid on the moist pavement and jolted to a stop short of a massive SUV's bumper.

The driver, sporting a black and white Pacific Northwest ballcap, opened the passenger window and yelled, "Pay attention. You're going to get yourself killed." Dylan held up both hands and apologized as she closed the window and accelerated away.

"Good advice," Dylan called in response. He shook his shoulders to release tension. Once his heart rate slowed to a sustainable pace, he started again but paused at each crossroad.

Soaked with sweat and exhausted, Dylan arrived back on the front porch an hour later. He held a quilted water-repellant hunting jacket under one arm—a hasty purchase from a second-hand store he had spotted a block from the house. He figured it would come in handy at the Sasquatch event.

Despite his earlier near collision, Dylan saw few moving cars in Destiny's neighborhood. Back in Chicago, he would dodge traffic until he gained access to a bike path that eventually took him to the Lakefront. The wind blowing across Lake Michigan could be brutal, but the views of whitecapped water made the journey worthwhile.

Thoughts of Chicago prompted Dylan to think about Tom. They had talked after Augie and Dylan arrived at Destiny's, but Dylan owed him an update. After a few minutes of rest on the wooden porch swing, the air cooled Dylan to the point of shivering. Time to warm up with a shower.

Augie was not on the sofa when he passed through the living room. Upstairs, Dylan grabbed clean jeans and a shirt from his duffle and made his way to the bathroom they shared with Trip.

Dylan started the shower to give the hot water time to journey from the basement to the showerhead before he climbed in. After the room filled with steam, he stepped over a basket hooked to the tub's rim. The basket overflowed with plastic battleships, ducks, and water guns. *Trip is a lucky boy,* concluded Dylan as the hot water warmed his chilled skin.

Scrubbed clean, dried, and dressed in fresh clothes, Dylan trudged downstairs to find Augie. He found him sketching in a notebook at the kitchen table. Four pencils, a sharpener, and a pink pearl eraser lay next to Augie's elbow.

Gray midmorning light trickled through the window over the sink. The scant daylight provided insufficient illumination. So Augie huddled over the paper and drew shadows with swipes from a nearly horizontal pencil. Dylan flipped a switch by the door. A tethered fixture cascaded light onto the table. Augie looked up at the lamp and then at Dylan. He nodded his thanks before he returned to work.

"What are you drawing?" Dylan asked.

"Destiny."

"May I see?"

Augie slid the notebook across the table toward Dylan.

Dylan looked at the pencil sketch of Destiny's face. The shading to accent Destiny's cheeks and eye sockets mimicked a photograph. Not merely a flattering portrait, Augie's artistic skill captured Destiny's character. Destiny's emotions were exposed in her eyes and expression.

"May I look at the rest of your drawings?" Dylan did not dare to turn a page without permission. Augie nodded agreement.

Dylan parked himself at the table and closed the notebook to examine the cover. Augie's name and a date five years past were on the top right corner of the red cardboard cover. "Is this when you started sketching?" Dylan asked.

"Nope. That's when I started this book."

"Where are the other books?"

"No others. I used to draw on loose paper. My aunt bought this for me."

"I'll be careful with it." Dylan rested a palm over the cover to acknowledge its value.

He opened the cover to the first page. The first drawing featured an older woman with shrunken features and tired eyes. Salt and pepper hair flowed away from her face as if a weighty braid or ponytail pulled from behind. Inner beauty and kindness escaped from the lines hewn from life's struggles. Dylan assumed she must be Augie's deceased aunt.

Dylan absorbed each drawing before he turned the page. Augie watched as Dylan poured over the portraits and admired the detail in each one. After a dozen pictures of Augie's aunt, the next section contained a mixture of sketches of Destiny and Jen.

Dylan's breath caught in his throat when he paused at one capturing Jen's thin-lipped smirk. He knew it well. She had displayed that expression on several occasions in response to one of Dylan's insensitive remarks. Apparently, Augie had been a recipient of one of Jen's smirks, too.

A sketch near the back of the book included both Jen and Destiny. They laughed with their arms wrapped around each other. Dylan could feel their affection and merriment in Augie's rendering. The drawing made him long to be in their moment and its embrace. "How do you decide what to draw?"

Augie paused thoughtfully. "I draw what I remember."

Dylan assumed Augie could recall his experiences in such detail he could recapture variations of light, skin texture, and hair placement, as well as the emotions reflected on a person's face. What a gift.

"I've noticed your subjects are all women." Dylan pushed the notebook across the table and good naturedly scolded his friend. "What's up with that, Augie?"

"I like to draw nice people."

From the response, Dylan gleaned men had not played a positive role in Augie's life. Sad, but not surprising, as Dylan figured most men would be engrossed in sports events or business matters. Those types of guys would have little patience to engage with soft-spoken Augie. Grateful for Jen's encouragement to spend time with Augie, Dylan knew his life was better for having him as a friend.

"Do you have one of Trip?" asked Dylan.

Augie opened the book and turned to the last page with the unfinished picture of Destiny. She leaned over an open book cradled in her arms. Her downcast eyes were nearly closed, and Destiny's glasses slipped down her nose. The details of her face and hair were complete, but a few curved lines and shading represented her unfinished body and the background.

Augie pointed to a corner of the page with the end of his pencil. "I can put him here."

"What would he be doing?"

"His homework," Augie said, matter-of-factly.

"And what's Destiny doing?"

"She's tired from so much work." Augie added, "Being a mom is hard."

Dylan jumped at the cell phone vibrating in his pocket. He removed it and looked at the screen. "It's the Sheriff's office in Salida."

Augie looked up from his notebook, forehead creased with concern as Dylan answered the call.

Chapter 22

Dylan and Augie waited in the living room until Destiny came home from work. Dylan paced while Augie sat on the couch and held a pillow. Augie's heels tapped with anxious energy but stopped when he heard Destiny's car pull in front of the house.

She arrived breathless. As she closed the front door and hung her keys on a vacant coat hook, she asked, "What's happened? Nothing's wrong with Trip, right? The school would have called me directly."

Dylan crossed the room and gave Destiny a firm hug. He pulled back and held her at arm's length. "Destiny, I'd like you to sit down."

"No way. You tell me what's happened," said Destiny, wide-eyed with anxiety. She looked to Dylan, then Augie, and back.

"Trip's fine." Dylan chose his words with care. "But I'd like you to sit down."

She released a long sigh and followed Dylan into the living room, where she sat on the edge of a side chair. "Don't scare me like this. Tell me what's going on."

Dylan sat next to Augie on the couch. He leaned forward—elbows on knees and chin on steepled hands. "We got a call from Sheriff Austin in Salida."

Destiny stiffened in alarm. "Did Nate find out about us? Is he sending someone to arrest me?"

"No, no, no. Neither Nate nor the Sheriff knows I'm here with you. The call came on my cell."

"Why the drama? Tell me why the Sheriff phoned you."

"Nate's dead." As soon as the words left his lips, Dylan considered whether the statement was overly abrupt.

Destiny's shoulders sunk as if all the air escaped from her body. She shook her head in disbelief. "What did you say? Nate Stewart? He's dead? How? When?"

Dylan crossed to kneel at the foot of Destiny's chair. He took her hands in both of his. "They found him today, but he was killed last night."

"Found him? Killed by whom?"

"They assume animals attacked him."

"That doesn't make any sense. Nate wouldn't spend time outdoors. Where did the attack happen?" Destiny's voice squeaked. Her words spilled out in double time.

Dylan patted her hand and hoped to calm her. "Jen's cabin."

Destiny yanked her hands away and shook her head. "That's just crazy. He wouldn't go up there on a bet. Start at the beginning."

"Last night Cynthia Waters, a woman who was dating Nate, called Merle Hodges at the Police department to say that Nate hadn't shown up for dinner. Merle immediately suggested Nate may have found a different dinner companion."

"I'll bet that didn't go over well."

"Nope. After Cynthia gave Merle a few choice words, she hung up and called the Sheriff's office. She spoke with Erle Hodges. He offered to take her report but told her they would wait until morning before convening a search party."

"For real?" Destiny cocked her head.

"Not precisely, but his point was they didn't plan to send anyone to look for him until morning. Everyone knows Nate. They expected he'd show up sometime that night or in the morning. That's when Cynthia admitted Nate had left early in the afternoon for Jen's cabin. Because of the attacks last summer, she wanted to be sure Nate didn't run into the same animals."

Destiny interrupted with, "Why would Nate go up there?"

"That's exactly what Erle asked Cynthia. She told him Nate went to collect some of Trip's stuff from when Jen babysat for him. Nate had said he wanted to get them before Kate put the cabin up for sale."

"Sounds like a thin excuse to me, but okay." Destiny motioned for Dylan to continue.

"Erle stuck to his position and told her the Sheriff's office would send someone to the cabin if Nate did not show up by 10:00 the following morning. At 8:00 in the morning, Cynthia called again. The Sheriff said she was frantic and demanded they do something."

"Why didn't she just drive up there herself?"

Dylan shrugged. "Great question. I didn't think to ask. At any rate, Cynthia admitted Nate had a reputation for unreliability, but he never spent an evening away from *her*. After talking over the circumstances with Sheriff Austin, they decided to send a car to investigate." Dylan nodded solemnly. "Austin found Nate's body in the front yard. Based on the looks of his wounds, his killers were likely the same animals that killed Jen four months ago."

Dylan watched as tears welled up in Destiny's eyes. Were the tears for herself or Trip? Based on her situation, she may have even felt relief from Nate's death.

She took off her glasses and swiped a cheek with the back of a hand. "What am I going to tell Trip? He's been okay hiding out here with me in Oregon, but he probably figured this was temporary. Trip couldn't have imagined he'd never see his dad again."

Augie moved to stand next to Dylan. He repeatedly clasped and unclasped his hands. "You'll know what to say. You were there for me when Aunt Peg died."

Destiny looked up at Augie. "Sweetie, I was stronger then."

Dylan interjected, "Augie's right. You'll know how to tell him. Assure him you'll face this together."

Destiny stood and walked to the bookcase. She picked up a framed photo of Trip and touched the picture with an index finger before she slammed it back on the shelf. "What the hell was he doing at Jen's cabin? I don't believe that bullshit story about Trip's stuff. Like he would care about a few toys or kid's clothes."

Dylan sighed, his face slack with compassion for Destiny and her son. "I'm not sure. But when I saw him right before Augie and I left Salida, he asked me questions about whether I thought Jen's father might have left valuables at the cabin."

She scoffed. "It's not enough for Nate to torture the living. Now he's stealing from the dead?"

"Sounds pretty bad when you put it that way."

"What other way is there? What a bastard. I was a fool to stay with him as long as I did."

"Not foolish, only under his spell." Dylan understood her mental struggle between facing the tragedy of untimely death and wanting to be free of Nate's magnetism. "The past aside, we'll need to work out with the Sheriff what to do about your situation."

"Shit. I hadn't thought of that. Everyone in Salida still thinks Trip's missing." She straightened. "And I'm dead."

Chapter 23

SALIDA, COLORADO
KALEV

From the position of the sun, I knew it was far past midday. Yet nothing could tempt me to rise from my bed. I had spent the night cowering in the bushes. The vicious beasts were long gone, but their shredded prey lay only a short distance away.

I could smell the blood that poured from his body into the earth and the waste he released as they tore him apart. I wanted to rise and cover him with dirt or leaves to dampen the stench but knew I must leave him untouched.

Scores of individuals had arrived in the morning to investigate and clear the area. From my perch in a high pine tree, I watched as they handled his body with a gentleness I did not understand. Why did they methodically lift him, piece by piece, onto the gurney? Clearly, he was dead. He did not appreciate their painstaking compassion.

They stayed for hours to search the woods and talk incessantly. What could they possibly need to discuss? Animals attacked and killed him. They must have seen death before.

I thought about the murder I had witnessed in the summer. An older male had approached a man shoveling dirt into a hole filled with trash. The man with the shovel had attacked and beaten the older male to death. The survivor had certainly felt no compassion as he hastily buried the dead man in a shallow grave.

As I watched the people scurry around the cabin, I wished they would leave me in peace. After more hours of chatter, they finally left.

I climbed down from the tree and nestled into my bed, concerned whether this debacle might derail my plans. What if the target heard about the assault and decided never to return?

Slowly, I rose and walked to the creek. I splashed water on my face and stared at my reflection. How could I let this happen? Maybe I should have raised an alarm before they attacked. The killers would have fled into the woods, and the trespasser would be alive, none the wiser.

But what if he continued to defile the cabin? He broke windows and dug holes. Would the target be fearful of returning?

At that moment, I recognized how the trespasser nearly jeopardized my mission. I was *right* not to stop the predators. They did me a favor by killing him.

I leaned forward to drink from the stream. As I gulped mouthfuls to quench my thirst, the frigid water chilled my throat. A headache crept across my forehead. Disgusted with the brutal conditions of the dreadful place, I spat the last bit of water back into the creek and swiped my mouth with the back of my hand.

How could I accomplish my mission with everything fighting against me? The weather and wilderness were sufficiently demoralizing. But individuals, with no business interfering, came to disrupt my carefully laid plans. With a huff, I stood and stomped back to the yard.

I stopped in front of the spot where his blood had stained the earth. I kicked the dirt—not to cover the evidence but in frustration over the event. I hated this place and everything it threw against me. My fists clenched. I released a howl that would have drawn dozens of my colleagues if they could hear me. But they were far from here.

I ran with abandon to the edge of the woods and grabbed fists full of grass and threw them to the ground in hopes the aggression would dispel my anger. The action only fueled my frustration. With two hands, I yanked on a knee-high sapling and pulled it from the ground to heave it over my shoulder. I needed more.

The adjacent tree, with a trunk thinner than my wrist, looked promising. I braced my feet on the ground and my shoulder against the stem. I pulled and knew this tree would not be the last one to feel my wrath.

Chapter 24

GROVERTON, OREGON
JAMES WHITED

James helped Joann arrange furniture in the church's stark white community room. They had set out five circular tables with six folding chairs at each table on the gray wall-to-wall carpet.

"Think we've put out enough chairs?" He twisted the curled end of his handlebar mustache as he looked at their work.

Joann joined him to survey the room, her hands poised on the hips of her St. John black pantsuit. "There have been twenty-eight confirmations, and a few more may show up." She paused. "Do you think some might be no-shows? The weather could be an issue. They're predicting rain tonight."

"They'll come prepared for any weather. Most of the folks are from around here. They're used to the rain. I don't think it'll keep them away."

Joann placed a hand on her husband's forearm. "You know how people can be when the days are short and bleak weather gets them down. They'd rather stay indoors with a cold beer and watch the latest reality TV show than sit outside in the cold rain."

James nodded in agreement. "I want this year's search to be even better than last year. Remember all the excitement when the crowd came back to the church? Everyone was impressed by the sounds in the woods. I've never heard anything like that in my life."

"Do you think it might have been from a Sasquatch?"

James leaned toward Joann and closed his meaty arms around his petite wife. He liked the way her tiny five-foot frame made him feel taller than his average height. He pulled back and placed a finger under her chin to tilt her face toward his and looked straight into her caramel brown eyes. "Honey, I don't know for sure, but I'd like to think so." He kissed her on the forehead. "Funny, though. I've been into the same glade a dozen times since last year's search and never heard those sounds again."

"Well, whatever happens tonight, it'll be fun to reminisce about prior searches and hope for something new tonight."

"True that." He stood back and appraised his wife. While he cherished watching her walk around the house in one of his old shirts, James admired her work clothes. Joann took pride in dressing stylishly. She spent extended time in their bathroom with makeup and hairstyling goo, but the results were spectacular. His wife always looked like the day they first met. James adored Joann from the moment he spotted her in the school auditorium, all proper and in charge as their class secretary.

He knew how she would respond but asked anyway. "Are you coming out to the woods with us tonight?"

"I'd love to be out there with you, but I haven't had time to go home and change. I'll stay at the church this time and be here when you finish. Would that be okay with you?"

James recognized Joann had finalized her decision, but he still enjoyed their farce of letting him decide. He smiled at his wife. "I think it would be best. Folks will be cold and hungry after the search. They'll appreciate having the hot chocolate ready when they get back."

"My thought as well." She nodded in agreement as if it was his idea.

Joann walked to the bins they had brought from the church's kitchen and retrieved brown tablecloths dotted with fall leaves in red, orange, and yellow. She snapped one into the air and watched it fall across the table. Joann bent to smooth the creases with a wide sweep of her hands. "There's a man coming tonight, and I'd like you to watch out for him."

James' eyes narrowed. "Watch him in what way? Did he bother you?"

Joann tugged one side of the tablecloth to ensure a perfect drop. Then she closed the gap between herself and James and put her arms around his waist. "No, my darling. He did not. He's looking for information from the church and met with me a couple of times."

"What's his beef?"

She laughed, and her eyes sparkled. "Maybe I shouldn't have brought it up. I didn't know you'd be suspicious. He's looking for details about his birth parents. We handled his adoption about thirty years ago."

"Were you involved with that one?"

Joann paused and turned away from James. "Maybe, but there's been so many over the years. They've started to blend."

From her posture and response, James knew she kept something from him. Once she closed the vault, she would only release the truth at a time *she* deemed appropriate. "Why is he coming tonight? He's not a reporter, is he?"

Joann pulled collapsed tissue paper pumpkins from a bin. "No, nothing like that. Dylan and a friend from Colorado are in town for a couple of days. They are staying with someone about an hour north from Groverton." She unfolded a pumpkin and fluffed the honeycomb tissue. "It sounds like he was involved with a believer group last summer in Colorado. As far as I know, Dylan wants to experience a real hunt."

"I'll keep an eye out for him." James frowned. He was unsure of the visitor's motives to join the search but willing to keep the stranger close. "On second thought, maybe I'll take him along with me."

James grabbed several reconstructed pumpkins and set them at the center of the tables. Joann followed behind him and slightly adjusted the position of each decoration and the tablecloths. He smiled. The changes were imperceptible but vital to her.

"You might like to talk with him about his experiences in Colorado," she suggested.

James softened. "It could be interesting to hear if they've had sightings out there. I don't know much about the Colorado groups. We get focused on what's going on locally. Pooling information could be helpful."

Joann asked James to set up an oblong table near the wall for the coffee service. As he unfolded the legs, she fetched the last tablecloth. While she smoothed it into place, she said, "The girls will be here soon to help me set out the baked goods and start the coffee. You outdid yourself in the kitchen."

"Mostly pies, and more pumpkin than anything else." James mentally inventoried the cartons of sweets he had packed from home.

Joann walked up to him and stood on tiptoes to kiss his lips. "We're almost done here. Why don't you head outside to organize the searchers?"

James pulled a hooded hunting jacket from the coat rack adjacent to the door. With a nod of goodbye to Joann, he walked through the atrium and stepped outside to the church's lighted front entryway. The first searchers had started to arrive.

He knew many of the people outside and greeted them with handshakes and hugs. Heavy mist saturated the night air. He breathed deeply and relished the cold moisture filling his lungs.

The dampness accentuated the fragrance of wood stoves from neighbors' homes. James loved the smell. It prompted thoughts of the coming winter months, for him a time of rest, good books, homemade soups, and freshly baked bread. Life was good, and everything was prearranged for an exciting night.

Chapter 25

Dylan disconnected his call to the Sheriff and looked up at the anxious faces of Destiny and Augie. "Well, he's not sending a S.W.A.T. team and helicopter to pick you up. That's the good news."

"How did he take it?" Destiny asked.

"The Sheriff expects you to see him right away when you're back in Salida. You'll need to play along with him. To everyone in Salida, he will pretend to be shocked that you and Trip aren't dead."

"I understand. I won't let on that he knew." She tucked a strand of hair behind her ear. "Or at least suspected we were here."

"He's not sure if you've broken any laws. That being said, Austin's pretty pissed off at you and Nate for concocting a story about your suicide and costing taxpayer money and volunteer hours to search for Trip when you kidnapped him and brought him here."

Destiny bowed her head. "How will they ever forgive me?"

"I don't know what the legal ramifications are, but I suspect the locals will be relieved you and Trip are alive." After he glanced toward the stairs to be sure Trip had not chosen that moment to leave his room, Dylan added, "People in Salida knew how Nate treated you guys. Nobody will blame you for running away."

"Not one single person?" Destiny asked with a catch in her throat.

"I can't make any promises, but you should give them a chance. The

Sheriff said Nate's folks are on their way to Salida. They want to do services and cremation at a funeral home in town. They'll take the ashes back to Chicago for another ceremony in a couple of weeks. My aunt and uncle made plans before anyone knew you're still alive. As Nate's wife, you could change those arrangements."

"I can work things out with the Stewarts when Trip and I are back in Colorado. I'll call them tonight to let them know we're coming, right after I make flight arrangements for tomorrow."

"Let us know when you want to be at the airport. Augie and I can drop you off on our way out of town."

Creases formed across Destiny's forehead. "You don't have to go because we're leaving. You still have so many unanswered questions and are welcome to stay here at the house as long as you need to."

Dylan nodded. "I appreciate the offer, but I should attend one of Nate's services to show respect for my aunt and uncle. Frankly, I'd rather go to the one in Salida."

"It'll be great to have your support. I'll have to think of a good excuse for why my parents knew about my faked death, and Nate's folks didn't."

"Didn't they contact your parents to console them or ask about services?"

Destiny scoffed. "I didn't think they would and, true to form, they didn't. If they *had* called, my folks were supposed to say the services were only for the immediate family living nearby."

"Makes things easier when people are predictable." Dylan weighed his evening plans against his duty to stick around with Destiny and Trip. "I plan to bail on James' Sasquatch search. I should be here with you and Trip."

Destiny placed a hand on Dylan's shoulder. "You don't need to stay with us. I'm in a daze about whether to go into mourning or break out the champagne." She glanced at the stairway. "Don't tell Trip I said that."

"Understood."

"Joann's already given you information about your past. She or her husband might share something new tonight. Don't risk losing this chance to find out more."

Despite how he felt about supporting her and Trip, she was right. Once he left Oregon, he may not have another opportunity to speak with Joann.

He felt the tug of resolving his unanswered questions. "As long as you'll be okay, I'd like to go."

She gave him a playful shove. "You should join the search. We'll be fine."

Dylan nodded. "I'll pack up tonight when I get back." He turned to Augie. "Are you sure I can't convince you to sit out in the rain with me to look for Bigfoot?" Augie only laughed in response.

When Dylan pulled up at the church, he saw people huddled in clusters across the entire lawn. As the church lot was full, Dylan drove around the block to find a place to park. Once the car was situated, he walked to the church and looked for Joann.

Yellow-tinted torchier lamps cast an eerie glow over the white façade of the building and illuminated a circle of women who clutched red-checkered stadium blankets and laughed at a joke he would never understand.

Dylan spotted Joann in the group. She stood amongst her peers but looked like a movie star amid camo-clad amazons. A black curly-lamb coat draped loosely around her shoulders.

As Dylan approached, Joann broke from the group to give him a one-arm embrace. She clutched the wrap under her chin.

"Dylan, I'm so glad you came!"

"I wouldn't have missed this for the world."

"Where's Augie?"

Dylan smiled sheepishly. "He took one look at the weather and bailed on me. I think he'll be more comfortable with popcorn and a movie."

"Well, no matter. You'll meet some new friends tonight at the search." She tugged Dylan's arm as she pulled him away from the clutch of women. "Come, let me introduce you to my husband, James. He's been looking forward to meeting you."

Joann led Dylan toward a group of men outfitted in heavyweight jackets. Little piles of campstools and blankets stood neatly stacked by each man's feet. *These guys are experienced at nighttime ventures into the woods,* thought Dylan.

She stopped behind a stocky man and softly placed a hand on his upper arm. He listened intently to a slightly built fellow with an untrimmed beard that had taken charge of the man's face. Had the speaker hung with a motorcycle gang, or was he merely too lazy to care about his appearance?

At a tap of her slender finger, James turned and looked at her with every ounce of attention. James' obvious infatuation with his wife brought a smile to Dylan's lips. How many people still carried this type of passion after many years of marriage?

James leaned toward his wife and softly gripped her by the upper arms. Joann raised herself on tiptoe to speak into his ear. As she spoke, his head turned toward Dylan, and he nodded intently. She lowered her heels to the ground. James squeezed her shoulders and brushed a kiss on her cheek. Her head cocked in response as Joann unleashed a girlish giggle. James' waxed handle-bar mustache must have tickled.

Joann quickly slipped back toward the female commandos. James reached up to place a hand on Dylan's shoulder and drew him into the circle of men. After quick handshakes, they resumed their places and listened to the thin man with the scruffy beard finish his story about the previous year's search.

In a high-pitched voice, he explained he had not seen any of the elusive beasts but unquestionably heard a Sasquatch signal to other creatures by pounding a log against a tree.

While the stork-like man wrapped up his story, Dylan looked around the circle and appraised the group members. They ranged in age from mid-twenties to a few in their retirement years. All had their hands stuffed into jacket pockets and moved their feet in an attempt to maintain body heat as if shuffling to the beat of a rhythm only they could hear. When they spoke, their breath formed clouds of mist puffed into the cold, moist night air.

Most of the men wore camouflage hunting jackets, but about a third wore green and yellow hooded sweatshirts from the nearby university. Dylan speculated whether they were alumni or sports fans. Jen would have been disappointed at their decisions to come outdoors on a cold, wet night in clothes that would not shed rain. Grateful he had picked up the jacket and gloves earlier in the day, Dylan guessed this would be one chilly night.

Once the questions to the reedy man subsided, James turned to Dylan and brought him into the conversation. "Tell us about your experience with hunting Sasquatches in Colorado."

As all heads turned his way, Dylan felt like a fresh hay bale delivered to a herd of cows. The men looked hungry for tales from a new sect of their believer society.

Instead of mentioning his skepticism about the creatures, Dylan entertained his new compatriots with his experiences in Salida. He told them about Kate's Bigfoot sighting in her herb garden when she watched a hairy monster sip the nectar from her hummingbird feeders.

They were mesmerized when Dylan pulled out his cell phone and showed them photos of fourteen-inch footprints he had seen nearby Jen's cabin. As a finale, Dylan told a story about his cousin who found his barbeque grill in flames, presumably due to a Sasquatch cutting the propane lines with his claws.

He left out the stories of animal mutilations and deaths attributed to the monster by Salida's believer community. It seemed unfair to accuse the beast of atrocities that were excessively heinous and were more likely the work of real-life predators.

As he talked about his experiences, the group nodded and asked for more details. Their fidgeting feet grew still, and they hung on every word. Despite being a city boy among hearty rural men's men, Dylan felt his Sasquatch encounters had pulled him into their believer confederation.

"We'd better load 'em up and head out." James switched his attention away from Dylan and organized the group's exit. James straightened and headed to the stairs of the church to address the crowd.

As James passed, he tapped Dylan's forearm. "You're with me for the briefing."

Dylan followed James through the crowd and kept him in sight. James' camouflage cap and heavy jacket were identical to many other outfits. If Dylan's attention wandered for a moment, he would lose him in the sea of Oregonians.

When James reached the front steps of the church, he turned to face the crowd. His voice boomed and silenced the group. "Listen up, everyone. In a few minutes, we're headed out to Sullivan's Ravine. As most of you know, parking is limited. I want to take as few cars as possible. If you want to drive, be sure to have at least four people in your car or truck. We'll reconvene in the parking lot to walk to the viewing area. So don't start up the trail on your own. Plan to be outdoors for more than an hour. Don't forget to take blankets and camp chairs."

He motioned toward his wife. "Joann has copies of driving directions if you need them. Any questions?"

The crowd grew silent. Dylan scanned the crowd. Most faces pointed toward James, but a few panned the group to see if anyone dared to stall the search with a question. A hand shot up from a woman situated near the front. Dylan noticed a collective sinking of shoulders from the deflated crowd. "Can we bring flashlights?" She ignored the murmured groans.

James' ruddy face broke into a friendly grin. "Great question. We can use flashlights when we're on the trail. But once we've situated in the woods, I want everyone to be still and quiet. The Sasquatch will only come out if we're silent and unobserved. Flashlights would scare them off. Let's not limit our ability to see them tonight with excessive noise or light. Anyone else?"

Was everyone else clear about the process? Dylan had dozens of questions about protocol and what they might see. But he did not want to be singled out as the new guy that slowed everyone down.

James gave a final direction. "Anyone not wanting to join us can stay here with Joann. She'll prepare the community room for our debriefing. For everyone else, we're off." The crowd started to disperse. As James left the stairs, he paused in front of Dylan. "Wanna ride with me?"

"You bet." Dylan smiled, pleased to be on James' team.

From behind, he heard the shrill voice of the thin man who had talked about prior experiences. "Can I ride with you, James?"

"Absolutely, Kevin. Paul will ride with us, too. So that'll make four." James turned toward the church parking lot and stopped at a large, shiny pickup with an extended cab. Dylan walked to the passenger door behind the driver's side and jumped in. Shortly, Paul, a huge muscular man with dark-rimmed glasses and a full black beard, pulled open the passenger door for the front seat. Kevin joined Dylan in the back.

The drive to Sullivan's Ravine took about twenty minutes, with the last half of the ride along a smooth, well maintained dirt road. James drove with the stereo cranked up to a high volume. Rock music from the 1980s spilled from the speakers and drowned out any attempts at conversation.

Once they reached the trailhead, Dylan knew no more about the group than before they had entered the truck. As he stood outside, a loud ringing filled Dylan's head. His ears would need time to adjust between the silence of the forest and nearly 100 decibels of rock music. He speculated whether James suffered from hearing loss.

As cars and trucks arrived at the parking lot and disgorged their Sasquatch hunters, James called for people to assemble close to the trailhead. Once six to eight people reached the start of the trail, James sent them forward to walk for a specific length of time. He directed the first group to hike for forty minutes, the next for thirty-five minutes, and so on until the last group would only walk for five minutes.

After sitting for about a half-hour, the first and farthest group would start back to the cars. When the returning pack of people approached the next seated group, they would merge into one long line to walk back to the trailhead. Dylan and the other members of James' truck would form the final group. Thus, they would have the shortest distance to their observation point and, consequently, to the cars at the end of the event.

Dylan stamped his feet to warm them as each group left the parking lot. Twice he walked a short distance down the dirt road toward town and lifted his arms in a jumping jack motion to generate body heat. Finally, only a half dozen searchers remained.

Once James lost sight of the group designated to precede them, he clicked on a flashlight and motioned to Paul, Kevin, and Dylan to follow. The men turned on their beams but would darken them when they arrived where James would direct them to hunker down, watch, and listen.

James took the lead, and Dylan fell into the rear position. He tried to leave a respectful distance between himself and Kevin, as Jen had cautioned him about hikers who would annoyingly tailgate the person in front of them. A lead hiker with someone on his heels might feel pressured to walk at an uncomfortable pace as if the tailgater pushed from behind.

The broad path seemed generally clear of rocks, but tree roots crisscrossed the trail like massive dead snakes to create a slick tripping hazard for the hikers. Now and again, Paul or Kevin would comment or ask a question. At each transgression of the stealth-mode rule, James stopped to toggle his flashlight—from the trail to the offender.

James' tactic worked. The group settled into a quiet trudge up the path.

The only sounds came from rhythmic breathing, footfalls, and subtle rasps from rubbing fabric, all of which were dulled by the insulation of their hoods.

Dylan felt the darkness of the forest close around him. The mist created a gray cloud around his flashlight's beam but, thankfully, did not diminish his ability to see the trail. Layers of decayed leaves created a musty fragrance, periodically overpowered by the scent of fir and cedar.

As he let the gap between himself and Kevin widen, he felt a chill of solitude creep in. Faint sounds came from behind, and he jerked his flashlight beam to the rear to be sure no one followed.

The light cascaded over the receding trail and into the trees bordering the path. Dylan saw only tree limbs and the brush that glistened with moisture from the light rain. He shook his head to fling away the feeling of being observed. Maybe the excitement and drama of the search played into his imagination.

They only walked the designated five minutes, but the time seemed endless. Relieved when James stopped and motioned for the group to set up the camp chairs and blankets, Dylan looked down at the muddy mess made by feet tromping to more remote points. James' loaner chair would come in handy to keep him off the cold, wet ground. The group settled into a wide spot on the trail and sat.

Dylan heard James sigh each time one of them moved. The rustle of fabric and squeak of aluminum against the canvas disturbed the silence. The longer they sat in the darkness and drizzle, Dylan could make out the forest sounds. Insects chirped, and rodents rustled in the underbrush.

As the rain started to fall in earnest, Dylan succumbed to the hypnotic rhythm of drops plopping against his heavy jacket. As his head nodded, he feared falling asleep and pushed the edge of his hood behind one ear to improve his hearing. He pulled the other side across his face and covered his chilled nose.

What's that smell? He scowled and pulled the fabric away from his face. Dylan recognized the scent of wood smoke and sweat. An itchy shiver trickled across his shoulders. He hoped the thrift store honored its rule about accepting only laundered items.

As he squinted into the darkness, Dylan could barely make out his group, a collection of hulking shapes parked in a row on the trail. All faced the same way. If they had organized themselves to each face a different direction, then they might be more effective. Had James missed an opportunity?

A sudden movement snapped Dylan to attention. James reached out to nudge his neighbor, and the pattern dominoed through the others. The energy switched from mild boredom to high alert. Dylan strained to detect something in the blackness.

Then he heard it—a rhythmic thump. Dylan sensed the men straining on their chairs. *Where is the noise coming from?* Dylan pushed back his hood. The rain doused his already damp hair. He pivoted his head one way and then the other until he decided the noise came from farther up the trail. The pounding, low and constant, sounded more like machinery than from a person.

Tempted to stand and investigate, Dylan struggled to stay seated. He assumed any exploration would be frowned upon by the event's organizers. After all, they were in the woods to observe and listen, not to engage.

Chapter 26

GROVERTON, OREGON
JOANN WHITED

A few women stayed behind to help set up the post-event gathering. Joann was okay with that. With a short list of tasks, she did not want a bunch of controlling wives telling her how to organize her domain.

While most of the helpers were compliant, one rasped Joann's shell. Despite Victoria Arlington's good intentions, she annoyed everyone with passive-aggressive maneuvers. Joann managed to find assignments for Victoria designed to remove her from the room. The latest mission—to comb the storeroom for a box marked *mini pumpkins*.

Joann tapped an impatient foot and crossed her arms over the front of her fitted suit jacket to review their work. A commercial-sized, stainless steel coffee urn seeped the fragrance of roasted beans into the room. An adjacent pot held water for hot chocolate and tea. Platters of cookies, cakes, and James' pies, wrapped in clear plastic wrap, waited temptingly for the first searchers to return.

The wife of another avid Sasquatch believer and church member placed a friendly arm across Joann's shoulder. As they admired the room, Joann's compatriot said, "The sweets are out, and the drinks are nearly ready. I wish I had your knack for organizing these things. The tables look perfect."

Joann leaned into the hug. "Thanks for all of your help. I think we're good to go."

Victoria, an empty-handed polyester nightmare, plodded toward the pair with her head hung low. She said, "I've looked at each and every box. It's not down there. If you'd let Francie come with me, we could have searched in half the time and found it. But we'll have to do without."

Joann gritted her teeth. "Francie was busy with the coffee service. I was confident you'd manage without her."

"Well, you see how that worked out," Victoria mumbled.

Francie patted Joann's arm and smiled. "Don't worry. I'll fetch them. Be back in a jiff." She left the room with a self-assured gait.

Victoria stared at Joann and waited for new instructions. Joann knew she was unwilling to ask. So Joann returned her gaze. *Two can play this game.*

Joann maintained the silent standoff until Victoria finally succumbed. "Well? Do you have something else for me to do?"

Joann delivered a sugary smile. "The fliers for next Sunday's service are on the corner of my desk. Would you please bring them here? I'd like to place a few on the tables in case any nonmembers are interested in joining us for services."

Victoria nodded as she turned. "They'd better be easier to find than the pumpkin box," she muttered, loud enough to be overheard as she slunk from the room.

Moments later, Francie reappeared with the missing tote. "Right in front of the decorations boxes," Francie said in a stage whisper as she scanned the room for the absent Victoria.

Joann rolled her eyes as the pair scattered handfuls of miniature wire pumpkins onto the tables.

Joann glanced at her watch, an expensive Swiss model James bought her for one of those birthdays with a significant number. "They should be back soon. I think we're on time." As she spoke, the door to the community room opened.

James lumbered in, at the front of a long, wet line. His red-faced group shed their water soaked coats and shook them on the community room's tightly woven carpet. Joann glided to the entry and directed the searchers to hang their sopping gear over racks she had strategically organized near the doors.

Victoria approached. She held two fliers, one in each hand. "Are these what you wanted?"

"Precisely. If you'd fetch a dozen more and put them on the round tables, I'd be most grateful."

Victoria's shoulders slumped as she turned back to the entrance. "I would have brought more if you'd simply said so." Joann sighed in exasperation at the retreating Victoria.

After James removed his coat and cap, he hurried to Joann and gave her a warm hug. He leaned low to nuzzle his mustache against her neck and chin. She giggled at the tickle of his hair and icy cold cheeks.

Joann pushed him with both hands against his thick chest and playfully reprimanded him. "James, now stop! Your hair is sopping wet, and you're getting water all over me."

James let her escape but not beyond arms-reach. "Baby, we had an incredible time tonight. We heard the thumping sounds that happened last year, only this time they were closer to the trail, and they came from a bunch of directions. I think they may have been signaling to each other."

Joann's eyes widened. "Do you think it was them?"

"What else could it be? I can't imagine any humans would hide throughout the woods on a cold and rainy night. It was miserable out there."

She spotted the telling signs of deceit on his face. She gave him a tender smile. "Oh, James, I'm so glad this search was successful."

Apparently oblivious to her insincerity, he responded, "It would have been better if we actually saw one of them, but I'll take tonight's action as a step forward. Maybe they're more comfortable with being near us. There were nearly forty searchers out there tonight. Sasquatches are smart enough to know we were in the forest to watch them. I tell you, each year they're less reluctant to tell us they're there. It may take time before they come out in the open, but I'm sure they will eventually."

Joann looked at her husband and mentally questioned why he felt compelled to participate in the charade. No matter. His retirement hobbies were his own to design.

She glanced around the room. Had James invited the noisemakers to join the group for refreshments? No one would probably realize they were not part of the searcher group. The likely suspects were men from his old crew. They were loyal and willing to endure the torture of the elements without divulging their role in any deception.

As she admired her husband, Dylan approached—a wet mess with a mop of dripping hair. She speculated whether his rosy cheeks were a result of the cold or his excitement about the evening's events.

Nearly breathless, Dylan blew across the top of his paper cup filled to the brim with hot chocolate and a half dozen mini-marshmallows. "Joann, I'd fill you in on the Bigfoot sounds, but I'll bet James already told you what we heard. It was incredible."

"I've heard from James. It seems like there was more than one."

"I can't even explain it. Thumping sounds came from everywhere. There must have been a pack of them. It went on for at least ten minutes before the pounding slowed and then finally stopped."

Wide-eyed, Joann kept with the pretense and asked, "What did it sound like?"

"Like somebody smacking a log against a tree. Sometimes the thumps were in rhythm with eight or a dozen thuds. The next sound was from a different location, and there might only be one or two thumps. Then, another group with more. None of the patterns repeated." Dylan nodded like a bobblehead doll. I think someone recorded the noises on a cell phone. By the time I thought of doing it, the sounds had nearly finished."

"Somebody recorded the sounds? I'm amazed anyone had the presence of mind to take out their phone."

James interjected. "Kevin did it from our group, but there were others. They were higher up on the trail but recorded the noises, too."

"What are you going to do with them?" Joann asked James.

"Probably send them to one of the research groups analyzing Sasquatch data. This is a tremendous advancement in the evidence."

Dylan took a sip of hot chocolate. "Do you have plans to go back to Sullivan's Ravine tomorrow to see if they can find any clues about what made the sounds?"

James nodded. "I'll take a ride up there in the morning to set up a few motion detection cameras in the trees. Maybe I'll catch something on those."

Dylan looked intrigued. "You've done that before?"

"Yeah. I usually go out by myself at a time when nobody is around. I'd hate to have someone follow me into the woods and pick up one of my cameras. They're not cheap. I go back after a couple of weeks to change out the memory cards."

"What have you captured? Any signs of a Sasquatch?"

Joann smiled and thought about the hours James had spent organizing his wildlife photos on the computer.

He shook his head and said, "Unfortunately, no. But I've taken great photos of black bears and small mammals like weasels and raccoons. Of course, there is plenty of deer and elk in this area. So the cameras take pictures of them when they wander by."

"You must have an incredible collection. What do you do with them?" Dylan asked.

"I store them on my computer. Maybe one of these days, I'll make a show out of them. I don't know what I'm waiting for." James glanced into space. "Well actually, I do know. I'll be satisfied when I capture something extraordinary."

"Like a Sasquatch?" Dylan suggested.

James grinned. "Yeah. That would do it."

Chapter 27

DYLAN COX

As the evening wound down, guests ditched their used plates and cups in tall trash bins set up near the tables. Before they left, most searchers stopped to thank James for organizing the event. He vigorously shook their hands and asked them to be prepared for more excitement at next year's search.

While James dealt with the dwindling crowd, Dylan pulled Joann aside. "I need to thank you for the document you gave to me yesterday."

With eyes narrowed, she tapped a finger against her chin. "I'm not sure what you mean."

Dylan did not intend to play along. "I suspect you weren't supposed to give me the certificate, but I appreciate that you did. Don't worry. I won't tell anyone at the church about it."

She glanced around the room. "I don't think the *official* procedures are the best alternative for every situation. I hope you find peace in knowing your parents lived in Oregon."

"The certificate has led to more questions than it answered." Dylan told Joann about his trip to the university and his conversation with Dr. Breedlove.

Her forehead creased in dismay when he finished the tale of the Indian maiden. She patted his arm. "I assumed giving it to you would end your search. It doesn't seem like that happened."

"Do you think there's more information I could get from the church? Would there have been a written summary or interview document from when my parents came in?"

Joann shook her head. "We didn't write up anything like that back then."

"Back then?" Dylan straightened and realized she might have more to tell. "Did you work here back when my parents brought me to the church?"

"I had hoped you'd be satisfied with the information I gave you yesterday. I'm not really at liberty to say any more about your situation." She pulled a carton from under the coffee service table and started to transfer miniature pumpkins into the box.

Dylan understood she intended to close the subject, but he pressed further. He folded a honeycombed tissue pumpkin and laid it in the box.

Joann pulled it out and placed it on a table. She put a tender hand on Dylan's arm. "These will be stored separately." She took the box to the next table and gathered only the wire mini-pumpkins.

Dylan apologized. "I'm desperate to know more. I know you can help me to find out about my birth parents. Please, tell me what you know."

Joann straightened the front of her jacket with a tug. With a conspirator's stage whisper, she said, "Meet me in my office. I'm not comfortable having this conversation out here."

As she left, Dylan considered what information she might have concealed. Joann approached James, who was buried in an animated discussion with a half dozen stragglers. Dylan watched her interrupt his conversation, motion toward Dylan, and point to her office. He nodded in apparent understanding.

Before she left the community room, she turned and signaled for Dylan to follow.

Once inside her office, Joann shut the door. She asked Dylan to take a seat and sat in the chair next to him, rather than rounding her desk to the power chair.

Joann took a deep breath and placed a hand on Dylan's knee. "I was here the night she brought you into the church."

Dylan trembled. His past was shrouded in layers of secrets. Perhaps Joann held the key to at least part of the truth. "Why didn't you tell me when I first met you?"

"When you first came in, I couldn't place your name. But it sounded familiar." She patted his knee. "Once I found your file, the details flooded back to me. You realize I normally can't share details because of the Reverend's strict policy."

"I got that, but why tell me now?"

"Because we don't know who your birth parents are. They wouldn't be able to initiate contact."

Dylan imagined another giant stepping into his path as she continued. "You came to us long before Reverend Erwin became our pastor. That night, nearly thirty years ago, our minister called at about one o'clock in the morning and asked me to come to the church to help him deal with an emergency. When I arrived, I found him in the sanctuary with an older woman and a tiny baby."

While Joann looked at Dylan, he could tell her mind replayed a scene from long in the past. She said, "The baby was you—only a couple days old. You were swaddled in a soft gray blanket and looked warm and content. You had a startling amount of curly light brown hair, and your eyes were the palest green. They're darker now, but back then they were the color of spring leaves. When the woman handed you to me, you looked straight at me. I'm not sure if infants that young can make out what they see, but I believe you inspected every inch of my face."

"An old woman brought me here?" Dylan stood and crossed to the window. He muttered, "Why can't my story be simpler?"

Unwed teenagers gave up babies. Parents without the means to raise another child placed newborns in adoption centers. His history included myths and an old woman who brought a baby to a church in the middle of the night.

Outside, fog-encased streetlights cast an eerie glow on the nearly empty parking lot. Dylan watched a couple exit the church and walk to their pickup.

Joann joined him at the window. "She was definitely too old to be your mother. The woman came from a reservation and said they couldn't keep you there. She wanted us to arrange an adoption to a family who would take care of you. We assured her you would be placed in a good Christian home. She seemed comfortable with that, so we completed the certificate with the information she gave to us."

He turned toward Joann. "She gave you the names?"

"Letter for letter. I recall the woman thought for a while before she wrote them on a pad of paper. I asked her if they were first or last names, but she only nodded and wouldn't explain further. I put them on the certificate the way the woman gave them to me. The first word for the father and the second for the mother. When I finished typing, she reviewed the completed certificate and confirmed all the details were correct."

"That's it? She didn't say anything about how she came to walk into your church with a baby?"

Joann shrugged and ran her hands down the front of her suit. "She wanted to leave right away, but I told her we were obligated to call the Sheriff and report an abandoned child. The authorities would likely contact the tribe to set up a meeting to find out more about what happened. She looked scared, and I thought she might want to take you back and leave. But the Reverend intervened. He promised her full confidentiality. Later, he told me he was afraid of where you might end up if we didn't agree to take you and respect her need for privacy."

Dylan crossed his arms in front of his chest. His eyes narrowed. "Did she tell you anything about where I came from? What if somebody had kidnapped me?"

"That was always a risk. But I contacted every hospital and police station in northern Oregon. I kept an eye on the papers for months. I never discovered any hint of a missing child."

"That's it?"

"No, there's more."

"Now what? I was born into a family of wolves?" Dylan struggled with his frustration. "Sorry about that. Please, tell me the rest."

She nodded, her eyes full of empathy. "There was a story, but I don't know if it's true. Come and sit while I tell you."

Joann tugged at Dylan's arm and led him back to the chairs. "She told us you were found outside on a windy night at the edge of the forest near the home of one of the tribal leaders."

Dylan scoffed. "That's unlikely."

Joann shook her head. "I don't know whether she told the truth or not, but that's all she would say. After she left the church, the Reverend and I agreed not to report her or you to the authorities. That night, I took you home. James and I cared for you while we verified you weren't reported missing and arranged the adoption with your parents in Chicago."

Joann folded her hands in her lap. She leaned forward and whispered, "You were such a beautiful baby. Part of me wanted to keep you for myself, but it wouldn't have been our place. Your parents were on our waiting list for a long time. You were their baby."

"Why would the tribe give me away?"

"I don't know. There could have been any of a dozen reasons. Your coloring didn't match theirs, so you could have been a mixed-race child. I'm not sure that would have been acceptable at the time. Or maybe they *did* find you in the woods, left by someone who intended to have you raised by the Indians. If that was the case, I'm not sure they would have wanted to deal with questions about your heritage that may have come up later. These are possibilities. But we'll never really know the truth. I'm sorry, but we don't know anymore."

Dylan straightened and considered his next steps. "Did you take down her name or which tribe she was from?"

"I did not," said Joann sheepishly. "If we'd pressed her, I felt she would have lied. That was nearly thirty years ago. She had to be in her seventies or eighties. I'm sure she's long dead by now."

Dylan felt doors slam shut to stop his momentum.

Chapter 28

Destiny slid her key into the deadbolt of Nate's gallery. The dim evening lights lent a spooky air to the place as if the space were frozen in time and waiting for Nate to return.

As she stood next to the conference table where Trip used to play hide and seek as a toddler, Destiny scanned the gallery and corner studio where Nate created his work. Scents of turpentine and oil paints rushed her senses and brought back memories—some dear and familiar, others stressful and unkind.

She walked to his desk and sat in the stiff leather office chair. As Destiny rolled forward, she placed both palms on the desktop and drummed her fingers on the polished surface. The desk had been a gift from Nate's parents when the gallery opened. It sat orderly and pristine, a space forever off limits to Destiny and Trip.

A coarse cement letter tray lay on one corner. As Destiny dragged it to the center of the desk to flip through the contents, she straightened with a start. The rough edge of the tray left a faint gouge in the polished teakwood top.

Destiny leaned forward to run the side of her thumb across the mark. After a moment of thought, Destiny smiled deviously and tugged the inbox back and forth across the surface to leave gouges reminiscent of Zorro's slashing rapier. Nate would have been furious.

The box held unpaid utility bills, a three-month-old birthday card from an insurance broker, and a receipt for drywall repairs in Nate's upstairs apartment. Destiny scoffed. She speculated whether Nate had put a fist or piece of crockery through a wall.

At least it wasn't toward me this time. She dropped the correspondence back into the tray.

Destiny stood to browse the gallery. She started near the front door and slowly examined each piece of art. They were suspended from wires and illuminated with pinpoint lights from above. Dozens of new works hung displayed with only a couple in the style familiar to her.

"I gotta admit, I like this new approach better than the crap he churned out when we were together," Destiny whispered to an abstract piece, loaded with acrylic paint and dotted with wires, leaves, and feathers.

Destiny spun around as footsteps tapped down the stairs and entered the gallery. Cynthia clacked forward on stilettos.

"Who the fuck are you?" asked Cynthia, a spandex-clad Ninja, waving a baseball bat over her mass of auburn curls.

"I could ask the same of you, but I assume you're Cynthia Waters." Destiny straightened to her full height.

"You have me at a loss. You are…?" Cynthia raised a brow.

"I'm Destiny Kusik—or rather Stewart. I'm Nate's wife."

Cynthia pointed the bat at Destiny and sneered. "She's dead."

"Actually, as you can see, I'm not. I suspect Nate never mentioned it to you?"

Cynthia lowered the tip of her weapon to the floor. "That's interesting news, and yes, Nate neglected to inform me." She narrowed her eyes at Destiny. "He could be a real ass."

Destiny snorted. "You got that right."

Cynthia raised the bat and tapped it against her palm with the authority of a batter anticipating the first pitch. "Why fabricate your death instead of just leaving town?"

Destiny stepped forward to tower more than a foot above Cynthia's petite action-figure posture. "Extenuating circumstances. Why are you still here?"

"I live here."

"Not anymore. I'm asking you to leave by morning."

Cynthia raised her chin. "What if I don't care to?"

Destiny drew courage from her new circumstances. Earlier, she would have avoided confrontation at all costs. "I stopped by our attorney's office before coming here. We reviewed Nate's directives. I own this place now."

Cynthia scoffed. "That's unlikely. Nate and I had plans."

"You may have *had* plans, but Nate never made it official. If you don't choose to go, I'll have to get the police involved." Destiny looked down at her rival. "Wouldn't you like to avoid that?"

"I don't care who gets involved." Cynthia glanced around the gallery and toward the door. "Is Nate's spawn with you?"

As she drew her shoulders back, Destiny responded, "His name's Trip, and he's at a friend's house. I wasn't sure if I wanted him to meet you." She frowned. "Now that we've met, I'm glad he's with her. At any rate, I expect you to leave by morning."

Destiny walked back to the desk and scanned the adjacent pegboard laden with keys. She picked out a set of car keys. "I can't believe he kept my old Subaru. It must be parked out back."

Destiny pocketed the ring and ran her hand across the remaining clusters. She watched them rock back into place. Nate's precise penmanship identified each one—gallery, storeroom, BMW/spare, and M&D's house. She grabbed the last set and made a mental note to return them to Nate's parents.

"I assume Nate gave you a key to this place. Please leave it when you go." Destiny paused near the door where a stack of paintings leaned against the front wall. "What's the story here?" She pointed at the canvases.

With authority, Cynthia said, "Those are pieces Nate wanted me to have. Seal & Send will pick them up in the morning for shipment to New York."

Destiny crossed her arms in front of her chest. "Unless you can produce a receipt, they stay in the gallery." She twirled a finger to outline the perimeter of the room. "All of this, including the paintings, belongs to Trip and me."

She returned to the office chair and sat with a thud. Destiny defiantly clasped her hands on the desktop. "On second thought, I'd like you to leave now. I'll hang right here until you clear out your things. That's only *your* things. I've put up with bitches like you for my whole married life, but no more. Get the fuck out of my gallery."

Chapter 29

IDAHO
DYLAN COX

The sign blinked *Maricle Motel* in pink neon. A one-story brick building with twenty drive-up rooms shouted family-run establishment. Probably in his price range. Dylan pulled under the canopy to the door marked 'Check In.'

Besides being over halfway between Jamesville and Salida, Dylan could not resist a motel that advertised an *amazingly clean hot tub*. The illuminated sign had caught his eye on the way out to Destiny's place, not merely for the hot tub but also for their color TVs.

Augie stayed in the car while Dylan went inside to register. A country western tune, circa the 1980s, played on a portable AM/FM radio with a large numbered dial and a chrome telescopic antenna.

As he approached the counter, a tobacco-chewing, middle-aged woman spat into a white Styrofoam cup. She abandoned a dog-eared magazine to face him. The pages of the periodical lay open to a two-page glossy of men accompanied by hounds and rifles. Even upside down, Dylan could read the title of the story, *Novice Hunters Be Warned: Cover Your Scent*.

Tempted to start the conversation with a question about undesirable smells, Dylan took the high road and asked, "Do you have any rooms available?"

She closed the magazine with a sigh and placed both hands on the counter. "Did the sign say 'No Vacancy'?"

Basic customer service training might be needed. Dylan smiled and tried again. "I'd like a double room with twin beds. Do you have any of those?"

"Nah. I only have a double with two queens. Will that do?"

Dylan agreed. With nicotine stained fingers, she pushed a registration form and pen past the No Smoking sign and across a marred linoleum countertop.

Dylan looked at the pen that advertised Ted's Guns and Donuts. Might need to pocket this one—Tom would not believe it otherwise.

As he completed the three-part form in white, buff, and pink, Dylan reached to retrieve his wallet. "So how long have you had color TVs?"

The clerk's eyes narrowed. She snatched the document from Dylan. "I'm not the owner, and I didn't have anything to do with the sign out front. Bill thinks it's funny, but I'm tired of dealing with the smart-ass questions about it."

"Bill's the owner?"

"Bill Maricle. His family's had this place since the forties."

"Are you Mrs. Maricle?" asked Dylan with a boyish grin.

The corner of her mouth twitched. "Hardly. Bill's my husband's cousin."

"If you're married to Bill's cousin, you could still be Mrs. Maricle. Right?"

The twitch turned into a hint of a smile. "Not a Maricle. Name's Henson. Sue Henson."

"Glad to meet you, Mrs. Henson." Dylan handed her a credit card.

She nodded as she stuck his card into a chip reader and tore apart the registration form. After she stapled his receipt to the pink copy and returned it to Dylan, Sue slid the other pages into a metal file box.

Dylan leaned over the counter. "Mrs. Henson, I've had a long drive today and am looking forward to a soak. Is the hot tub as clean as advertised?"

Her eyes twinkled. "Maybe not amazingly clean, but at least surprisingly so."

After they unloaded their bags into the room, Dylan pulled his swimsuit and T-shirt from the duffel. "Wanna join me?" he asked Augie.

Augie sat on the bed with pillows propped behind his back. He reached for the remote and said, "Nope."

Dylan smiled. "We've had quite a day. Between seeing Destiny and Trip to the airport and driving all day, you might find it relaxing. Why don't you want to come?"

"They made me swim in school. I didn't like it."

Dylan envisioned the typical high school swim class filled with noise and boisterous youngsters. Dylan was not surprised to hear Augie would find the experience chaotic and disconcerting. "No worries. We can go some other time."

When Dylan left the bathroom dressed for the hot tub, he found Augie absorbed in a movie with gunfire and car chases. Dylan draped a towel around his neck and headed out into the night.

A wrought iron fence surrounded the spa and pool to separate them from the asphalt parking lot. Six chaise lounges made from aluminum tubes and white nylon webbing stood in a row between the fence and a kidney-shaped pool. It was empty except for a few dried leaves rustling around the bottom in the light autumn breeze.

In the far corner, Dylan spotted the in-ground hot tub, unoccupied and covered with a thermal blanket. He pulled the cover onto the concrete slab and spun the timer button full circle to activate the jets.

Dylan slipped into the swirling pool and settled back against one of the pulsing streams and succumbed to the massage. Tension from endless hours in the car eroded.

He stared into the night sky to pick out constellations he remembered from his youth. Jen had enhanced his repertoire with a dozen more, but his recollection of their names and locations had faded. He wished she was here to remind him. She would probably scold him for his forgetfulness. Jen had a way of teasing him about his lack of outdoor knowledge that fueled his desire for her. Most likely because the teasing commonly escalated into a wrestling match and ultimately sex.

To counteract the heat from the tub, Dylan pulled his arms from under the water. He braced them back on the lip of the spa and inhaled the mixture of chlorine-infused steam and chilled night air.

Suddenly, the pool area blurred, and shapes obscured his view. The migraine sent black and white triangles to dance in front of his eyes. He opened and shut them to clear his vision, but the gyrating shapes remained. *No brandy this time.* Dylan hoped the massaging water might help thwart his headache's intensity.

Dylan straightened as the shapes faded and morphed into an image. He strained to focus. Jen's cabin returned but in a scene different from his previous trip across Idaho.

Instead of a clear late afternoon with sunshine beaming through the pine branches, a misty fog enveloped the yard. Dylan guessed the image was from a rainy, post-dawn morning. In the driveway stood Jen's Jeep, a doorless mud-caked affair with knobby tires designed to ascend boulder filled roads with ease.

While Dylan recognized the place, he did not feel a sense of déjà vu. This picture was someone else's memory.

The vision faded, replaced by a new image—two footprints in the mud next to Jen's Jeep. *I've seen this before,* Dylan thought with a start. He tightened his grip on the rim to stop from sliding farther into the water.

Misshapen and large, the prints looked like the ones Jen spotted near the cabin last summer. She had photographed them after she laid a tape measure next to them. They were over fourteen inches long.

Only two days prior, Dylan had shown his photo of Sasquatch prints to James Whited's believer friends. But Dylan's picture differed from the vision and not merely from the lack of a tape measure.

On the bottom edge of the hallucination, nearly out of view, Dylan could see a tiny portion of a toe. The chestnut-colored toenail badly needed a trim and was encrusted with mud and fur.

Chapter 30

SALIDA, COLORADO—OCTOBER 16

Augie and Dylan sat at the dining table in Augie's trailer and shared a pizza from a cardboard to-go box. Consistent with his commitment to eat healthier foods, Dylan had ordered two medium pies—one pepperoni and the other vegetarian. The pepperoni pizza was long gone, but half of the veggie pizza remained. *So much for good intentions.*

Both he and Augie were exhausted from two long days in the car. Storms across Utah had slowed their progress, but otherwise the weather cooperated to keep the drive sufficiently uneventful.

Dylan finished his final piece of pizza and washed it down with a swig of beer. He wiped his mouth on a paper napkin. "I want to stay in town for a couple of nights to catch up with Kate and spend more time with you. Of course, I'll go to Nate's memorial service before I head back to Chicago. Are you fine with that?"

Augie's wide grin provided his answer before he responded. "Yeah. But I'm not going to Nate's service."

"Understandable." Dylan wished he had that option but wanted to be there for his aunt and uncle. Trip and Destiny might appreciate it, too. Before he took another sip, Dylan asked, "What did you think of Oregon?"

"Wet and cold. Why would Destiny want to live there?" Augie absentmindedly pulled at the corner of the pizza crust on his plate.

"You'll have to ask her. Maybe she'll move back to Salida once everything's straightened out with Nate's estate and her role in Trip's disappearance."

"I want her to stay here. Salida is better with Destiny here."

"Indeed, it is. When do you start to work again?" Dylan stood to gather paper plates for the trash.

Augie took the empty pizza box to the kitchen. After he shook remnant crumbs into a tall can, Dylan placed the container on the portion of the counter reserved for trash destined for the recycle bin. Augie said, "I'll go to see Kate at the school. She'll call my boss for me."

"That would normally work, but it's the weekend so she'll be off work tomorrow. How about I come by here in the late morning, and we can call Kate on my cell phone. Or, we could call directly if you have the work number. What do you think?"

Augie cocked his head as if evaluating his choices. "We can call my work on your phone. I've got the number."

Dylan suggested they still contact Kate and see if she could join them for lunch. Dylan wanted to talk with her about Augie's artistic talent. She might have some ideas about connecting Augie with a local artist who could help him fine-tune and promote his work.

Augie came around to Dylan's side of the table. He surprised Dylan with an awkward hug. "What was that for?" Dylan asked. He knew Augie's embrace was a special gift.

"I think you might be sad. Hugs feel okay when people are sad."

"Why do you think I'm sad?"

"Because you didn't meet your parents."

A lump swelled in Dylan's throat. "I *am* sad about that. It seems like we've got more questions now than when we left. But I still enjoyed meeting Destiny and Trip. I liked spending time with you, too."

Augie returned to his chair. "I liked taking a trip with you, too."

A sharp knock at the door silenced the pair. They glanced at each other before Augie stepped to the front and looked through the peephole. "Destiny!" He threw open the door and rushed into her open arms.

"Hey buddy, you're gonna knock me flat!" Destiny said as she embraced him.

Dylan stood to welcome her. "You're in time for some pizza. You'll be happy to know there's plenty of your favorite flavor."

Destiny grinned and stepped into the trailer. She stopped to unwrap a long woolen scarf from her neck and hang it and her denim jacket on a peg by the door. "Man, it's hot in here, Augie. Are you still keeping the temperature at 75?"

She took charge and walked to the thermostat to swivel the dial. Destiny scanned the room. "I can't believe I'm back. I thought I'd never see you in Salida again."

"Come, come, come," Augie stuttered, too excited for a formal welcome. He took her hand and led her to an empty chair at the table. Without hesitation, Augie placed his cushion on her seat.

Augie fetched a plate and cutlery from the kitchen. He tore a paper towel from the spool, folded it into four precise quarters, and slipped it under her fork.

Before he returned to his chair, Augie pulled the box with the vegetarian pizza in front of Destiny. He opened the lid. "We ordered this one with lots of vegetables. We didn't know you'd be here, but it's all yours now."

"I'm forever grateful—for the pizza and your friendship," Destiny said.

As she settled at the table, Dylan stood to open the fridge. He pulled out a brown bottle. "I assume you'll join me to drink a beer. We're dying to hear what the Sheriff said."

"More of a wine gal, but I'm up for a break in tradition. I'll join you with a beer. We've got a reason to celebrate."

"I'm guessing you're not expecting a lengthy prison term?" Dylan handed her a bottle and a glass.

"Sheriff Austin is my hero. He won't issue any charges against me. Since Nate and I were still married and hadn't filed any custody arrangements, I didn't break any laws when I took Trip to Oregon."

"What about charges for obstruction of justice or impeding the missing person investigation?" Dylan hoped they would be lenient.

"He said there would have been a problem if I'd lied to officials or actively tried to derail the investigation. Since they never contacted me, I'm in the clear. In the records, Sheriff Austin plans to implicate Jen as the person who masterminded the abduction, coerced Augie into helping her, and could have stopped the search."

"Is it fair to put all this on her?"

She leaned forward to lay a hand on Dylan's forearm. "I don't want to tarnish her legacy either, but the Sheriff said they would close the investigation based on this scenario. I've assured the Sheriff that Augie and I will each commit to 100 hours of community service in the coming year. He thought my suggestion sounded reasonable."

She looked at Augie and asked, "Are you okay with joining me to pick up trash along the highways and working for the county's social services center?"

"Will you go with me?" he asked.

"I said you'd be joining me. What to do you think?"

"You know, I'll help you."

"Good. I already told Sheriff Austin you'd help. I'm sorry for not asking you first."

Dylan interrupted. "How's Trip taking Nate's death?" He knew the boy hated change. Could he handle a tragic shift?

Destiny's face fell. "He's really gloomy. I hope their rocky relationship won't make him feel guilty. I've always tried to talk up his father's positive attributes. Never saw any point in poisoning Trip's mind against Nate. Now that his dad won't play a role in his life, Trip will have to make up his mind about how he wants to remember Nate."

"I assume you've talked with my aunt and uncle. What's the plan for a memorial service?"

"Nate's parents are on their way from Chicago and will be here tomorrow. I've spoken to them over the phone. But we ignored the elephant in the room."

"The story about your faked suicide and why you took Trip to Oregon?"

"Yeah, that one. It'll come up when we meet face-to-face, but up to now, we've only talked about plans for Nate."

"How are they taking it all?"

"Your aunt seems strong—all business and handling arrangements. Your uncle's a basket case."

Dylan took a sip of beer and watched the foam head slither back down into the glass. "I thought it would be the other way around. My uncle is more the take-charge type. But you never really know how people will react in these situations."

Destiny nodded. "His folks still want to have a service here and another in Chicago. I'm not fighting them for custody of his cremains. They have a family crypt in a cemetery near their home and will keep his urn there. Our service will be at Ark Valley Funeral Home with a celebration of life afterward at the gallery. I haven't finalized anything yet."

"Where will you stay?" asked Augie.

"At the gallery. That's been a surreal experience."

Dylan imagined Destiny in Nate's sterile bachelor pad. "To be there without Nate?"

"Well, that and evicting Cynthia. She didn't intend to move out."

Dylan chuckled. "She must have been shocked when you showed up."

"To say the least. First off, Nate never told her I was still alive. Her attitude morphed from surprise into territorial banshee in a heartbeat. Once she heard the gallery and Nate's apartment were still jointly owned by him and me, she threw a fit."

"Nate never changed the ownership when you left?"

"I talked with his lawyer and found out he didn't modify any deeds, titles, or his will. I suspect he hadn't gotten around to it and never imagined we'd be in this situation. The inheritance will help me fund Trip's college reserves and pay for us to resettle."

"Here in Salida?" Augie chimed in.

Destiny shrugged. "Maybe. There's a lot to think about. I don't know the first thing about running a gallery, and there's a lot of bad memories in Salida." She looked at Augie and smiled. "There are good reasons to stay, too."

She gulped the last sip of beer. "I've got to run. Trip's at the gallery with a friend of mine. I wanted to stop by to welcome you back from your long drive and tell you the news. I'll be tied up with Nate's parents tomorrow, but maybe we can meet up in the next day or two."

After Destiny left, Dylan joined Augie to clean up from dinner. He wanted to ask a favor but hesitated about how to say it. Based on Nate's attack, Augie might turn him down flat. While staying at the cabin could be reckless, he longed for the comfort of feeling connected with Jen. Additionally, he felt drawn to her home after the visions he'd had at the motel in Utah.

Finally, he asked, "I'd like to stay at Jen's cabin while I'm here if that's okay with you."

Augie stiffened, his concern apparent in his knitted brows. "No. It's not safe. Both Jen and Nate were killed there."

Dylan reached across the table to place his hand over Augie's. "Nothing happened when I stayed at the cabin before our trip. I should be okay for a couple of nights. I promise to be very careful."

Augie did not look convinced but reluctantly agreed.

Chapter 31

KALEV

Another day had passed without gaining further intel. I stayed on the trails near the cabin, convinced the location was the key to meet my objective. Consistent with my daily pattern, I policed the perimeter by skirting the adjacent meadows. All the while, I stayed cautious not to alert the deer and elk browsing on grasses and seeds. Normal conditions would create an atmosphere of calm and tranquility to lull my target into complacency.

Earlier, I had watched the sun rise and dry the trails. Typically, larger mammals sought cooler confines to rest and escape the traffic along the paths. The day was drastically different from a few months earlier when trails choked with hikers forced me to find shelter in a cave. But the summertime crowds diminished as fall progressed. So I sat for hours on a hillside to monitor foot traffic.

Birds and animals provided little distraction, as they behaved in predictable ways. The birds collected food on their journey southward, and small mammals gathered nuts and materials for their winter dens.

At midday, my interest piqued when I spotted a group of birds collaborating to chase off a potentially lethal predator. These small events added to my collective knowledge of the area and terrain. I wanted to understand how animals interacted, as their behaviors could potentially derail the mission once everything fell into place. I overlooked not even the smallest details.

Recreators' patterns seemed, at first, unpredictable. But after I watched them for months, patterns emerged in their activities.

Hikers, who smelled of insect repellant and sun protection, hurried along the path. They talked among themselves and were oblivious to all who watched them pass. The mountain bikers sped along the trails at a blistering pace—focused only on the inches immediately in front of their tires. A few of the bikes were motorized, which obliterated all sounds of nature. These individuals were bundled up in protective clothes and helmets, which insulated them from the subtle movements of mountain breezes and the sounds of bird songs and squirrel chirps.

Why did they bother to be outside? Perhaps they only attempted to conquer nature and not experience it.

Hunters had not wandered the woods in the first couple months of my mission. In the recent past, as shadows lengthened and daylight hours grew short, I spotted them daily. Typically alone or in pairs, they stalked the trails dressed in clothes imitating woodland hues. Hunters believed they blended into the environment despite their smells and noise.

Once I saw a pair of them take down a deer. After that experience, I enjoyed thwarting their efforts by warning the game. The animals would flee far from the reach of arrows and bullets.

As daylight transitioned to dusk, animal activity shifted from those ambivalent about being seen to those seeking the protection of the darkness. I followed my routine and walked to the cabin shortly after sunset.

Nothing looked amiss, except for the stacks of uprooted trees piled in the yard behind the house. That devastation had happened days earlier and could not be undone. While I played a part, I refused to take full credit for the explosion of timber. I blamed circumstances beyond my control.

I inspected the exterior of the building and chased away a small pack of rodents that intended to take up residence. At the stream behind the cabin, I sloshed frigid water over my hands and raked a fingernail under the other nails—an inadequate attempt to rid myself of dirt.

Despite my frustration, I dipped my cupped hands into the flow and splashed water on my face. As I rubbed my grubby cheeks, gray, grit-filled drops fell back into the stream. This place was covered with unrelenting filth.

My campsite lay only a short walk from the cabin, and I reached my bivouac well before the final minutes of daylight. The overhang of brush provided shelter from peering eyes, and my stash of soft juniper boughs afforded insulation from the hard ground. If the evening turned cold, I planned to huddle under the branches. I longed for the moderate temperatures and soft clean covers of my bed at home.

As I wriggled my hips to find a comfortable position on the hard ground, I recalled events witnessed earlier in the summer. From behind a barrier of bushes and pine limbs, I had watched silently as the target searched frantically and finally found his mate's dismembered body, anguish apparent from his grief-stricken face and the primeval sounds he released.

I wanted to comfort him and let him know her death was the work of a bear and mountain lion. I could not be held responsible for their vicious attack. But the timing was wrong—far too early to make contact.

When uniformed males arrived to remove the female's carcass, the target seemed immeasurably distraught. I expected him to stay at the cabin to rest and grieve, but he disappeared for the rest of the summer and into autumn.

First bewildered at his response and then insurmountably angry, I cursed my arrogance to assume he would remain after she was gone. Would he ever return? If not, the sacrifices I had made to come here were all for naught.

When the target finally reappeared, he slept inside the cabin for two nights. While brief, I took his stopover as a sign he intended to make regular visits. All thoughts of defeat were vanquished. My plans were back on track.

I knew the target could not resist the cabin, a place offering familiarity, comfort, and a bond with the female. He would be lulled into feeling protected and secure. Besides, the isolated location provided a perfect place to implement my plan.

Nearly asleep, I heard a car turn from the dirt road into the driveway. The crunch of tires was unmistakable. I sat up at immediate attention. Would the visitor be another person coming to degrade the cabin?

In my experience, only those familiar with the location came at night.

Did I dare hope the target had returned?

I hated to be disappointed. Whenever events fell short of expectations, my mood exploded and turned to anger, which prompted aggression. After these episodes, I felt great remorse and longed for the sanity and comfort of those who knew me.

The car stopped, and the engine noise ceased. I rose to peek around the cabin to see whether the caller looked worthy of my attention.

Chapter 32

DYLAN COX

Dylan pulled the rental car to the front porch. He felt braver than the last time at the cabin and turned off the vehicle and extinguished the lights. He shut the car door and stood in the yard to let his eyes adjust to the meager light from the nearly full waxing moon. Nothing moved, and nothing rustled.

He juggled Augie's door key, a flashlight, and a small duffle with his necessities. When he reached the porch, Dylan dropped the duffle and clicked on the light. He scanned the beam across the front and spotted the boarded-up window. *Must be where Nate gained access.*

The blemish looked like a plywood pirate's patch on the face of Jen's home, a cruel reminder an uninvited guest pawed through her belongings. He tracked the light back to the entrance. Dylan unlocked the deadbolt and pushed his duffle into the cabin with his foot.

A dozen stacked moving boxes sat inside, all taped and identified with "Woman's clothes" in black marker. Kate must have started to clean out Jen's things.

He stepped to the bedroom and shone the light in the closet. It stood empty except for a pair of abandoned wire hangers. Dylan tugged open a dresser's middle drawer. The pull offered little resistance as the bureau, once jammed with yoga tights and fleece, was brutally bare.

Surely the bathroom still held evidence of Jen's existence. He opened the medicine cabinet to chipped paint and empty glass shelves streaked with old toothpaste crumbs. Dylan pulled the shower curtain across the rod.

He smiled with satisfaction and opened the nearly empty shampoo bottle. With eyes closed, Dylan inhaled the rosemary and mint fragrance to bring Jen into the room. He could almost feel her damp hair rest against his chest, as it had when he held her after she had showered. When he returned to the great room, Dylan slipped the shampoo bottle into his duffle.

He set the flashlight on the kitchen counter to splay a beam across the living room. Dylan spun the light toward the piled boxes and then to the boarded window. If he had felt Jen's calm energy on the previous visit, he now sensed irritation at the violation of her domain. Maybe it was a mistake to stay here.

Broken glass shards caught the light and twinkled like discarded glitter on the rug. Dylan grabbed a broom from the mudroom to sweep errant bits of windowpane into a dustpan and deposited them into the trash.

Dylan wanted to preserve his batteries. He lit candles and knelt by the hearth to start a fire. After the starter-cube ignited, Dylan sat cross-legged in front to transfer fuel between his shrinking woodpile and the fireplace. He added the thinnest pieces first.

The little blaze grew and gave off much needed warmth. Dylan held his hands toward the flames to take advantage of the meager heat escaping into the living room. Once he warmed up, Dylan rose to rummage in Jen's liquor cabinet. He poured himself a brandy and returned to the floor in front of the fire.

Dylan stared into the flames and enjoyed the silence of the night, only broken by crackling wood and sporadic settling of the ancient log walls. He inhaled the aroma of smoke, which brought back memories of lying before the fire with Jen. They made love in this very spot, and Dylan recalled the patterns of light flickering across Jen's toned, naked body.

She was an incredible lover, attentive to his desires but willing to succumb to his advances. Dylan felt physical pressure from his romantic thoughts and considered an escape to the bathroom to take care of his pent-up need. Or maybe he could take care of business here in the living room.

He glanced toward the uncurtained windows and scoffed at his modesty. Who could possibly be watching? He stood and took a wad of napkins from the holder then returned to sit on the loveseat in front of the fire. He unzipped and stroked himself. Dylan drifted into memories of Jen's firm and welcoming body.

Without warning, the flash of pre-migraine shapes danced into his vision. "What the fuck," he said aloud. Dylan zipped his pants with an exasperated yank, then cradled the sides of his head and rubbed his temples. The familiar black and white flashes blocked his view of the fireplace. He lay down on the loveseat and curled into a fetal position to wait for the shapes to transition into stabbing pain or a vision.

The shapes dissipated as they had in the Idaho spa. He continued to massage his temples and sat up. The gyrating outlines faded with only the corners of his vision obliterated. Dylan wanted to dull his senses further. Peripheral vision helped him walk to the kitchen and refill his drink.

When he returned to the loveseat, an image replaced the flashing shapes. Not a snapshot like before, but a streamed video. He saw himself and Jen walking in the woods. She wore hiking shorts that flattered her tiny waist and exposed her tanned, toned legs. In the lead, Jen's mouth moved as if she explained some specific aspect of wildlife or folklore. She wore a bulky, sky-blue backpack, which might have been filled with feathers, as its weight did not hamper her pace.

Dylan could see himself moving several feet behind her. He wore jeans and a sweaty T-shirt and gasped for breath. Dylan, in the vision, appeared scarcely able to keep up with her and focused myopically on the back of Jen's boots.

He felt torn between shaking the vision from his head and enjoying the scene with Jen—a voyeuristic view of their first hike. Back then, he had been ill-equipped without proper clothes or a pack. Dylan recalled showing up and carrying only a water bottle. Dylan relied on her preparedness for his lunch and her purification pump to refill his bottle with clean mountain lake water.

Besides his immediate physical attraction to Jen, this hike had fostered his appreciation for Jen's self-sufficiency in the wilderness. She did not brag about her extensive knowledge. It showed in her awareness and willingness to share tidbits about what they saw along the hike. Jen could identify birdcalls, plants, animal tracks, and scat. The image faded slowly, and Dylan's feeling of loss refreshed.

As the room came back into view, Dylan noticed the fire had started to fade. *That's not good.* He stood to feed more logs into the fireplace. After he added the reserve, Dylan picked up the log sling and went outside to gather wood from the pile.

The night felt chilly and still. A nearly full moon cast beams through the thick, dense forest. Shadows formed intricate patterns on the dry, rocky ground beyond the porch.

Dylan took several deep breaths that made the thin air chill the back of his throat. He thought about his promise to Augie. Was he wrong to act cavalier and head outside in the dark? Jen's attack came at night. When did they come for Nate? He needed wood for the fire. That was a certainty. The current location of the predators seemed uncertain.

He straightened and pulled his headlamp from a pocket. After Dylan positioned the beam in the middle of his forehead, he clicked on the light and adjusted the empty sling over a shoulder. He moved quickly past the boarded window and stepped off the porch to round the corner of the cabin.

While he strained to hear anything amiss, Dylan only caught an occasional owl hoot and a sole hearty cricket. As he transferred logs from the woodpile, a branch snapped. Dylan stopped with the last one held above the sling.

Dylan kept the weapon in his hand as he straightened and turned toward the sound. He scanned the beam of his headlamp across the yard's perimeter. Nothing moved. With silent toe-first steps, Dylan moved to the rear of the cabin and shined the beam across the backyard. Huge uprooted trees and bushes, their root balls caked in mud, filled a space that a few days earlier contained only dried grass, rabbitbrush, and yucca.

"What in the world happened here?" asked Dylan as he walked from the house to the edge of the debris pile. He panned the beam across the jumble of tree limbs and then turned to inspect the roofline. How did the house not sustain damage with a massive blowdown only a few feet away?

Dylan shook his shoulders and concluded the noise must have come from the uprooted trees settling. Or perhaps squirrels had scampered in the wreckage. He slapped his defense log against the palm of his hand. As he rounded the corner, he heard another snap.

His heart raced as he spun toward the pile of tree trunks and limbs.

Beyond the wreckage, he spotted two sets of reflecting eyes. Dylan could not make out who or what headed toward him. But by the height of the eyes, he assumed they were not raccoons or rodents.

"Hey, go away," Dylan called to the intruders and hoped his voice would scare them. He tried to recall Jen's direction on what types of animals could be chased off through aggression and which responded better with submission. He knew there was a difference but could not recall the details.

Undeterred by the light or his voice, the creatures drew closer and approached the edge of the debris pile. Dylan hefted the log in front of his body, hoping the animals perceived his action as a threat. He wanted to run. But maybe the movement would entice them. As the pair steadily closed the gap between Dylan's position and the woods, he decided running was not an option. They would undoubtedly beat him to the safety of the front door.

The animals cleared the security of the downed timber and came into full view—a mountain lion and a massive black bear. Dylan froze. His leaden feet felt doused in concrete. The pair slowly advanced as if they knew speed would not be an essential factor in capturing this prey.

First Jen, then Nate, and now me. How could I be so arrogant? Dylan dropped the log, tensed his muscles, and closed his eyes, succumbing to the inevitable attack.

Seconds passed. The assault did not come. Dylan cautiously opened one eye. As slowly as they had approached, the massive predators had retreated.

After holding his breath through the encounter, Dylan gasped great gulps of air. He straightened and rotated his head to scan the yard with his headlamp. The beam spotlighted another creature who remained near the treeline.

It stood erect and watched the break in the undergrowth where the bear and the cat went back into the woods. The beast stared as if it orchestrated the predators' departure and ensured they did not return.

Slowly, the hairy bipedal being turned toward Dylan. It nodded its head in a single crisp movement. Piercing ice-blue eyes stared at Dylan from behind threads of chestnut hair. Was the animal acknowledging its power to direct the killers to stand down?

Chapter 33

KALEV

Once the mountain lion and bear retreated, the target stopped trembling, and color returned to his chalky white face. I hoped he was sufficiently intelligent to figure out I had saved him. Without my intervention, they would have torn him to shreds.

As I expected, the target did not immediately run to the cabin when the predators left. His reaction was reasoned and not an irrational instinct to flee when the threat had already gone. While he did not return my nod, he bent to place firewood on the canvas. His eyes never wavered from my position.

The target hoisted the sling to his shoulder and slowly turned toward the front of the cabin. After he took a couple of steps, he pivoted to face me again. His eyes scrunched as if puzzling over what had happened. Slowly, he sidestepped to the front and backed up along the porch. The target concentrated on me until he reached the front door.

Once inside, I heard him bolt the door. I planned to give him time to think about our first contact before I approached him further.

Pleased with the progress, I walked to my campsite and replayed the day's events. While confident the target would return after his previous visit, seeing him in the car had felt exhilarating. It took all my strength to stay hidden behind the trees and not rush forward to engage him. Waiting for the right moment to demonstrate peaceful intentions would be paramount.

If frightened, he might arm himself, or worse yet, return with others in an act of defiance or to attempt my capture. Yet I knew our next meeting must come quickly. What if he only intended to stay one night? I set my plans in motion.

The bear and mountain lion slept nearby, but not close to each other. While the bear spent the night in a nest carved into a pile of fallen decomposing logs, the cat preferred a protected, rock-strewn ledge overhanging a canyon. They were not willing colleagues.

The first time I called on their services, their aversion to pooling strengths surprised me. Both were powerful predators. They could combine their skills and down massive game with plenty of food to share. But they were hardwired to avoid contact and respect territories. Perhaps they were too primitive to understand the power of collaboration beyond their family units.

They were the perfect actors for my introduction to the target, and I called them. As they had done on previous ventures, they came when summoned and approached from opposite directions into a clearing not far from the cabin.

They looked at me with indifference. To each other, the beasts exchanged low growls, narrowed eyes, and snarled lips to expose deadly teeth. Both stood before me with aggressive postures and displayed their contempt and envy at the status of the competing animal.

I ordered them to be calm. In response, the beasts lowered their heads in deference, but tension remained. Finally, the mountain lion relaxed and walked behind the bear. After two sniffs, the cat rubbed its neck against the hindquarters of the other animal. I assumed the lion's display signaled its intention to cooperate if asked.

We approached the cabin, and I directed the killers to wait. They stayed nearby, and the lion rolled on its side, stretched, and licked a paw. The bear flipped a rotting log to search for grubs. I smiled at their primal behaviors and turned to face the cabin.

What type of vision should I transmit to the target? I understood the danger of sending too much information. Earlier, I sent a blend of still and motion-filled thoughts. He looked to be in excruciating pain and held his head, moaning. His actions made me consider whether earlier transmissions were similarly painful. I did not want to hurt him, simply communicate.

Perhaps a single discrete vision might be the safest way. If a minimalist approach worked for the initial communication, the target's ability to absorb transmissions might improve over time. I marveled at these incredibly primitive and delicate creatures. Infants in my homeland could absorb far more information than him.

Something pleasing might work best. Several times, I watched the target and his mate while they hiked. Based on their laughter and intimate touches, they must have enjoyed those occasions. Their first hike likely held the strongest memory. I held back all other thoughts and sent a single discrete vision, hoping not to overload his simple, underutilized brain.

While I waited for the target to absorb my transmission, I knelt to scratch behind the lion's ear. These beasts seemed to enjoy physical attention, and I provided this small compensation for their assistance. I glanced at my hand and saw cat hair clinging to my palm and nails. How vulgar. I did not know what was worse, their offensive odors or infestations of insects. Once I sent them on their way, I would spend hours plucking off bugs that jumped from their fur to mine. I cringed at the thought.

As predicted, shortly after I withdrew the vision from the target, the front door opened. He carried the empty canvas sling over a shoulder. I had seen him use the sling to transfer wood from the stacked supply into the cabin. So I marshaled my compatriots to the edge of the blowdown pile and waited in the side yard. I wanted a full view of the predators' approach and the target's reaction.

Once he had nearly finished loading logs, I tempted him into the backyard by snapping twigs and tossing a handful of stones into the mound of uprooted trees. Then I directed the lion and bear to approach slowly. They were warned not to intimidate the target with growls or other aggressive actions.

When they saw him, isolated and vulnerable, I could tell the pair wanted to take an easy meal. They glanced at me and hoped I would give the command to attack. Without wavering from my instructions, they approached until within an arm's length of the target, their noses and neck hair twitching from the scent of defenseless prey.

I directed them to retreat, and they slowly retraced their steps past the blowdown pile and entered the woods to go their separate ways. They flawlessly played their parts. Right before they disappeared from the target's view, I stepped from behind a tree so he could watch as I commanded the killers to stand down.

My first contact had been a great success. I was convinced the target would spend the evening thinking about my identity and why I had saved him.

Step one complete. In the morning, I would implement step two.

Chapter 34

DYLAN COX

Dylan entered the cabin and flipped the deadbolt. Was that a waking dream, or did he really see a Sasquatch? He dropped the sling near the hearth, and the logs clattered in every direction like pick-up sticks falling in random disarray.

In a daze, Dylan sunk on the loveseat and shook uncontrollably. He pulled a throw from the back of the seat and bundled into the blanket to thwart his shivers.

As the tremors subsided, a wave of nausea clutched his stomach. He glanced at the door. *No way. I'm not going out there.* He ran into the kitchen for a pot. *Just in time*, he thought as he wiped his lips and reached for the water jug to rinse out bile and bits of dinner.

Confident the mountain lion and bear would have killed him if not for the intervention of the giant hairy beast, he thought about how it controlled them. He heard no verbal message or saw no physical signs from the creature. The pair of predators simply turned around, sauntered around the blowdown, and slunk into the woods.

How could this being have influenced them without any outward interaction? Clearly, he commanded them to move away. Who was this creature with power over lethal animals? Was he a man? A beast? Or something in between?

Dylan delved into his duffle to retrieve a spiral notebook and pulled out a few sheets. He needed a pencil and rummaged through Jen's junk drawer until he found one with a serviceable eraser. After he recorded the time and date at the top of a page, Dylan began to sketch.

Starting with a full-body view, Dylan outlined the physique. Lanky and lean. He struggled to recall if the arms were disproportionately long. No, his whole body was long, with the hands that fell to right below the hips.

Dylan held the picture at arm's length. Something wasn't right. The shoulders—he had drawn them too narrow. They were broad, like a swimmer's body. He erased his first attempt and expanded the shoulders and narrowed the waist. Better.

He laid the lead flat against the paper and added fur with flowing lines. Wrong again. Dylan shook his head. He erased all but the initial strokes and added strands to curve along the form.

The body hair seemed fine and wispy like it would move with a breeze, not coarse like an ape or the matted hide of a bison. Dylan reviewed the sketch. It seemed close, so he flipped the page and started on the head.

Dylan stared toward the front window and imagined the details of its face. Was the nose crooked or straight? How thick were the brows, and how prominent the chin?

He drew an oval. The face had a long forehead and evenly spaced eyes with shaggy brows. The fullest part fell below the eyes and caused the cheeks to indent slightly. High cheekbones and a chiseled jawline, recalled Dylan as his pencil swept across the paper. The nose seemed Nordic, straight and pointy with narrow nostrils and a long nasal bridge. He remembered the Sasquatch's sapphire eyes, expressive and calculating every movement and counter-movement.

Dylan scrutinized the bald figure in his drawing. He felt at a loss to capture the hair. While the features looked human, the beast's facial hair was animal. Completely different than a Lhasa Apso or StarWars Wookiee with long hair sprouting from everywhere, the face was covered with short, trim hairs like a hound. Lengthy hair grew in places where humans have longer hair. Dylan shaded the cheeks and nose with soft strokes and added elongated wavy lines around the face to flow toward the shoulders.

Ears. Had he seen the ears? Dylan did not notice them poking out from underneath the long hair. Maybe they laid flat like a gorilla, rather than sticking out like a chimp.

He tipped the pad toward the candlelight to review his work. *I wish Augie were here to do this. He'd get it right.*

The sketches were crude but captured much of what Dylan remembered. But he'd drawn the expression flat and lifeless, while in reality, the creature seemed intelligent. Dylan recalled Kate had the same comment when she encountered her Sasquatch last summer. Could it be the same creature?

In the summer, Dylan had been convinced Kate's creature was an actor, perhaps the same man who Cynthia had hired to pose for publicity shots. But based on what he saw outside, maybe he and Kate had seen the same beast. Or maybe, his Sasquatch was an actor. It seemed unlikely. Why would an actor come out to Jen's remote mountain cabin?

Dylan recalled Merle's announcement about the Sasquatch convention scheduled for mid-November. Merle and the other organizers might orchestrate sightings to promote the event. It seemed reasonable, but a developed area would attract considerably more attention.

If the being *was* an actor, he must have spent hours in makeup and a fortune for the costume. The get-up looked convincing, especially when teamed with a lion and bear to legitimize the fantasy. And what *about* the bear and the mountain lion?

How on earth could an actor arrange that? Even if the animals were tame, why create such an elaborate ruse? Particularly on a night when Dylan had come alone and unannounced to the cabin. It didn't make any sense. But Dylan searched for any logical alternative besides the one haunting him. What if the Sasquatch was real?

Dylan put the sketches aside and caught sight of the firewood jumble. The fire needed attention, or he'd have a frigid night. Dylan stacked the logs and laid in a few to stoke the fire. He poked the orange and red coals to intensify the heat.

He sat cross-legged in front of the hearth and stared into the flames. As the adrenaline rush ebbed, Dylan's head nodded forward. His eyelids sank and closed.

Thankful to be safely indoors and for the lack of visions or a headache, Dylan returned to the loveseat in a daze. He curled under the wooly throw. Lulled by the crackling fire, he fell into a sound sleep and dreamed of mountain streams, meadows teeming with wildflowers, and Jen.

Chapter 35

OCTOBER 17

Early morning light streamed through the cabin windows, and Dylan stretched to relieve his cramped muscles. He prodded the fire with an iron poker to see if there were any live embers. After Dylan discovered none, he debated what to do. Should he pack up to leave for Chicago and abandon thoughts of whatever had happened to him?

He could stay in Salida, and Destiny might put him up at the gallery. But she was already dealing with Nate's death and his soon-to-be-arriving aunt and uncle. Dylan deferred the decision on short-term plans. He decided to take what he needed into town for a run and a soak at the municipal hot springs pool. The exercise would clear his head and give him time to think about choices.

Dylan sniffed. A pungent odor rose from the kitchen and forced Dylan to decide his first order of business. Clean up the puke.

He picked up the pot and held it far away from his body to avoid gagging. Dylan paused before he opened the door. Could the beast still be nearby? No matter. A creek flowed only a few yards beyond the backyard. That would be an excellent place to rinse the pot.

Dylan gave the blowdown pile a wide berth and entered the woods to kneel next to the stream. The difference between the water flow now and what he had seen last summer seemed astonishing. A stack of logs spanned the creek to form a makeshift bridge, a necessary structure to cross the stream in June. The lack of rain and spring snowmelt relegated the flow to a mere trickle.

Dylan submerged one side of the pot into the paltry flow. He swished and dumped the contents into the frigid water. The current carried off pieces of partially digested pepperoni pizza. Dylan lifted the pot to tip the bottom side up and shook out the final drops.

Dylan placed the pot on the ground and rubbed his hands across the front of his jeans. The feeling returned to his numb fingers. Dylan rose and rounded the downed-timber pile. He marveled at the power of the microburst. A half dozen thirty-foot trees lay in a pell-mell heap. "Glad I wasn't here when that happened," Dylan said to no one.

As he neared the front porch, Dylan caught movement out of the corner of his eye. He dropped the pot and jerked to face the stand of pine trees.

Right in front of a shaggy, blue-gray juniper, the creature stood. Dylan's chest tightened as he drew a sharp breath. The beast watched him, not in an aggressive posture or ready to attack, merely watching. Before he could react, the giant nodded his head, as if to acknowledge Dylan's presence.

Dylan exhaled slowly to calm himself.

In the daylight, Dylan could see its features more clearly. The creature's hair was the color of chestnuts with the longer body and head hairs lighter than the short hair on the face. The longer hairs looked like they were bleached from the sun. Flat ears. Dylan recalled his uncertainty from the night before. The eyes never shifted from Dylan. They were a brilliant blue.

Dylan scanned the perimeter for any sign of the mountain lion or the bear. Neither were in sight. But how dangerous was the Sasquatch? Could it have killed Jen and Nate? The Sheriff blamed the cat and the bear, but who had ever analyzed a Bigfoot attack?

He squinted to see whether the creature had claws. None were visible, but some superhero beasts had retractable claws. While Dylan's mind raced, the Sasquatch watched, still and unafraid.

It did not seem threatening. Dylan opted for a friendly initial approach. "Hello?"

Without returning the greeting, it took several hesitant forward strides. *Is it scared of me or afraid of spooking me?* Dylan replicated the movement and took two cautious paces toward the creature. They traded advancing steps.

Once the initial distance closed by half, the beast lowered to the ground and sat cross-legged to face Dylan. It extended an arm toward Dylan and pointed toward the ground, as if indicating Dylan should be seated, too.

Dylan hesitated to consider the invitation. It probably could have killed him right away if it wanted to. Dylan's curiosity surpassed his fear. He stepped forward to a spot a few feet from the creature and sat. The cold, hard ground chilled the back of his thighs.

Feeling short for the first time in his life, Dylan tilted his head back to gaze a full two feet upwards into its eyes. The creature took a long breath and relaxed its shoulders. It absentmindedly stroked the fur covering its thighs. The beast's calm and hospitable gaze never wavered from Dylan's face.

It wants me to make the first move, but how in the world should I begin? Ill-prepared and at a loss for ideas, he tapped his chest. "I am Dylan." He pointed to the creature and asked, "Who are you?"

The creature gave no verbal response but placed a hand on its throat and with the other pointed to its mouth. Did it want something to eat? Dylan shrugged in confusion, then repeated his introduction.

The creature shook his head. Dylan jerked when he realized the animal understood the concept of yes and no. He was sitting with a sentient being.

"What can I call you?" Dylan attempted again. The creature raised an eyebrow and touched its furry neck.

"I know you can hear me. Are you mute?" The creature squinted and tilted its head to one side. Dylan assumed it did not understand.

"If you can't tell me your name, I'll pick one for you. I'm not even sure if you're male or female. But, to avoid poking around where I'm likely not welcome, I'm going with male. You'll need to trust me. This name is consistent with your strength and stature." He had borrowed a name from royalty in an ancient culture.

He directed a finger to himself and announced, "I am Dylan."

He pointed at the creature and said, "You are Kalev."

Chapter 36

KALEV

I looked at the small primitive man in front of me. He grinned like a proud child who had taken his first steps. I guessed the target gave me a name in his crude verbal language. Well, so be it. I accepted whatever he wanted to call me if it helped to move us forward.

The previous night, I had held back the urge to engage and allowed him to rest until morning. To distract myself, I had fallen into my routines. Not wanting to stray far, I walked the property in concentric semicircles and turned each time I reached the road.

Several hours after the target went into his house, a car approached and slowed to a stop at the driveway. I took cover in the trees and crept forward to investigate.

The car made no effort to enter the drive and idled on the far side of the road. Its lights illuminated the dirt and embedded rocks. As the driver opened the window and leaned out to look up the cabin's driveway, a cloud that smelled of roasted leaves spewed from the car. His tongue rolled across stained teeth and made a sucking sound as he stared toward the cabin.

After he extended a gnarled hand out the window and tapped the end of a burning cigarette with a bent finger, he drew a long puff and exhaled. He sat, watched, and thought.

I recognized this male. A few months earlier, I watched him in the woods. He had clubbed another male to death with a shovel. I did not trust him. He seemed even more brutal than others of his kind.

I glanced toward the cabin to confirm what this uninvited visitor saw. I could make out the target's car parked up the drive. Between the trees, faint light flickered through the cabin windows. Smoke billowed from the chimney and glowed in the moonlight. I was not certain but assumed the acuity of the driver's eyesight could not compare to mine.

After another draw from the cigarette, he flicked the butt into the dry weeds only feet from my hiding place. He put the car in gear and pulled into the driveway to turn around. Once back on the main road, the vehicle spewed gravel and fishtailed until it straightened and sped away.

As I listened to the noise of the engine fade, I watched the orange ember of the discarded cigarette smolder. Encouraged by the evening breeze, withered stalks of grass caught fire.

According to protocol, I was obliged not to intervene. I glanced at the cabin and then the growing blaze. If I woke the target to alert him to the danger, he would most likely escape harm. But a compromised location could derail the plan. Surely these circumstances deserved flexibility.

Without further deliberation, I grabbed handfuls of dirt and buried the fire. The flames dwindled, and smoke dissipated. I patted the scorched earth with my palms to ensure no sparks remained.

Afterward, I had visited the creek to scrub the cinders and ash from my hands. To detect any additional threats, I had stood vigil the rest of the night until I heard the cabin door open in the morning.

Oblivious to the calamity that might have destroyed his domicile, the target smiled at me with eager innocence. At that moment, I realized how difficult communication would be with an entity limited to a verbal exchange of ideas.

On the trails, I listened to these beings as they chatted incessantly. I never made sense of what they said. But tones were understandable.

Arguments were the easiest to recognize. Raised, aggressive voices usually accompanied bold gestures. The interactions often resulted in subsequent periods of silence, or one of the hikers would distance himself from the others. They appeared happy when their actions included smiles, playful taps, and hugs.

These types of expressions and emotions existed in my culture as well.

But they would have been preceded by transmitted feelings or perspectives, commonly embedded in visions to provide context, not merely a string of words. Misunderstandings must be common with a limited form of communication.

The target appeared small and unremarkable. He sat before me and grinned like a child. That image helped me to understand how I might interact with him. After all, his undeveloped intellect was childlike. I would treat him commensurately.

I decided it was time to send another message. To warn him, I delivered a cautious look and tapped my forehead. After I pointed a finger toward the target's brow, I sent him the same memory of his mate that I had transferred the previous night. By repeating the vision, he might understand the images came from me.

At first, he sat relaxed, with forearms resting against his thighs. His smile deepened as the vision progressed. With a start, the target jolted upright. He placed both hands on the ground at his sides. Slowly, I withdrew the image and watched his reaction.

The target vigorously nodded his head and spoke with a questioning tone, an undecipherable message. I tried again, first making the gestures and then transmitting the vision. He jumped to his feet and pointed at me with a stabbing motion—his words punctuated with enthusiasm. He did not appear angry or upset, more as if he had a revelation. I assumed the target understood who sent the message.

He knelt on all fours and closed the distance between us. When he settled on the ground in front of me with crossed legs, our knees touched. Ever so slowly, he placed his hands on my thighs and peered deeply with his pale green eyes. I trembled at the familiarity.

He extended a wary finger toward my face. Tempted to nip at him, I held back—not a good time to test his sense of humor. The target lifted to lean forward and touch the hair on my cheek. He touched my ear and stroked my neck before he sat back and replaced his hand on my thigh.

I smiled and slowly nodded my head in approval. *Now we are getting somewhere.*

Chapter 37

DYLAN COX

Dylan marveled at the Sasquatch who teemed with human features but looked far from human.

"I get it that you don't understand me, but what are you?" The creature smelled like a park bench jammed with vagrants, but the fragrance did not imply Kalev was primitive, as he seemed intelligent and thoughtful. Besides, Kalev had saved Dylan from an attack. If the Sasquatch had sent the visions of Jen, then perhaps he was telepathic.

"How can I ask you to send another?" Dylan pointed at Kalev's forehead and then to his own. He intended to welcome another message, and Kalev nodded in response.

The world in front of Dylan blurred. As it cleared, he saw Jen spread a blanket on a grassy patch next to an alpine tarn. The pond sat at the base of a mountain cirque with school bus-sized boulders dotting slopes that funneled into the treeless drainage. Bits of fine-leafed grass and veins of snow streaked the mountainsides. Above the lake, stunted deformed krumholtz gave way to barren earth.

On her knees, Jen smoothed the throw and unloaded food from her backpack. Ziploc bags with meaty sandwiches, chilled grapes, and carrot sticks hit the fabric. Her lips moved, and she glanced over her shoulder, which suggested a conversation with someone who would emerge from the trail.

Shortly, he saw himself breaking free of the stately pines along the path below the lip of the lake. He dragged his feet across the grassy meadow and trounced on fuzzy violet Pasqueflowers before he plodded over a bouquet of brilliant scarlet gilia.

Jen called out and pointed to the damaged wildflowers, which caused Dylan to hop from toe to toe until he reached the blanket and flopped to the ground.

As he gasped to catch his breath, Dylan sheepishly showed Jen his empty water bottle. A sarcastic smirk spread across her face as she delivered a verbal dig, no doubt something about his city-boy background. He raised himself on an elbow to smile in response and watch her finish laying out their lunch.

As the vision faded, Dylan wanted to grasp it back and relive the scene. Sadly, the past disappeared, replaced by the giant seated in front of him. "Thank you," said Dylan as he laid a hand on Kalev's forearm. The visions of Jen were a generous gift. He wanted Kalev to understand his gratitude.

The Sasquatch cradled Dylan's chin in a cupped hand and rubbed a thumb against the side of his face. Dylan saw compassion in his eyes and decided the beast knew about emotional love.

Kalev offered his massive furry hand for Dylan to investigate. He took it in both of his and stroked the top before he turned the palm upward to inspect the other side. While long hairs covered the back of Kalev's hand, his palm bore fine, thin fur like the belly of a mouse.

Dylan touched the end of each brown fingernail. They were long and caked with dirt. Kalev released a heavy sigh—his face clearly showed dismay. Dylan's lip curled into a sly smile. He asked, "Shall I take you to town for a mani-pedi?"

Kalev's head tilted inquisitively. Dylan patted the back of Kalev's hand. "Making an appointment for you wouldn't be a good idea." Dylan chuckled as he imagined Kalev's feet in a foot bath with a manicurist filing his unkempt fingernails.

As they exchanged smiles, Kalev ran his fingers through Dylan's hair. He took a lock from the top and rubbed it as if evaluating the thickness and texture of the strand.

Dylan said, "You've never been close enough to a human to touch one, have you?" This could be the first encounter for both of them.

Dylan reached to stroke Kalev's face. The creature responded with a brisk slap. Dylan jerked back his extended hand and searched Kalev's face for an explanation. The beast grinned from ear to ear, and his eyes grew moist with tears. He rocked onto his back and shook with mirth—his feet bicycled in the air. When he resumed his seated position, he took Dylan's hand and placed it against his furry cheek.

"Could my Sasquatch be a jokester?" Dylan asked.

Kalev allowed Dylan several minutes to feel the texture of his fur before he leaned back to give an appraising look. "What now?" Dylan asked. Kalev touched his furry forehead to let Dylan know to expect another vision.

As the scene came into focus, Dylan could see several Sasquatches sitting in a tight circle. They huddled together, and their heads nearly touched. He could not see their faces, as the point of view came from outside of the ring, and everyone faced the center. Quickly the image faded.

When Kalev came back into focus, the beast nodded and stood. As Dylan jumped to his feet, Kalev motioned for Dylan to stay put.

Kalev took several long strides and paused at the edge of the woods. Torn between wanting to follow the beast or remain behind, Dylan watched as Kalev turned to give a single nod. Then he disappeared into the forest.

Dylan assumed Kalev intended to return to others of his kind. *Would he ever see the Sasquatch again?*

Chapter 38

Dylan parked the car in the lot at the hot springs pool in the last available spot. Moms exited SUVs and shuffled their preschool tots into the building as they passed dozens of damp-haired seniors on their way out. Dylan smiled at the juxtaposition of beginner and seasoned swimmers.

After he dodged cars and pedestrians, Dylan paused to stretch his calves against a low brick wall bordering the lot. The morning air chilled Dylan's skin, but he came prepared with running tights, a fleece jacket over a thin polypro shirt, and lightweight gloves. He figured he would warm up quickly once he started uphill and began with his hat in his pocket.

Right decision, he decided, as his breath deepened and blood surged to feed thrusting muscles. His planned route took a warmup pace along I Street, turned right on 14th and left on F Street, then straight to the base of Tenderfoot Hill.

In autumn, the neighborhood looked bleak with leafless trees and brittle brown lawns. A few overachiever homeowners had decorated for Halloween with plastic pumpkins and fake spiderwebs. Dylan realized the end of October was less than two weeks away. He ran along the sidewalks and glanced at homes filled with people living their lives, drinking coffee, and reading the paper. *His* morning had been anything but normal. He felt desperate to tell someone.

Dylan ran past several blocks of houses before he reached the commercial buildings. Despite a lack of traffic in either direction, the red-light at the corner of F and First forced him to stop. A block down on his left, he could see the brushed steel façade of Nate's gallery.

Should he stop in to talk with Destiny? Her perspectives on Kalev could be helpful, but Dylan shook off the idea. She had enough on her plate.

Dylan scanned the cross-streets and contemplated civil disobedience when the light changed. The problem solved itself without rules violations.

At the Sackett Avenue intersection, Dylan paused to glance into the lobby of the impeccably renovated Palace Hotel. An artfully stamped metal ceiling, overstuffed leather couches, and Asian influenced casual tables begged guests to loiter in the lobby with a newspaper and cappuccino. Within his first minutes in Salida last June, Dylan met Jen, who worked at the front desk.

As he passed the hotel and approached the door of Ferraro's Italian restaurant, scents of garlic and freshly baked bread met his nose. The next window, a liquor store, held dozens of posters advertising future events. Dylan paused to scan the fliers.

He spotted an advertisement for the November Sasquatch conference. The flier listed workshops, vendors, and nationally recognized speakers for the symposium. It promised to be the "event of the year" in Salida that would start on November 18th, with an opening ceremony in Riverside Park, a favorite public spot next to the Arkansas River.

Next to the conference poster, Dylan saw a yellowed flier from last summer with a sketch of a ferocious Sasquatch monster. The notice attributed several atrocities to the creature, including a kidnap, livestock and wildlife deaths, and property destruction. "Not a good likeness of Kalev," said Dylan to the poster.

He squinted at the list of crimes. Kalev definitely didn't kidnap Trip, but what about killing animals? Sasquatches had long taken the blame for eviscerating cattle. Dylan hoped Kalev preferred vegetables for dinner.

Based on his two encounters with the creature, Dylan figured Kalev was intelligent and peaceful. But the poster reminded Dylan of how little he knew about Kalev. What was he capable of?

Dylan tipped an ear toward each shoulder to stretch his neck muscles and abate growing tension. Before he restarted, Dylan pledged to keep up his guard, in case Kalev's motives were less than diplomatic.

After he crossed the Arkansas River on a road bridge, Dylan started the ascent up the little peak. He felt his lungs burn as he pushed to maintain a robust uphill pace.

He weighed options. Sheriff Austin knew of Dylan's anxiety over Jen's death. If Dylan confided in Austin about meeting Kalev, the Sheriff would assume he had gone completely nuts.

As an alternative, Dylan could engage Salida's believer community to meet with Kalev. But that decision might result in hordes of Sasquatch followers and the press invading the woods near Jen's cabin. When faced with a mob scene of disciples desperate for an audience, Kalev would undoubtedly disappear.

Dylan turned on a switchback and pondered why Kalev had approached *him*. There must be some motivation for a Sasquatch to engage with a human and specifically to pick Dylan.

Websites and television shows interviewed people who claimed to have spotted one along a highway or near homes in rural areas, but the creatures immediately fled. Other encounters were indirect, like the signaling sounds he experienced in Oregon or whooping noises.

Since Kalev was mute, Dylan questioned whether whooping noises were even possible. Dylan snorted and realized his presumptuous assumption. There must be more of them, and maybe not all Sasquatches were mute.

He paused to pick up a discarded glove from the trail. Sun-bleached and dusty, the fingerless palm-padded garment probably slipped out of a biker's jacket pocket. Dylan stuffed the glove in his waistband with a plan to leave it at the trailhead on his way back to the aquatic center.

As Dylan started again, he thought about his migraines and recent visions. Certain Kalev caused them, he realized the scenes must have originated from Kalev's memories. But if that was true, then Kalev had watched Dylan hike with Jen. They were oblivious to being observed. Had Kalev inadvertently surveilled or intentionally stalked them?

Dylan recalled his vision of Kate in her garden. Perhaps Kate's frightened expression sprang from her discovery of Kalev. If the image came from Kalev, then it had to be *him* drinking from her hummingbird feeders.

As Dylan rounded the final switchback, he skidded to a stop with his running shoes skating sideways across loose gravel. A coiled prairie rattlesnake snapped to face the sound. It flicked a forked tongue and pulled into a tight circle while hissing and rattling a warning.

Dylan's heart pounded. He leaned back and held up both hands. "Whoa, little fellow. I won't invade your space. Give me a minute to back up."

The agitated reptile continued to tremble as its tail emitted a succession of staccato sounds. The head stayed in place as the coils grew tighter to hide all but the last few dark brown bands on its tail.

Dylan backed down the trail until he crossed a shortcut path. He muscled up a steep incline and pressed his toes into loose dirt and low-growing prickly pear cactus. Dylan scanned shrubs for signs of the rattler's family or friends. Soon he reconnected with the main route and avoided another confrontation with the solitude-seeking snake.

As Dylan approached the concrete steps to the tiny summit house, he slowed to a walk and took the stairs at a deliberate pace to the white concrete block building. Dylan paused at the doorway, buttressed on either side by two paneless window frames. Full of dried leaves, the structure stood open to the elements with no door or windows.

To get the most out of his workout, Dylan retraced his steps down the stairs and climbed them twice more before he stopped in front of the summit house. He bent to rest his palms on his knees and pant. Dylan straightened to look at the town below, a grid of roads and homes.

What did *he* want to gain from this experience with Kalev? If he told anyone, he would minimize chances to see the Sasquatch again or find out why Kalev had approached him.

Dylan compared meeting Kalev to his encounter with the rattlesnake. He saw value in keeping a respectful distance, yet he lost the ability to inspect the reptile and appreciate its unique attributes. While the snake made clear its disinterest in Dylan, Kalev initiated the contact.

Drawn by the prospect of learning more about the Sasquatch, Dylan decided to keep his meetings with Kalev a secret. He did not want this morning's encounter to be the last.

Chapter 39

After a long soak at the hot springs pool and a quick shower, Dylan stopped at Café Dawn to pick up bagels, a latte, and hot chocolate before he drove to Augie's trailer. Augie opened the door and spotted the drink tray. "I already ate."

"I figured by now you'd already walked to the grocery and had breakfast." Augie nodded with a smile. "Maybe you'd join me for second breakfast?"

"Second breakfast?"

"A tradition made popular by hobbits, but we can borrow from them. Alternatively, you can have hot chocolate and watch me eat while we plan out the day."

"I can, but this is my drawing time," Augie responded and reached for the cardboard cup marked "HC."

Dylan followed him into the dining area and hastily unwrapped and took a bite of his bagel. Augie closed an open notebook and scooped pencils and an eraser into a tray before he moved them to the far end of the table. After he placed the placemats perfectly parallel to the edge, Augie folded two napkins into precise rectangles. He handed one to Dylan and said, "We should call my boss when you finish your breakfast."

After he wiped the remains of cream cheese from his fingers, Dylan handed his phone to Augie.

His boss needed Augie back to work the following evening. Augie promised to be at the mine site before six o'clock. Once Augie returned the phone, Dylan tapped Kate's number to check her availability. She agreed to meet them for lunch after the noon rush.

Dylan looked at Augie. "What should we do for the next few hours?"

Augie shrugged.

"How about we look around downtown? You might want to take your sketchbook along, in case we talk with some artists."

Without hesitation, Augie finished off his hot chocolate. After a thorough rinse, he placed the cardboard cup and plastic lid on his recycle pile. Augie slipped a ring of house keys from a hook near the door and tucked the notebook under an arm. He tapped his foot as he waited by the door.

Dylan threw crushed bakery paper into the trash and placed the second bagel into Augie's fridge. As he approached Augie, Dylan slapped his shoulder and said, "No keeping you back once you've made a decision."

They left the trailer and walked a short distance to F Street, past a mixture of small homes, prefabricated structures, and trailers. Augie's side of town built out before building codes homogenized the developments surrounding Salida. While the residences were understated, the pair passed neatly kept yards.

In stark contrast to the tidy homes, they reached a twelve-unit apartment building with boarded-up windows on half of the second floor. The six front stoops lay cluttered with discarded children's toys and trash in various stages of decay. Two young, unsupervised children sat huddled by the front door of one of the units. One held a bright red plastic truck while the other pried the side open with a screwdriver.

Dylan thought they seemed underdressed for the chilly October morning, and his judgmental glance must have lingered too long. As he passed, one shouted, "Take a picture—why don't cha?" Dylan smiled at the reprimand and issued a quick apology to the aggrieved tot.

Augie turned to the boy. "You don't talk that way to adults."

The boy lifted a grimy proud chin toward Augie and announced, "You can't tell me what to do."

"I will when you've disrespected my friend. Respect for ourselves guides our morals—respect for others guides our manners."

Baffled, the boy stared. The screwdriver drooped in his hand. Dylan placed a hand on Augie's forearm. "Is that a quote from your aunt?"

"No, from Destiny. She said Laurence Sterne said it."

"Good memory. Do you know who Sterne is?"

Augie shrugged but continued to watch the children for signs of remorse or an apology. Ambivalent about the adults and the reprimand, the children resumed the truck dissection. Augie looked at Dylan. "That little boy shouldn't have talked to you that way."

"I agree, but I'm not sure teaching manners are foremost on his parents' minds."

Augie appeared to lack empathy and shook his head. "Kids should respect their elders."

"Did your aunt teach you that?"

"Yeah, but mom said it before Aunt Peg."

"They were wise women." Dylan realized Augie had never spoken about his mother. "Sounds like your mom wanted you to act like a gentleman."

As Augie slid his hands into his pockets, his lips formed a flat hard line. "She had a lot of rules but didn't follow them herself."

"Like what, for example?"

"She said it was wrong to hit people when you're angry." He looked back at the children before he turned toward Dylan. With narrowed eyes, he said, "But she did it when she was angry."

Dylan placed a hand on Augie's shoulder as they resumed their walk. "Did she get angry with you?"

"Yeah, sometimes. Aunt Peg said my mom did the best she could to be a good mom. Sometimes people don't have enough goodness in them to be good all of the time."

Sensible words. Dylan asked, "Why did you move in with your aunt?"

"Mom said she wanted her own life and couldn't deal with me anymore. So she sent me to live with Aunt Peg."

Saddened by this revelation of abandonment, Dylan asked, "How did you feel about moving in with your aunt?"

Augie gave a start, as if surprised by the question. "I liked living with

Aunt Peg. We had fun. She told me she loved me. Mom didn't tell me stuff like that. She mostly talked about herself and how I made her life *difficult*."

Dylan thought about Augie's aunt and how she sacrificed independence and finances to care for Augie. Dylan's parents had also changed their lives when they adopted him. He recalled Nate saying, "Not everyone is cut out to raise children." Dylan agreed. Some people should not be parents.

Dylan compared Nate's lack of parenting skills, Augie's mom's inability or unwillingness to raise Augie, and his own birth parents' decision to abandon him. *Sometimes children are better off without their real parents.* If he agreed with the sentiment, then why did he feel driven to find out about his birth parents?

To Augie, he said, "Well, I'm glad your aunt loved you and took you into her home. I wish I could have met her."

"But she's dead."

"Yes, and that's sad."

"Yeah."

They reached F Street, and Augie scanned each corner with a smile. "This is my favorite street," he announced.

"Because of the stores? Because the width is exactly 28 feet?"

Augie shook his head. "Nope. All of the addresses on both sides are F Street addresses."

Dylan tilted his head. "Other blocks include some addresses on the cross streets?"

"Yeah."

Dylan smiled and patted Augie on the back. "Cool. Only you would notice that."

They turned onto Salida's main drag, and Dylan glanced at the first gallery's storefront. Bold white letters splayed across the window and welcomed everyone to join weekly pottery lessons and reserve kiln time. Inside, shelves and showcases lined the walls to display ceramic vases, bowls, and sculptures.

A stout middle-aged woman stood behind a counter. She glanced over a pair of tortoiseshell reading glasses and caught their hesitation before she motioned for them to come inside. As they walked through the door, she greeted them and quickly resumed her paperwork. Dylan figured she intended to provide uninterrupted time to browse.

After a few minutes of strolling around tables and shelves with pieces from local artists, Dylan moved toward the counter to engage the clerk. "Is your work on display?" he asked with a warm smile.

"I'm not an artist, but I married one," she responded with a faint Wisconsin accent.

Dylan cocked his head. "No slam intended, but are you a cheese-head?"

"Born and raised in Green Bay. Go Packers." She pumped a fist in the air.

"I heard a hint of Wisconsin in your voice. I'm from Chicago. Is your husband from the Midwest, too?"

"No. He grew up on a farm east of Salida. We met thirty years ago in Africa when we both served in the Peace Corps. After our stint, we played hippie for a couple of years in California. Then we decided to settle in Salida. It's nice to be near family and away from the brutal Green Bay winters."

"Well, that's a great story. I assume his work is here somewhere?" Dylan looked around the shop.

She motioned toward a side wall. "His pottery is on those shelves. He uses local materials but learned his mixing and firing techniques from craftsmen we met overseas."

Dylan left the clerk and wandered toward the wall display with ceramics strategically clustered in groups of three and five. Earth-tone vases with sides formed in machine-like precision stood a foot high. Their high-gloss glaze speckled with flakes that caught the natural light streaming from the windows. The effect reminded him of shimmering mica that glittered at the bottom of a stream bed.

He'd first seen mica while on a hike with Jen. Naively, he had asked if the flecks were the famous Colorado gold. After she chuckled at his romantic notion, Jen told him about mica, a crystallized mineral that was scattered all over the Rocky Mountains. Dylan speculated whether this artist had found a way to incorporate the abundant but generally valueless mineral into his work.

"These pieces sparkle," he called to the clerk. She set down her pen and abandoned a stack of receipts to join him.

She pointed an index finger at the base of a glimmering vase. "That's his signature treatment. He adds crushed crystals to the glaze to create the effect. It's striking. Don't you agree?"

Augie joined them to admire the pieces. While he remained silent, Dylan could tell by Augie's concentration he appreciated the craftsmanship. Dylan turned to Augie. "What do you think? Does this make you want to start making pottery?"

Augie raised a brow, likely to imply Dylan might have lost his mind. "No," was all he said.

Dylan turned to the clerk. "My friend Augie is an artist, too. He has an exceptional portfolio of drawings."

The clerk looked at Augie with interest as Dylan continued. "His work is amazingly lifelike. He does a lot of portraitures. It would be nice to find an artist in Salida who would look at his work and see if there is any commercial value to his drawings."

The clerk turned from Augie to Dylan and suggested he connect with an artist with similar interests. There were several in town who worked with pencils and charcoal. She named a few, the last being Nate Stewart.

Dylan started at the mention of his cousin. "Do you know Nate?"

"Everyone in town knows Nate. Salida is a small community, you know."

"Did you hear that Nate died four days ago?"

"That can't be. I just saw him, but maybe it's been a week." She lifted a hand to her mouth. "My husband and I got back in town last night. October is our slow season, so we closed the gallery for a couple of days to visit friends in Arizona. Nate didn't look ill last week. Was there an accident?"

"Animal attack, they think. Sheriff Austin says the case is still under investigation."

The clerk gazed out the window. "There's been a lot of attacks this year. I hope they catch him."

"Him?"

She turned to face Dylan and, without hesitation, said, "The Sasquatch."

"Seriously?"

"They're vicious primitive animals. Now that he's tasted human blood, they'll be no stopping him until he's dead."

Dylan sighed, unsure of how to respond. "Last I heard, they assumed a bear or mountain lion were the likely predators. But, if a Bigfoot is to blame, I hope they find him." As they left the gallery, Dylan felt akin to Victor Frankenstein, protecting his Creature from a gathering mob.

Dylan and Augie browsed another gallery before they paused outside a bookstore. Dylan motioned toward an inviting bench in front. Augie sat and placed his notebook across his knees. Dylan sat next to him and stretched both arms across the back rail. He patted his friend's shoulder as they relaxed and took in the street scene.

A woman with a curly beige labradoodle on a leash strolled past. She allowed her pet to take a drink from a stainless steel water bowl next to the bench. Dylan reached down to scratch the dog's ear.

The animal paused to sniff the air and then Dylan's hand. As the animal moved its charcoal black nose to the leg of Dylan's jeans, the owner pulled the leash to no avail. The dog resisted her insistent tugging, its nose glued to Dylan like an elephant discovering a banana cache. She apologized to Dylan. "Max is usually better behaved. You must have a dog or cat at home?"

He smiled. "Never have, but I've been around an animal that your dog might find interesting."

In a layered crescendo, she called her pet and pulled his lead until he complied. The owner continued her reprimand until the pair disappeared around the corner at the end of the block.

Augie and Dylan sat in silence and watched occasional shoppers, some with bags and others yet unburdened. Dylan figured these holdouts would soon join the ranks of consumers. Hard to resist the offerings on Salida's main street with galleries, two bookstores, and specialty shops with irresistible treats like locally made honey—either plain or infused with flavors such as caramel, lemon, or chocolate. Dylan recalled Jen pouring caramel honey over vanilla ice cream and berries. His mouth watered.

Sporadic gusts of wind blew down the block and carried autumn leaves and the occasional tumbleweed. Dylan imagined the Salida of a hundred years in the past. Many of the old storefronts still stood, like the A.T. Henry building at First and F Streets and the antique shop at 112 ½ East

First Street that formerly housed the Salida News Printing Shop. In the past, these buildings overlooked dirt streets with hitching posts and carriages rather than paved roads lined with SUVs and pickup trucks.

Behind his sunglasses, Dylan's eyes started to close right when a shadow blocked the sun. A brash voice stifled the serenity of the bucolic scene.

"What the hell are you doing back here?" Junior Deputy Erle Hodges stood in front of Dylan. Same reddish-brown crewcut, but fifty percent of the body was missing.

"Erle, is that you? You look like a completely different person."

Erle looked down the front of his baggy uniform shirt and back at Dylan. "Yeah. I've lost some weight since last summer."

"Some? You've dropped at least fifty pounds. Are you okay?"

Erle straightened. "I've lost close to eighty. Ever since Jesse left town last summer, I've been eating better and riding my bike."

"Well, you look terrific. You should keep it up."

Erle nodded and placed his hands on his hips. He stood with his feet wide apart and shifted his weight from side to side. Then he turned enough to display the sidearm hooked to his belt. Did Erle think the stance made him look authoritative?

"Great news about Trip Stewart, huh?" Dylan asked.

Erle's eyes narrowed. "His mother cost us countless hours on the investigation. I can't believe she's getting off *Scotch-free.* We should have given her jail time."

Dylan ignored Erle's mispronunciation. "Now that she's back in town, Destiny intends to resume her volunteer work at the food bank and the adopt-a-highway program for trash pickup. The Sheriff may have some other ideas about ways to help. Augie will join her, too."

"She deserves stiffer punishment."

"Isn't it better for everyone to have her volunteering? That way, she pays for her own food and shelter, rather than giving her three hots and a cot." Dylan tsked. "Anyway, what would they do with Trip? Hoist him off on social services? That's a fine way to treat a kid who's just lost his father."

Erle stared at Dylan, with pursed lips. Dylan decided to change the subject. "Any more evidence in finding Bigfoot?" Dylan knew Erle to be an avid believer.

"There continues to be a lot of Sasquatch activity. While he's cleared from involvement with Trip's disappearance, we still have the unresolved goat slaughter and Juble Lee's steer mutilation last June. He's also a suspect for the murders of the hiker from Kansas, Jen Rickard, and now Nate Stewart."

Why did everyone want to blame Kalev for these killings? Dylan deflected. "Any more sightings since the one Kate Meyers reported?"

Erle sighed and solemnly shook his head. "Things have been pretty quiet. There've been no more sightings or typical signs like footprints or signaling. But some hikers have reported unusual situations in the woods."

Dylan pulled his sunglasses from his face to the top of his head. He squinted to get a better read on Erle's expression. "Like what?"

"Shortly after you left, someone called in about a terrible blowdown on Church Mountain. Trees blocked the dirt road to the summit and lay scattered in every direction. It took the forest rangers about a week to clear the road."

There was a mound of downed trees in Jen's yard. Dylan had assumed a blowdown caused it, but what if it was Kalev?

Erle continued. "Another time, some campers got spooked in the middle of the night when they heard animals fighting. They identified cat sounds, but they weren't sure what was going on. Once morning came, they got out of their tent to look around. Couldn't find any evidence of what caused the noises, no sign of blood or an injured animal."

"Does the Sheriff have any thoughts about it?"

"Not that he mentioned to me. But I wouldn't be surprised if a Sasquatch stirred up the wildlife near those campers."

"This Bigfoot sounds like a pretty destructive character."

"These animals are nasty. They mutilate their kill to get to the tastiest organs. Once they eat the parts they want, they leave the carcass to rot."

"Are you certain they're carnivores?"

Erle shook his head with conviction. "They're not just meat eaters. They're omnivores, but they like meat the best. People have seen them eat leaves or saplings. They also eat shellfish and catch small animals in their dens, mostly squirrels and chipmunks. Sometimes they go after big game or steal another animal's catch. They've been known to eat an easy meal like roadkill."

"How do you know this?" asked Dylan.

Erle shrugged. "My dad tells me about what the researchers say. When Sasquatches are hungry, they'll tear into anything. If one of them got to Nate, I hope he was killed quickly."

Dylan grimaced. "Let's hope so. Hey, I went to a Sasquatch search when I traveled out west. Do you know if they have events like that around here?"

"Nothing official in the past, but there's a believers conference coming up in about a month."

"Your dad mentioned it when I saw him about a week ago, and I've seen the fliers around town." He paused. "What's the difference between a search and a conference?"

"The conference has workshops and presentations about research, sightings, and detection innovation. We have speakers lined up from all over the States—real experts." He smiled. "There'll be a boatload of vendors selling paraphernalia, too."

"But there won't be any people going into the woods to look for Bigfoot?"

"Nothing organized. But since Kate Meyers had a sighting last June, there might be casual groups who go out at night to look around."

"Sounds like a snipe hunt to me." When Erle delivered a blank stare, Dylan added, "It's a rite-of-passage prank where you convince youngsters to go out into a forest at night and chase around to catch a nonexistent type of bird."

Augie interjected, "Why would you do that?"

Dylan chuckled. "You're right. It's not very kind. I went on my first snipe hunt in Scouts. Frankly, it's harmless fun." Dylan turned back to Erle. "Have you been to a Bigfoot search?"

Erle contemplated for a moment. "I went to a hunt in New Mexico once, but I've never heard of an organized hunting party in this part of Colorado. The one in New Mexico was pretty cool. They took us in Jeeps way out into the wilderness. We sat out all night and listened to the Sasquatches making whooping sounds. One of my best nights ever."

"That's sad on a few levels." Dylan considered his next question. "Did you see one up close?"

"Are you kidding? They're wild animals and smart enough to avoid contact with humans. Some of the men on the hunt carried rifles. I'm pretty sure they would have gunned down any Sasquatch coming close to our group."

Appalled, Dylan asked, "They would have killed it before an attempt to capture or communicate?"

"Well, yeah. These creatures have evaded us for centuries. Anyone able to kill one and prove they exist would be a hero in my book."

"They'd be a murderer in my book," Dylan snapped as he imaged a dozen rednecks with hounds chasing after Kalev.

Erle scoffed at Dylan's response. "It'd be better to have one alive, but I'd be satisfied either way. Countless men have searched for Sasquatch, and the evidence is limited. A carcass would finally put an end to the debate."

Chapter 40

KATE MEYERS

Kate loved the fall. Crisp, clear nights and oversized moons made up for the shortened days. She longed for even colder weather to signal the start of downhill skiing. To take full advantage of the preseason discounts, she purchased her Monarch Mountain season pass in the summer. It sat idly on her dining table and waited for the snow to accumulate on the mountain and the chairlift operators to dust off the seats.

Skiing on the weekends gave her a mental reprieve from her intense work with first-graders. She needed the all-day workout of cruising the nearly vertical slopes combined with a sprinkling of hardcore, knee-pounding moguls to clear her head and face another week of class with her young charges.

She arrived at the restaurant about fifteen minutes before the appointed time. Since they were not busy, the hostess seated Kate at a booth. Kate slipped into the side with a view of the front door. When the waitress placed three settings of cutlery on the table, Kate moved the double set to the opposite side of the table. Better to have them sit across from her. She wanted to avoid an awkward moment if the men needed to decide who would share her side.

Kate reviewed her agenda. She had heard Destiny and Trip had returned to Salida. Dylan could provide the skinny on that. But her main interest lay in understanding how Dylan knew where to find Destiny and whether she could persuade him to extend his time in Salida. Dating in a small pool had pitfalls—particularly once she eliminated her students' single parents from her prospects.

Nearly finished with her first glass of iced tea, she saw Dylan and Augie enter the dimly lit restaurant. She stood and waved until Dylan spotted her. He nodded to the hostess and pointed toward Kate.

When they approached the booth, Kate gave Dylan a warm hug. She turned to Augie and held her arms wide to see if he would accept her contact. He nodded and leaned toward her. She embraced him with a delicate touch with respect for his desire for distance but to let him know she appreciated being with him. She hoped he received the message.

After ordering drinks, Kate looked directly at Augie. "How was your trip?"

"Fine," Augie responded.

Kate smiled good-naturedly and turned toward Dylan. "Got any more details?"

"You've probably heard we found Destiny and Trip."

"I've seen her." Kate's lips pressed into a straight line. "I had no idea you were going out there to look for her. You told me you were taking a trip to spend time with Augie."

"We had an idea she might be in Oregon, so we went to check out some leads. It didn't take a lot of effort to find her. I'm glad we did. Otherwise, I'm not sure how she would have found out about Nate's death."

Kate lowered her eyes. "I'm sorry for the loss of your cousin."

"Thank you for that. There wasn't a lot of love lost between Nate and me, but I'm sad for his folks and Trip."

Kate sighed and clutched her arms around her midriff. "Nate's passing wasn't a great loss for many people, but I'm certainly feeling for Trip. Destiny said he's handling it well, but she won't see the full toll for a while. When Trip is a few years older, he'll face the trauma of living without his father. It's a good thing he and Destiny are so close."

Kate took a sip of tea, and Dylan used the break to change the subject. "I've meant to ask you. Why are there stacked cartons of Jen's things at the cabin? There weren't any boxes when I stayed there last week."

"Sheriff Austin knows I'm taking care of the cabin for Augie. When they found Nate's body outside the cabin, he asked me to meet the deputies and see if anything had been disturbed."

Dylan's eyes narrowed. "And?"

She hesitated. "Somebody rummaged through her stuff, but I don't know if anything is missing. If Nate's the one who broke the window, then he probably searched the place."

She cleared her throat. Touching Jen's personal belongings had made Kate uncomfortable. "I didn't see any reason to reorganize her clothes and put them back in the drawers and closets. So I straightened things out and packed them into boxes. I'll clear out the rest for sale in the spring, but there's no point in handling everything twice."

Kate looked at Augie. "If I find anything of value, I'll take it to the consignment shop. They can give you a check once everything sells." She turned back to Dylan. "I'll leave the furniture to sell with the cabin. I thought you might want to stay there again. So I left the kitchen stuff in the cabinets."

"I appreciate that. But when I'm there, I bring paper plates and plastic cutlery. Since there's no power or water, I can't wash dishes or use the stove."

"If you're thinking of staying a while, I'd be happy to have the utilities turned back on." Kate gave her most encouraging smile.

"I haven't decided yet, but I'll probably be here a few more days."

"You don't need to stay out there. I'm sure there are places closer to town that might suit your needs. I've got a spare room. You're welcome to stay with me."

Dylan's deadpan face made her question if she'd made the proposition too quickly. Without addressing her offer, he changed the subject. "Let me get back to our Oregon trip. After we found Destiny and Trip, we wanted time to decide how to handle Nate. So we checked out the Pacific Ocean. I assumed it might be blustery and wild, with waves crashing into the coastline. It didn't disappoint us."

"Sounds nice." Kate managed through her disappointment.

Dylan straightened. "You may not know about my recent discovery. I was adopted through a church in Groverton, Oregon. We stuck around to do a bit of sleuthing about my birth parents. I *am* a detective, after all."

His wide grin softened Kate's mood. "Did you get to meet them?"

He dismissed her question with a wave of his hand. "Hardly. We left with more questions than when we started. It seems like I might have been abandoned at birth and given to a church. While I'll probably never meet my real parents, we met the couple who took care of me until the Oregon church arranged my adoption through a sister congregation in Chicago. Too bad my folks died before they could tell me what happened. It would have been good to hear it from them."

Stunned, Kate asked, "They never told you?"

"Nope."

"That's unconscionable. I can't imagine withholding that type of information from a child. What if an adopted person needs background about inherited health risks? They would erroneously rely on the health profile of their adopted parents."

A look of surprise crossed Dylan's face as he said, "I assume the secretism was consistent with the times. Thirty years ago, parents may not have been keen to tell children they were adopted."

Kate huffed with indignation. "Well, that attitude wouldn't go very far today. Keeping secrets from your kids doesn't tend to end well. Kids believe it's their right to know their heritage and about their parents' personal lives. You'd be surprised."

"Kate, give me details. What are you talking about?"

"During this school year, one of my colleagues had a third-grader who found out his father had a previous marriage."

"So, the kid's mom was his dad's second wife?"

"Yes. The boy found out about the first wife from a schoolmate with an older brother who had a big mouth. The older brother knew about the earlier marriage and forwarded the information to his younger sister. He assumed third-graders could keep a secret. I don't think the older brother knew that passing this information to his little sister would have any consequences. Well, it didn't take long before his sister used the information to take her classmate down a peg."

"What did she do?"

"The boy routinely teased kids from blended families. That's families with children from multiple marriages. He'd taken an arrogant approach and bragged about his own family coming from a single set of parents who'd never faced the *shame* of divorce. The little girl piped up with accurate information about his father's first marriage. This revelation devastated the kid. We managed to keep him calm at the principal's office until his father could pick him up. The boy was furious with his father for keeping the secret. As I said, honesty is the best policy when it comes to children. This type of betrayal can impact a parent-child relationship forever."

Kate watched Dylan as he considered the story. Finally, he spoke. "I'm not sure it's that simple. I can see the father's perspective not to divulge personal information about his past. It wasn't any of his son's business to know about the first marriage. Maybe he wanted to wait until the child grew old enough to understand relationships before he exposed him to details about a failed marriage."

"You might be right. However, I can't help but question *why* the boy teased the other children about being from broken homes. More likely than not, the child's elitist rhetoric stemmed from something he'd heard at home. If he mirrored his parents, who disparaged divorce or children from blended families, then finding out about his father's divorce would've made his father a hypocrite. Kids at that age believe their parents are infallible. After such an event, the boy might question anything his father said."

The waitress interrupted their discussion with beverages. They took a moment to review their menus. Kate asked for her standard chef's salad with grilled chicken breast, while Dylan and Augie ordered burgers. After the waitress left the table, Kate asked, "I hope you run every day to keep your arteries clear. Junk food will catch up with you one of these days."

Dylan laughed. "You're not the first person to let me know I should adopt a better diet."

As they waited for their lunch, Dylan told Kate about the Sasquatch search he'd attended in Oregon. While intrigued by the sounds they'd heard in the woods, Kate decidedly announced they were not from a Bigfoot.

After the waitress placed their plates on the table, Augie removed the pickles and lettuce from his burger and pushed the discarded garnishes to the far end of his plate. He compressed the bun with a palm before he lifted it to his mouth and took a bite.

Dylan watched Augie's methodic and predictable adjustments. He picked up the ketchup bottle and offered it to Augie. "Want some? I know it's your favorite."

Augie grinned as he chewed. After swallowing, he said, "Ketchup and mustard are for sissies."

Kate asked, "Private joke?"

Dylan lathered his burger with liberal doses of both condiments. "Definitely." He turned to Kate. "Why don't you tell us more about your sighting? I don't remember all the details, and Augie's never heard the story from you."

She turned to Augie and said, "Dylan's convinced me that my sighting was an actor dressed in a Bigfoot costume. So there isn't much to tell."

Dylan interrupted. "Well, it's still a good story. Tell Augie about seeing him drink sugar water from your feeders and how you ran out to protect them. What did he look like? It must have been a convincing costume."

"You know, the outfit had to be outrageously expensive. The hair was all different lengths. His short facial hair looked more like a hide than fur. Long, wispy hair covered his entire body. It seemed like it would be soft to touch."

Kate raised a hand to her hair and rubbed a lock between her fingers. "It seemed fine, like mine. Not coarse or thick. He had to be three feet taller than me, but with an athletic build, like a swimmer. His eyes were the most amazing feature. They were an incredible shade of light blue."

Dylan nodded. "It's funny, whenever I've seen drawings of a Bigfoot, they have monkey faces with dark eyes."

"Yeah well, I'll never forget this guy's eyes. They were clear and thoughtful. That's the other reason I'm convinced he had to be a man in a costume. His expression clearly showed surprise when I came out of the door and into the garden. I would swear he was considering his options. Animals don't respond that way. They simply react."

"In your case, it reacted by running away."

Kate scoffed. "I've never heard of a sighting that ended up in an exchange of phone numbers."

"Do you ever think about why they wouldn't be curious enough about us to make contact?"

"Who?"

"Sasquatches."

"Have you drunk the Kool-Aid? You're the one who convinced me I saw a man in a costume."

"I'm not saying you saw a real one. But if they *do* exist, then why might they want to engage with one of us?"

"Probably the allure of tasty organ meat."

Dylan wagged a finger at her. "Why does everyone think they are hungry predators? Don't you think they may want to meet us?"

"If there was such a creature, living alone, virtually undetected in the far reaches of the woods, do you think he'd come here to play a round of golf or go to the movies? I think he'd be after food."

"You're probably right," said Dylan before taking a big bite of his cheeseburger.

After they finished their meal and the waitress picked up their dishes, Dylan asked Augie to show his notebook to Kate. He nodded and passed the drawings to her.

She opened the front cover with care, as she assumed Augie felt his artwork personal and valuable. Astonished at Augie's work, she paused to examine each page.

Kate felt Augie captured the essence of his subjects' souls and emotions as well as their features. The faces personified sadness, happiness, kindness, and loneliness. Kate remarked on the realism in his work. Her critique prompted a grin from Augie and a confirming nod from Dylan.

As she continued to leaf through the pages, Dylan shared his idea about connecting Augie with a local artist for tutoring. Kate agreed his talent should not be ignored. Even if his work resulted in little commercial value, he enjoyed the hobby.

Kate believed Augie would respond well to thoughtful mentorship. Perhaps he might try some other mediums, such as watercolors or oils. With more diverse methods, Augie might further develop his already impressive talent. She had a couple of ideas and would make some contacts.

Kate turned to the final portrait, incomplete but undeniably Dylan. She held the notebook to a level where she could compare Dylan's face with the unfinished work.

"What are you doing?" Dylan asked.

"Well, here's one of you. I wanted to contrast the drawing with real-life."

Dylan turned to look at Augie. "You're doing one of me?"

"Yeah."

"I thought you only did women's faces?"

"I said I only draw nice people."

Chapter 41

DYLAN COX

Augie and Dylan took a circuitous route to Augie's trailer to enjoy the exercise and each other's company. Dylan pointed out the houses with Halloween decorations, and Augie smiled whenever Dylan made comments about the inhabitants' lack of fear of what they'd created in their front yards.

Super-sized spiders and carved pumpkin faces might have raised concerns at any other time of year but were now commonplace for a holiday encouraging dress-up and candy exchanges. The Disneyesque celebration seemed a far cry from the original Celtic-based day to honor the dead. *Maybe it's all for the best.*

While still early in the afternoon, long shadows fell across the lawns, and an afternoon breeze held a chill absent a week prior. As they approached Augie's trailer, Dylan stopped at the front gate and waited while Augie stepped forward to unlock the door. Augie paused, presumably to see if Dylan planned to follow him inside, but Dylan stayed on the chipped sidewalk.

"I've got an errand to run before I go back to Jen's cabin. Can I stop by tomorrow to visit?" Dylan asked.

"Yes." Augie held the notebook wedged between his elbow and side while his hands fidgeted in the front pockets of his jeans. From his movements, Dylan knew Augie felt anxious. Augie asked, "Are you scared to stay where something killed Jen and Nate?”

"Not scared, but I'm extra watchful for signs of wildlife."

"Have you seen anything?"

Dylan did not want to lie outright but was reluctant to tell the truth. "I caught sight of a couple of animals that spooked me, but they took off and haven't been back."

"Why did they leave?"

"I might have a guardian angel."

Augie tilted his head. "A real angel?"

"The jury's still out on that. But I feel like I'm safe."

Augie frowned. "Too bad Jen didn't have an angel."

Dylan crossed the front walkway to give Augie a quick hug. "Yes. I assume my angel could have saved her, too. But at least he's watching out for me."

Dylan hoped his words rang true. He guessed that depended on whether Kalev remained his protector and did not turn into the vengeful monster that Erle, the gallery clerk, and Kate portrayed him to be. After goodbyes, Dylan started up the car and headed to the feed store.

When Dylan arrived at the cabin, he stood on the porch in the fading afternoon sunlight to scan the perimeter. The tops of the tall pines swayed from intermittent wind gusts that whistled through the limbs like wind blowing across the high-tension wires back in Chicago. Halfway up a tree, above the crotch of a branch, Dylan spotted a squirrel hustling a cone into a winter den. The end of its fluffy tail disappeared last. As Dylan walked inside, he felt Kalev watching him.

Dylan set his parcel next to the sink and went about lighting candles to counter the impending darkness. From a large brown sack, he pulled out a gallon jug of water and an orange box of hummingbird food concentrate. Dylan filled a cup with water and pushed it aside to use later for teeth brushing. He tore open a premeasured packet of hummingbird food. After pouring the concentrate into the jug, he vigorously shook it to dissolve the mix.

Dylan chuckled. "I hope Kalev appreciates I bought one with natural ingredients and no artificial colors."

He searched for the wicker chairs that sat on the porch in the summer. Dylan found them wedged on top of each other in a closet next to the back door. He dragged them outside and positioned them arm to arm.

When he reentered the cabin, Dylan grabbed the jug and a throw from the back of the loveseat. Once outside, he set the hummingbird food next to his chair, wrapped himself in a blanket, and sat down to wait for Kalev.

Chapter 42

KALEV

When I left the target in the morning, I intended to provide a short break. After a couple of hours, I would resume his training. I returned to the vacant cabin several times during the day and burned in anger at my arrogance.

Why had I allowed him to leave? What if he had grown frightened and left? Worse yet, the target could have returned with a pack of primitive beings. The opportunity to communicate with him alone would end.

To dissipate my frustration, I hammered fists on a thick pine until my knuckles were raw and bloody. As the tree swayed from the beating, bits of an abandoned flicker nest fluttered to the ground from a hole high in the branches.

Unsatisfied, I stood with a shoulder to the tree and wrapped my arms around the trunk. I pulled. The roots snapped under the strain. Dirt clods and decades of rotted pine needles rose from the forest floor as I separated the tree from the forces keeping it erect for the decades.

My heart pounded and lungs seared as the trunk broke free and forced me to step back to balance it between my neck and shoulder. With knees bent for leverage, I heaved the tree forward to release both it and my anger into the woods. It bounced twice and fell with a thud. A squirrel chattered a reprimand, no doubt for the noise and disruption of topography, until I silenced him.

I had spent the day alternating between striding through the forest and passing the cabin. At midmorning, three female deer crossed the yard. They stopped to nibble branches sticking out of the blowdown pile. They browsed, oblivious to my distraught mood. I signaled them to move on. They complied and skittered through the trees. Good thing, as my patience eroded with each moment the target stayed away.

Finally, near dusk, I heard tires on the driveway. I crept into the woods within sight of the cabin and peeked from behind a shaggy juniper bush. He had arrived alone.

I resisted the urge to approach him immediately and stayed hidden to watch. I drew satisfaction as he hesitated on the porch. He scanned the tree-line to look for me. Let him wait until *I* decided to re-engage.

As the target carried chairs from the cabin to the front porch, he reminded me of how weak these creatures were. He struggled to align the chairs by awkwardly dragging them into place. I could have placed them with a single hand.

Before he sat, the target wrapped a blanket tightly around his shoulders. Despite their clothes, they must be continually fighting a chill. They could not possibly survive in nature. I clearly understood why they spent so much time building shelters to protect themselves from the world around them.

I stepped forward from behind a stout pine. Slowly and cautiously, I approached, not wanting to frighten him. He stiffened, then relaxed. Tension showed in his expression but also familiarity.

When I reached the porch, he motioned for me to sit in the vacant chair adjacent to his. It seemed like the target believed he was taking charge. I smiled at the gesture and recognized the invitation as a sign of welcome and a cultural sharing.

My kind did not sit on objects. Where we lived, there were plenty of comfortable, clean places to sit without a need for artificial structures. These creatures spent inordinate resources making objects to soften the harshness of their lives. Even hikers, who I assumed spent time in the forest to enjoy nature, sought logs or flat rocks to rest on while they talked or ate. Some brought pads to cushion the surface before they sat down. At least I believed they were softening the surface. After further consideration, perhaps the pads were designed to buffer them from the bugs or dirt.

I turned in front of the chair and lowered my backside to the seat. The wicker pulled at the hair along my legs. I found the tugs annoying—anger built inside me.

My first inclination was to jump up to fling the chair across the yard, but I took several deep breaths. This was not the time to lash out. I smiled at the target and imitated his posture with an ankle perched on my knee. At that moment, I decided diplomacy was all about being unprepared and uncomfortable.

We sat together without engaging and experienced the retreating light. Once the sun's rays wholly hid from view and the sky shifted from light gray to deep blue, the target went into the cabin to retrieve a lantern. While not up close, I had seen them before, outside of buildings and on picnic tables when evening fell. The lack of sunshine probably challenged their ability to see. Or perhaps, their fear of the darkness prompted them to create artificial light.

The target dragged a match across the side of a box to make it sputter and flame. He pumped a lever and coaxed the lantern to glow. After he hung it on one of the posts supporting the porch roof, he returned to his chair. The light flickered softly, and the mechanism gave off a hissing sound, loud enough to drown out the insect noises driving me crazy. Despite casting unneeded light, I appreciated the lantern's side benefits.

As the target snuggled under the blanket, I reached forward to examine the fabric. His eyes followed my hand as I rubbed the dense, soft material between a thumb and finger. I tucked the end under his shoulder to keep cold away from his body.

He smiled. Then he turned toward me and pointed to his forehead. I shook my head from side to side—not this time. I indicated toward his chest to advise him. He should send a message to me.

He sighed and gazed beyond the yard, seemingly puzzling over my request. Slowly, he nodded and closed his eyes.

Not fully formed and grainy, his message included a female in her garden with a look of shock on her face. I smiled with recognition. The target had returned the vision I had sent a week earlier.

While he selected an image that was not his own, he likely sent one I might recognize—an appropriate choice for such a primitive being. The transmission included words: Kate, fear, and garden. While the meaning of these words was not clear, I understood the target had attempted to transmit language as well as the concept. To encourage him, I smiled and nodded.

He grinned and reached for a container next to his chair. After he opened the jug, he took a drink. Then, he passed it to me.

What was he thinking? If it held something harmful, he would not have drunk first. I sniffed and recognized the fragrance immediately. The container held the sweet fluid I drank in the female's garden. Smart fellow—send the vision first and then give me the familiar food.

With sustenance difficult to find, I constantly battled hunger. Occasionally, I took seeds or liquids from bird feeders but took only enough not to attract attention. However, there were times when my desperate need for food overcame restraint. When famished, I threw caution to the wind and emptied the feeders.

The evening in the female's garden was one of those times. I had stayed too long and ignored the click of the door handle. She discovered me. From that point forward, I avoided her feeders, despite their abundance and appealing flavor.

The target stared at me as I took several long gulps and wiped my mouth with the back of my hand. The nutrients calmed my rumbling stomach, and I realized the day had passed without eating. Reluctantly, I returned the container. Perhaps meeting him would have benefits beyond merely a completed mission.

Chapter 43

DYLAN COX

Dylan pushed the cap on the jug and placed it near his guest's giant feet. He hoped Kalev understood more was available whenever wanted. After his conversation with Erle about Sasquatches' preferred meals, Dylan could not stop thinking about Kalev's diet.

He glanced at the creature's nails, dagger-sharp and stained brown from either dirt or blood. Dylan hoped the former. Kalev's teeth provided minimal clues. He did not have overly defined canines, designed for tearing meat. Kalev's mouth seemed like a human's with straight, white incisors in the front.

Wanting a better view, Dylan turned to Kalev and delivered a toothy grin. Kalev mirrored the action and smiled while he lowered his head to Dylan's eye-level. Dylan opened his mouth and issued a long, "Ahhh."

Kalev opened his mouth wide enough to win a pie-eating contest. Abruptly, he snapped it shut. His brow furrowed as if he questioned the activity.

Dylan said, "Your orthodontist would be proud. I'm glad to see you have lots of molars. It makes me hope you're a vegetarian."

Kalev reached for the jug to take another drink. He flipped the top off with his thumb and caused the lid to sail beyond the porch. Dylan jumped from his chair to fetch it.

Dylan cleaned the lid against his jeans and slipped it into his pocket before he sat back down. "No need to make things complicated. I'll cover the jug later if there's any syrup left. You should eat as much as you want. You won't be able to find more in the gardens until spring." Dylan knew hummingbirds were only in Colorado between April and early September. By autumn, bird enthusiasts would have stored their feeders.

Based on his success in sending the first message, Dylan wanted to try again. Perhaps this time, he could send one necessitating a response and make their exchange feel more like a conversation. After he signaled an intended transmission, Dylan closed his eyes and conjured thoughts of the Sasquatch search in Oregon.

He envisioned himself with James, Kevin, and Paul as they slogged up the trail and set up the camp chairs. For each person, Dylan interrupted his message to give background on what he knew about the man.

When he thought about James, Dylan diverted into views of Joann with her sophisticated clothes and introspective artwork. A picture of the intake certificate flew through his memory.

With each digression, Dylan's thoughts grew disjointed. The voice in his head tried to unscramble the visions and reorder thoughts logically. Chronological did not work, but neither did grouping by topic. Dylan felt Kalev's hand touch his shoulder.

When Dylan opened his eyes, he saw Kalev shaking his head. He knew the message had derailed. "Help me," he said and held both hands out front with palms up.

Kalev leaned forward. He stretched open his fur encircled eyes with fingers and thumbs. Dylan grunted. "I get it. I don't need to close my eyes to send a message."

Kalev moved his mouth and shook his head. Dylan said, "Okay. So I'm still relying on my language to communicate."

Dylan reconsidered the topic. "This is going to be hard, but maybe I can teach you something, too." He conjured an image of Kalev and thought his name. Not the letters in the written word—Dylan merely verbalized the name with his mind. In the next vision, Dylan pictured himself in front of a mirror. When the image became clear, he thought the word, Dylan.

Kalev sat upright with a start. Immediately, he returned the images with the names attached. Dylan beamed with satisfaction. "You might have learned your first words."

The beast's eyes narrowed as if he contemplated the value of knowing more. He reached a skeptical finger toward Dylan's body and touched the fabric of his fleece. "Jacket," said Dylan.

With a nod, Kalev laid a hand on the side of Dylan's cheek, and Dylan responded with, "Face."

As the word left his lips, Dylan's sight blurred, replaced with a bombarding vision of hundreds of faces that flew at light speed. When the stream of mugshots stopped, Dylan heard the word "face," as clearly as if Kalev had said it aloud.

"You got it," Dylan confirmed with a nod.

Kalev rose from his seat, and his head grazed the porch ceiling. He scanned the surroundings. Without vigor or enthusiasm, he touched the chair and looked at Dylan with faint curiosity.

"Chair," Dylan said aloud and did not bother to transfer the word with his thoughts.

Kalev returned to sit. He waved a dismissive hand and took another drink. Why did the creature seem ambivalent about a pathway to communication?

"I still want to send a message needing a response," said Dylan. Kalev reacted with a shrug but nodded when Dylan signaled his intention to send another vision.

Dylan had learned from the disastrous muddle of images and words in the previous message. He focused on a discrete event at the Sasquatch search and imagined himself on a camp chair in the dark Oregon woods. Rhythmic thumping echoed through the forest.

As Dylan allowed the vision to dissipate, he pointed toward Kalev and raised an eyebrow.

Kalev's mouth curled into a smirk as he shook his head. He leaned toward Dylan and sent a vision of men, dressed in plaid flannel, in the woods. They pounded logs against trees.

Dylan burst out laughing. Asked and answered. Now they were getting somewhere.

They continued to exchange messages on Kalev's terms, mostly short visions used as a framework for understanding each other's cultures. Dylan discovered Kalev slept in the open air at night.

Each attempt to find out what type of meat Kalev ate was met with vigorous shakes of his head. Dylan sent images of a person eating pork chops, sushi, and steak tartare. Kalev grimaced and returned visions of juniper berries and seeds. Dylan grew blissfully convinced his new friend ate only plants. So much for Erle's theories.

Dylan wanted to increase Kalev's knowledge of the human language and sent visions with actions. He transmitted one or two words, usually a noun and a verb. When Kalev needed clarification, he selected one item or activity from the vision and sent it back to Dylan with a single word to clarify its meaning. Kalev had a remarkable memory, as he never asked twice.

When Dylan's stomach started to rumble, he realized he had skipped dinner. He glanced at the cabin and figured it would be a cold night if he did not start a fire. Dylan decided to take a break.

As he stood to start his chores, Kalev rose with him. Did he want to follow Dylan inside? He questioned the wisdom of inviting Kalev into the cabin.

He decided to throw caution to the wind. "Well, why not? Want to come along? I could give you a tour."

Dylan opened the door and swept his arm to motion for the Sasquatch to step inside. Kalev leaned low to peer into the cabin. Then he straightened and scanned the yard. While Kalev sent no messages, Dylan knew he was weighing his options.

"Maybe you've never been inside a home before?" Dylan asked but did not expect a response. "I would teach you how to use the shower and the toilet, but they've winterized the place."

Kalev cocked his head as Dylan continued. "You could use a shower, but even if it worked, I'm not sure I'd let you use it. You'd probably clog the drain with all that hair, and how would I explain it to Kate?"

The Sasquatch narrowed his eyes. Maybe he did not understand the words, but could he tell that Dylan was poking fun?

Once again, Kalev leaned into the doorway, a bit further this time. Slowly, he scanned the room before pulling back and straightening to his full height. Kalev stared at Dylan as if he speculated Dylan's motives.

Was Kalev concerned about an escape route? After all, he had hidden in the woods for a long time—without discovery by a human.

Dylan stepped inside and propped the door open with the chair. "Come in if you feel comfortable. Otherwise, stay outside."

After he laid logs in the fireplace, Dylan stacked kindling and lit the fire starter. A clatter outside the door drew his attention. Dylan went to investigate and slowly poked his head beyond the doorframe. Kalev was not on the porch, but a jumbled pile of logs littered the threshold.

He scrambled to organize the sticks into the canvas sling and transferred them to the rack next to the fireplace. As he stacked the logs, Dylan heard another delivery. He rushed outside.

"Stop!" Dylan shouted as the Sasquatch stepped from the deck into the side yard. Kalev paused to turn, and Dylan continued. "Thank you, but I don't need anymore. I don't want bugs to infest the house. Jen drilled that into my head, and I'm going with her edict."

Kalev tilted his head, and Dylan laughed. "What makes me think you might understand?"

Dylan took Kalev's hand and pulled him to the chairs. The Sasquatch offered no resistance and sat to watch Dylan move the remaining firewood from the deck into the house.

Once the fire seemed under control, Dylan pulled a Styrofoam container from a paper bag on the counter and went outside. Still parked on the wicker chair where Dylan had left him, Kalev acknowledged Dylan with a nod.

Dylan wrapped himself with the blanket and sat, before he lifted the lid and inhaled scents of chili powder, garlic, and cayenne.

"Room-temperature chili isn't my favorite, but smells delish." Dylan tipped the open container toward his guest. Kalev sniffed and scowled.

"Too spicy?"

As Dylan savored a bite, Kalev took a pull from the bottle of hummingbird food.

"Our first meal together," said Dylan as he motioned to the Sasquatch with the grease coated spoon. Kalev lifted the jug toward Dylan as if to acknowledge the moment.

Dylan smiled. "Here's hoping it's not our last."

Chapter 44

KALEV

Since few vehicles passed the cabin each day, I was surprised to hear one ascend the road and slow to a stop at the driveway. One glance at Dylan's shocked face told me he did not expect a visitor. I placed the nectar container on the porch and moved with haste behind the building.

Headlamps filled the yard with light as I ducked behind the pile of downed timber. The tree limbs still held their needles, which allowed me to peek without being seen.

I knew this vehicle, a two-toned affair with racks on the top. After a door opened, I heard shoes crunch on the gravel. A female strode to the cabin, the same one who spotted me in her garden last summer.

She had been to the cabin only a few days earlier—after the most recent attack but before Dylan came back. On that day, she brought a male who boarded the broken window while she attended to the inside.

I did not perceive them to be a threat to the mission as they seemed dedicated to returning the domicile to a safe condition. Their actions were contrary to the male who broke the window days earlier. He deserved the swift attention given to him.

The female held a tiny, nearly hairless dog in one arm. Dylan uttered a string of meaningless words to the animal and reached to scratch its head. I tensed as the beast nipped toward his hand. Should I intervene?

No need. The female pulled the dog away and admonished it with a wagging finger. Despite her grip, the animal wriggled, as it wanted to free itself. She acquiesced and lowered the creature to the ground.

After it barked at the pair, the creature scampered at its full speed to the woodpile, only feet from my hiding spot. It yapped incessantly. While tempted to call a hawk to dispatch with the pest, I decided to invoke a less violent measure by directing it to be silent and return to his owner.

The pet complied and sat at the female's feet with its mouth closed. The pest's tail dutifully wagged. The female seemed surprised, but she grabbed the creature and shut it in the car.

Dylan's voice had a friendly cadence as he and the female engaged in a conversation I did not understand. I heard the words *chair* and *cabin*, but without context, I lost the meaning. Dylan's lessons on language gave me some idea of how they communicate, but full comprehension would take time—a luxury I did not have.

Mastering communication was not part of my mission. But I wondered whether this new skill could increase my value with the upper echelon back home. They might even forgive me for taking on this operation without their explicit permission and preparation. However, to learn single words without context or action seemed an inefficient approach to comprehend their speech. I decided to find a more straightforward method.

I glanced toward the cabin and thought back to the recent incident at the doorway. Without pre-operation preparation, I had felt entirely unprepared when the target invited me to come inside. Tempted to follow him, I could not be sure his motives were sincere. What would have happened if I stepped inside and Dylan took me captive? While I could undoubtedly overpower him and escape through a broken window, I could not risk that type of encounter.

He seemed to appreciate my firewood delivery. But I still did not understand why he did not store the logs indoors. Why would he continue the repetitive task of stacking it outside and running to retrieve small amounts of wood? But his lack of efficiency did not surprise me as his kind mostly focused on survival. They would not have time to reflect on thoughts such as efficiency or serving society's greater good.

Despite Dylan's clumsy ways, a relationship had started. As trust strengthened, he would become increasingly unguarded.

The cabin door shut with a bang, and I no longer heard their voices. I knew better than to step on the creaky porch. So I moved to the front of the house and stretched tall to see inside the windows.

The female stood close to Dylan and talked with both her mouth and hands. She repeatedly touched his arm with affection. At least the gesture would have been considered affection in my society. Dylan nodded and stood with his arms folded across this chest. Each time she moved forward, he took a step back. I assumed he did not return her feelings.

When the cabin door reopened, I retreated to my post behind the timber. Dylan and the female hauled boxes to her car. They stacked them in the rear and twice took them out to accommodate more cartons.

The little dog yapped until I sent a message for it to be silent. The female gave her pet a startled glance before she shrugged and said something involving the words *dog* and *behaving*. I planned to ask Dylan their meaning once she left.

Once the car was packed full, Dylan closed the rear door and extended a hand to the female. She laughed and embraced him while he stiffly accepted her hug and glanced nervously toward the woods. I assumed he speculated whether I had stayed near enough to watch.

Dylan took a few steps toward the porch before he turned and watched her drive in a circle and down the driveway. I followed her to the main road and slipped behind trees to stay clear of the headlights. I watched her through the car's side window as she paused at the end of the drive.

My pulse quickened as I spotted a massive tree across the road. This could be an opportunity to be free of her interruptions. After all, what if Dylan asked her to stay with him at the cabin? I had no idea how often males teamed up with a new mate. Better to deal with her right away.

As she swiveled her head to check each direction before entering the main road, I transmitted a vision from the night she saw me in her garden.

No response.

I tried again and sent a barrage of sounds and actions. It was consistent with regular communications between beings of my kind and the type that caused Dylan incredible pain.

Oblivious to my transmissions, she cranked the wheel to the right and drove away.

Chapter 45

DYLAN COX

Dylan shook his head and watched through the trees as Kate's headlights traveled down the main road and out of sight. He returned to the porch and sat. While he drew the blanket tighter, Dylan hoped Kalev would return. Moments later, the hairy beast approached the porch and plopped onto the adjacent chair.

Dylan turned to him. "I'm sad Kate's taking away Jen's things but relieved she's gone. I think she's got a crush on me. While she's incredibly fit and not bad looking for her age, I'm about twenty years younger. She ought to know someone like Jen is more my type. Maybe she's having a mid-life crisis." Kalev raised a furry eyebrow. "I'll take your silence as agreement."

As they sat, Dylan thought about Jen's discarded clothes. Kate planned to take them to a consignment shop where the owner would pick through the boxes. She'd look for lightly used shirts, jackets, or shoes—anything someone might appreciate. Kate would donate the rest at the Caring & Sharing Thrift Store. Dylan imagined seeing one of Jen's favorite outfits on someone else. Would that trouble him?

Kalev tapped his forehead. Dylan shifted in his chair and prepared for an incoming message. As the vision focused, Dylan saw a burgundy 1994 two-door hardtop Monte Carlo stop along the main road in front of the driveway.

Despite the dim light, he could see the sun-damaged paint with peeled sections across the hood and roof. Dylan marveled at Kalev's exceptional night vision.

A tinted car window opened to reveal the driver's identity. Kirk Steadman rested a bony elbow out the window and tipped the frayed brim of his baseball cap with a thumb. As he squinted to see in the darkness, sun-induced cracks around his eyes deepened into furrows.

Steadman drew on a cigarette, and the end glowed to a brilliant crimson. Through pursed lips, he blew blue-gray smoke into the night air and stared toward the cabin. Watching. When did this happen? If this criminal scoped out the cabin, then he might have nefarious plans for the place.

Dylan thought back to when he ran into Kirk last summer. While never on Dylan's suspect list, his son Jesse had come under scrutiny for a time. Right before Dylan returned to Chicago, the County Sheriff's office brought Kirk in for questioning about a methamphetamine lab in the forest on Church Mountain. Two hardened criminals ran the lab in a camouflaged tent and made lucrative white crystals to distribute in Salida and the surrounding towns.

As far as Dylan knew, Kirk never helped to cook or sell the drugs. To score free meth, he hauled away their trash. Per his deal with the operators, Kirk dumped the empty fuel cans, bleach bottles, and blister packs in dumpsters or buried it in the next county. In exchange for testimony against the operators who set up the lab and murdered an old drifter, Kirk had remained uncharged and free. Why was this low-life scoping out Jen's cabin?

The vision continued as Kirk flicked a burning cigarette out the window and drove away. The butt smoldered in the breeze and ignited the dried grass. Withered leaves caught fire, and the little blaze grew in intensity.

Moments later, Kalev's furry hands and feet entered the image. He frantically pounded to extinguish the growing flames. As the fire subsided, the vision faded. Dylan saw Kalev's sullen face.

Dylan stood and indicated down the driveway. "Would you show me?"

Kalev rose and left the porch. He strode past Dylan and glanced over his shoulder before beckoning Dylan with a single finger.

Dylan followed. He noticed that Kalev walked like an athlete with arms, legs, and hips moving effortlessly in concert. His agility must contribute to his speed and stealth.

When they reached the road, Kalev pointed to the dirt next to the driveway.

In the pitch blackness, Dylan saw no evidence of the fire, but one whiff of the acrid smoke scent told him a fire had recently burned. He knelt to inspect the dirt and drag his fingers through the charred brittle grass. Dylan spotted a hint of white between the blades and picked up a discarded cigarette, now cold and impotent.

Dylan cranked around to look up at the creature. "You saved my life twice yesterday?"

Kalev's head tilted. His brow scrunched as Dylan stood to question him further. "Who would have figured you for my guardian angel?"

Dylan placed a hand on Kalev's arm, then hugged the woolly creature. He felt Kalev's arms wrap around his shoulders to return the embrace. As Dylan stepped back, he chuckled. "Now *I* could use a shower. You smell rough."

Chapter 46

KALEV

As we returned to the porch, I thought about Dylan's increasing trust and gratefulness. I initially assumed instinct solely drove their behaviors and was surprised at their complex feelings. According to our observations, their focus on survival steered most of their actions.

They spent inordinate amounts of effort to build habitats, cultivate food, and operate factories for clothing and transportation aids. How much time could remain for higher thought about society, personal interactions, and research?

Yet, there was so much we did not know. Dylan received my transmissions, but the female visitor did not. Could Dylan possess a superior intellect? Not superior in a broad sense, as these entities were clearly inferior to us, but their defects might vary among their kind.

Dylan held some telepathic ability, but I doubted whether he could ever communicate as quickly as me or any of my peers. However, his meager attempts at telecommunication helped us avoid talking as a sole method of communication.

Their spoken language was outrageously cumbersome and slow. That understood, maybe learning their language could prove beneficial. Without prior direct contact, my colleagues had only guessed at what drove behaviors. There were so many unanswered questions. Like, why did they honor lower animals with statues and images on their clothes but also tortured and ate them?

We continually sought a deeper understanding of these primitives. The ability to listen to their discussions or read their texts could help us to dispel myths and widen our knowledge. Earlier in the day, I had learned some rudimentary words and concepts. If I put my mind to it, I would become fluent.

If I went home with a complete understanding of their language and culture, I could bridge our research gaps and vastly elevate my status. The council would rue the day they rejected my application. I would return a hero, my objective fulfilled.

I turned to Dylan as he sniffed at the remaining food in the container. He shook his head and sealed the lid before he smiled at me. Dylan's breath smelled beastly. His food included a muddle of odiferous plants. I assumed they added fragrances to hide the scent of animal meat.

I appreciated my nectar's simplicity and sweetness and hoped Dylan would make another batch before he went into the cabin to sleep. As if he could read my personal thoughts, Dylan stood and pointed at the nearly empty container next to my foot. He asked something indecipherable, except for the word *food*, their generic term for sustenance.

Dylan took his refuse and the jug through the open cabin door and returned shortly with a full supply of nectar. I accepted the replenished container with an appreciative nod, and we exchanged smiles.

Dylan needed rest. So I tapped my head to signal a final outgoing transmission. I visualized a group of Sasquatches as they discussed a topic. They sat on the ground and faced the center of their circle. Unbeknownst to Dylan, this group simultaneously addressed a multitude of subjects, such as politics, recent matings, and news from a distant colony. The information would have flowed freely with visions and other cues, but this would have been far above Dylan's comprehension. I assumed the image was sufficient for him to understand I am not the only being of my kind.

After I withdrew the image, Dylan looked at me and raised six fingers to represent the six Sasquatches. I nodded to affirm his assumption. He asked, "Where?" and glanced around as if looking for them. I pointed toward the summit of Church Mountain.

When he stood and headed off the porch, I pulled his arm to stop him and shook my head from side to side. He looked at me questioningly. I pointed to the cabin and imitated sleep with closed eyes and resting my head against a palm.

"Show me." He insistently pointed to the peak, then placed both hands on his hips—feet planted firmly. Dylan pounded a fist on his chest, then indicated toward the mountain. "Take me," he said. I could not be more pleased with his willingness to join me.

I tapped my forehead and sent a time elapsed transmission of the sky. First, the night sky filled with glowing planets and stars. Some moved in rotation, and others streaked across the inky blackness. Gray dawn replaced night and morphed into daylight with the fierce sun tracking across the brilliant blue sky. After a pink-streaked sunset, the darkness returned, and a full moon rose to undermine the carpet of gleaming stars.

Once the transmission ended, he nodded and said, "Okay. Tomorrow night."

Dylan waited at the door to the cabin and watched me return to the forest. Once behind the trees, I turned to see him step inside and close the door.

I believed nothing could stop my forward momentum. In one more night, when the moon was at its fullest, I would take the next step of my mission by bringing Dylan to meet the others.

Chapter 47

OCTOBER 18
DYLAN COX

Dylan selected a seven-grain muffin with raisins to accompany his latte at Café Dawn. The chilly morning air nearly chased him back indoors, but he sought privacy for his phone call. So Dylan took breakfast outside at one of the wire mesh tables. He did not want any roving ears to hear his conversation. No problem, as none of the other patrons sat outside. Prepared for the weather, he had dressed in a fleece hoodie and a down vest.

As he sipped coffee and dragged his cell phone back and forth across the metal mesh tabletop, Dylan debated what to say to Tom about the recent events.

Still early, long shadows and commercial two-story buildings blocked the warming rays of the sun. Dylan suppressed a shiver as he gazed down G Street toward Tenderfoot Hill and the brush covered ridges beyond. A lone mountain biker, legs pistoning in low gear, made uphill progress on Spiral Drive.

He glanced toward Nate's gallery, kitty-corner across the street, and imagined that Destiny and Trip still slept. They deserved time to recharge before hosting Nate's parents.

He picked up the phone. Should he confess about the interactions with Kalev? Would Tom assume Dylan had lost it?

As Dylan touched the screen, he smiled at Jen's photo. Taken on a hike last summer, Jen grinned with boundless energy and posed with one hand on her slim hip. The other hand rested on the rough bark of a tree trunk that grotesquely bent into two ninety-degree angles. The first bend forced the trunk parallel to the ground and second resumed the tree's upward path. She had claimed the odd shape originated from Native Americans marking the trails.

Finally, he tapped the button for Tom's number. He answered on the first ring as if waiting for the call. Dylan gave Tom an update about the events in Oregon. After he reported the forward momentum and subsequent screeching halt on the adoption front, Dylan talked about the Sasquatch search.

Tom listened without judgment or comment, then said, "We're low on cash. What's your plan?"

Dylan sighed. "Sorry to leave you hanging out there without a detective for the agency."

"I've had two requests for your services, but I told them you weren't available until the end of next month." Tom laughed. "Once they heard you were in high demand, they decided to wait until you're back. Funny how everyone wants what they can't have."

"Are we okay with the bills for a couple of weeks?"

"Not really, but I might have a short-term solution. When I searched the attic for your adoption papers, I ran across a box of comic books. I didn't know your dad collected. Did you?"

Dylan chuckled. "Nope. It doesn't seem like something he'd do."

"They're all related to the Walter Langkowski character. I've taken them to a broker. He said the collection includes every issue with a Langkowski appearance up until your dad passed away. Based on a preliminary estimate, the collection could keep us afloat for months without additional income from the agency. Are you okay if I sell them, or do you want to see them first?"

"I don't know anything about comics or Walter-the-Polish-guy. But if the sale helps us through the next couple of months, go ahead and sell them."

Dylan sighed. "I need to tell you about what else has happened here. Hear me out before you comment. I'm not even sure I believe it myself."

He wrestled with how or if to tell Tom about Kalev. Finally, Dylan blurted the story without taking a breath. He started with the first sighting and recalled his near-death experience with the mountain lion and the bear. He insisted Kalev saved his life not once but two times in the same day. Dylan explained how they communicated, sometimes telepathically and other times with hand signals or expressions. Lastly, he described how he'd given Kalev a name.

Dylan's monologue droned on until he felt prepared to hear Tom's thoughts. "Well? What do you think?"

Slow to respond, Tom finally asked, "I don't know what to think. You're not pulling my leg, right?"

"Nope. This is the truth. I don't know why it's happening to me, but it is."

"Well, what's your next step?" Tom's pragmatic approach calmed Dylan's nerves. While he wanted Tom's assurance that his encounter could be authentic, Tom offered him something better. He didn't question the reality of the situation. He jumped to what needed doing to keep Dylan grounded in the process rather than defending the circumstances.

"Last night, Kalev left to spend the evening with other Sasquatches. I didn't see him this morning, but I'll bet he's around when I get back to the cabin. He hasn't directly said so, but I think he'll want to introduce me to his family or gaggle or whatever you call a group of Sasquatches. I think they have a camp not far from Jen's cabin. Maybe he wants me to help them organize contact between them and humans."

"You know I think the world of you, Bro. But it seems like they'd be better off to find someone in politics, the military, or a scientific field to make their first contact. Why do you think he picked you?"

Dylan laughed. "Well, that's the big question. Maybe my ability to communicate telepathically with them isn't universal among humans. I'm not sure they've ever tried to do this with anyone else. Come to think of it, I don't know how he figured out *I'd* be able to communicate with him. But if I'm one of only a few who can send and receive messages, then I'd be a good ambassador."

"That makes sense, but this whole deal brings up so many questions. Like do they want something from us, and why have they made contact now?"

"I suspect I'll find out more after I meet the others. Based on our cryptic communication, I assume Kalev plans to take me tonight or within the next couple of days."

"I smell an ambush. Maybe the daytime would be better. Don't let him take you in the middle of the night."

"It seems a bit spooky to meet at night, but if that's the offer, I might agree."

"Do you trust this guy?"

Dylan smiled at Tom's anthropomorphism. He seemed comfortable attributing human terms and characteristics to the Sasquatch. "I assume they've been living among us, virtually undetected, for centuries. They must have something in mind more important than to kill a single human. I don't believe they want to hurt me. If so, Kalev could have killed me right away. He's a powerful creature. I'd be willing to meet them on their terms."

"I'm glad you told me before you left. We should make a plan for you to call me every day. If you meet them tonight, you can tell me the story tomorrow. At least I'd know you're safe. If I don't hear from you by noon, I can call the authorities."

"Would they take you seriously?" Dylan doubted anyone from the Sheriff's Office would give Tom the time of day about a Sasquatch abduction—except maybe Erle.

Tom laughed. "Not likely. But I could take the bus to Salida to look for you. What do you think?"

"I'm not sure how remote their camp is. If we left tonight, we might walk a good distance to reach them. While Kalev has learned a few words and is teaching me at the same time, we don't talk in full sentences. So I can't confirm the details."

"I understand, but I don't plan to wait around indefinitely. What seems reasonable to you?"

Dylan weighed his curiosity about the Sasquatch against potential risks. Kalev chose him for a reason. Even if Dylan had no idea why, he felt the Sasquatch would protect him from harm. After all, he'd already saved Dylan's life, and Kalev did not seem interested in eating him.

For an instant, Dylan speculated whether Kalev might be a scout with plans to lure unsuspecting humans to a midnight Sasquatch feast. *Sounds like the perfect plot for a B-movie*, Dylan thought with a chuckle before he dismissed the notion.

Dylan needed time to find out what they wanted but knew setting a deadline with Tom was important. He decided. "If we go tonight, give me 48 hours. Let's plan for me to call at noon on the day after tomorrow. If we don't go tonight, I'll phone again tomorrow."

"It's your choice, but know I'll be worried sick until I hear from you."

"I'd feel the same if our roles were reversed. Thank you for watching out for me."

Dylan sipped his coffee. What would Tom do if Dylan ended up not making the call? "If you don't hear from me in a few days, come to Salida. Destiny will help you figure out what happened. I'll leave my rental car keys at Jen's cabin, and my stuff will be in the trunk."

"I'm not thinking about that until I need to. I know you'll call." Tom hesitated before he said, "Please, be careful. This sounds like a big adventure, but it's incredibly dangerous. Kalev may not be what he seems."

Chapter 48

Before he went back to the cabin, Dylan stopped at Augie's trailer. He figured Augie would leave for work in the afternoon and hoped to catch him before he left for his shift. He wanted Augie to know he may be away for a day or so.

Augie answered the door before Dylan had a chance to knock. He assumed Augie had been watching and waiting for Dylan to pull up. Augie twitched with excitement as he ushered Dylan into the living room. Dylan took his usual spot on the sofa, and Augie sat in the worn recliner. Augie's feet tapped, and his hands patted the tops of his thighs.

Dylan understood the cues. "Okay, spill it. I know something exciting has happened."

The words tumbled out without censorship or sequence. "I'm meeting Max in the morning. He's gonna look at my drawings. Kate says I can make money. What do you think?"

While Augie oozed infectious enthusiasm, Dylan remained unclear about Max or Augie's unbridled excitement. "Slow down, my friend. Tell me what happened."

Augie tilted his head to one side. "What don't you understand?"

"Well, first of all, when did you talk to Kate?"

"This morning."

"Did she stop by here, or did you meet her in town?"

"Here." Augie pointed at the floor to emphasize his point.

"Okay, did she bring bagels?"

Augie laughed at Dylan's question but responded earnestly. "No. You bring bagels. Kate doesn't."

"Well, I didn't bring bagels today. Did you have breakfast?"

"Yeah. I went to the store yesterday."

Dylan noticed Augie's fidgeting had slowed. "Good. Even though Kate did not show up with bagels, she must've brought you information. Out with it."

"She talked to Max. He wants to look at my drawings."

"May I assume Max is an artist in Salida?"

"Yeah."

"Does he have a gallery in town?"

Augie thought for a moment. "On Third and D, with other artists, too."

"Wow, Augie, this is great news. How do you feel about showing him your work?"

A puzzled look returned as if Augie could not understand why it would be a problem to share his pictures. *He's not shy about showing anyone what he's done*, concluded Dylan. Familiar with Augie's reluctance to embrace or to divulge information about his past, he wondered about Augie's ambivalence to share something as intimate as his art. Dylan supposed there was still much to learn about Augie.

Dylan said, "No worries. Your pictures are amazing. I know Max will appreciate them. If you think you could work with him, maybe he could teach you some new techniques or methods. Would you like that?"

Augie leaned toward Dylan. "Techniques? Like what?"

"I don't know. Max may suggest better quality paper or show you how to use charcoal rather than pencils. He's the artist, so he'd know how you can further your craft."

Augie nodded and rubbed his thumbs against his thighs. "I'll let him show me."

"Good idea. Hey, I wanted to tell you that I'll be away for a couple of days."

Augie grabbed the arms of the chair and frowned. "Are you going home to Chicago?"

Dylan did not want to lie to Augie. But he was unwilling, just yet, to share information about Kalev. "Not Chicago. Tom called about surveillance work I can do in Colorado Springs. It should only take me a day or two. Then I'll come here for a few more days before going back home."

"Can I go with you?"

Dylan smiled. "I assume you mean to Colorado Springs? No, you already agreed to work today, and this job needs my full attention."

"What about Chicago?"

Surprised but heartened by the request, Dylan said, "I hadn't thought of that. I figured you'd want to stay in Salida with Destiny and Trip. Plus, you're planning to work with Max. Why would you want to move to Chicago?"

Augie returned Dylan's smile. "I didn't say I'd move there."

"You're right. I jumped to that conclusion. Are you talking about another road trip?" Augie nodded.

"You'd love to see the Lakefront and the art museum. Plus, you and Tom would get along great. He's much nicer than I am." Dylan laughed. "Let's talk about it when I get back from this trip."

Dylan stood. But before he stepped toward the door, Augie asked him to wait and left the room. He returned with his sketchbook and flipped to the last page. Augie handed the book to Dylan.

Dylan's throat tightened as he took in the full meaning of the drawing. Augie had completed Dylan's portrait in profile. The angle came from Dylan's right side. His eyes fixed in a squint, both nearly closed. His mouth gaped open and contorted to the side. His right hand poised above a steering wheel as if he was pounding it with the fleshy part of his palm. The picture froze the actions mid-beat.

Augie had captured a moment from their road trip. They spent hours listening to music, and frequently Dylan would burst into song when one of his favorite road tunes came up. Augie never joined in, but he would nod his head to the rhythm and grin at Dylan's off-key renditions. Dylan felt honored to be the first male in Augie's notebook of *nice people*.

Dylan decided to grab lunch at the Boathouse before going back to the cabin. One of his favorite haunts in Salida, the pub offered incredible views of the Arkansas River and a backdrop of magnificent snow-covered mountain peaks. Since the lunch hour had only started, Dylan grabbed a parking spot in front of the restaurant. A gangly hostess seated Dylan at a table with one of the best views.

Dylan ordered an autumn brew from a local micro-brewery and the fish tacos. As he waited for his food, Dylan leaned back into his chair. As his fleece jacket stretched across his chest, a piece of paper crunched in the breast pocket. He unzipped the flap and pulled out the forgotten copy of Cynthia's article. Dylan smiled as he unfolded the document.

Could she have given him the commentary only a week earlier? So much had happened since then. Dylan took a sip of his beer and started to read.

Merle's assessment seemed right on target. The unbalanced article leaned light on the Bigfoot movement and heavy on those who attempted to profit from national attention. While Dylan disagreed with her thesis, he thought her arguments were well supported.

Dylan didn't believe the local restaurateurs and hoteliers were simply after a quick buck. He preferred to assume Salida's Bigfoot believer business owners had faith these creatures existed. They weren't specifically interested in national acclaim, but the countrywide attention might attract experts who could help them evaluate evidence. Among the believers, a blurred line separated facts to support Bigfoot's existence and misleading fallacies.

Impressed to see Cynthia had cited statistics about Sasquatch sightings, Dylan noted a surge had occurred in late spring when Salida hit the national news. By far, the most frequent reported sightings occurred in Washington and California. But Florida, Ohio, Oregon, and Texas were not far behind.

These areas must have something in common. Was it the extent of secluded terrain or the proportion of residents with good imaginations? Based on Kalev's vision of lumberjacks who rhythmically pounded logs, how many of the sightings were real?

Cynthia's quoted sources asserted Sasquatches were omnivores with a preference for meat. While they ate leaves, berries, fruits, and other vegetation, they consumed fish, small mammals, and occasionally large mammals such as elk, bear, and livestock. Further, Sasquatches' tastes weren't overly refined as they sometimes took a meal at the garbage dump. Researchers concurred the beasts were elusive, dangerous, and predominantly nocturnal.

As Dylan's lunch arrived, he pushed the article to the side and gazed at the churning river. A lone man with long greasy hair and a baggy plaid work shirt threw a stout stick into a lazy eddy. His eager yellow Labrador ran in two concentric circles before plunging into the water after the branch.

Dylan took his first bite of taco. The picante sauce trickled from the soft corn shell and dripped down his chin. With his free hand, Dylan wiped the sauce with a napkin.

As he ate his meal, Dylan thought about how Kalev would feel about Cynthia's portrayal of Sasquatches.

Chapter 49

KALEV

I spent the morning exploring Church Mountain. The little peak stood above the cabin, at the northernmost end of a range separating the cabin from a grand valley sporadically dotted with ranches and hastily built shacks. As I approached the summit, I thought back to my earlier explorations of the adjacent valley in midsummer.

In the long days while my target left me to await his return, I had reconned the area to seek broader knowledge of this species and the landscape. If by some remote chance he did not return, my mental terrain maps could be my consolation contribution to my superiors.

One night, I snuck over the treeless ridges and made my way southward until I found an expanse of fine sand nestled up against the mountains along the range in massive wind-carved dunes. I could not investigate during the day, as the area teemed with activity, mostly parents accompanied by their young. So I spent the day hidden in the trees above the sand piles and watched. I needed to determine the best time for investigation.

They laughed and made their way up the soft hills by taking two steps forward and sliding back to halve their progress. Some strapped boards to their feet and skimmed down the slopes before they lost their balance and tumbled most of the way to the bottom. Once stopped, they retrieved their boards and followed the same pattern, their faces carved into maniacal grins.

I planned to visit the dunes after dark when the risk of detection would diminish. Once the visitors left to shelter in their tents and trailers, I imitated their actions of the day. While the sun had set a few hours earlier, the surface of the sand still held the heat of the day and scalded my feet. I pushed them deeper into the sand to find cooler temperatures and wriggled my toes into each step. This technique helped ease my ascent to the top.

For the next hour, I loped up the steep sides of the tallest dunes and rolled down the other side. Sand coated every strand of my hair. On the first roll, I made a grave error by keeping my mouth open. Sand clung to my lips and tongue. Once my tumble ended, I spent considerable time spitting and wiping my mouth against an arm to clean out the sand. I never made that mistake again.

On my way back to Dylan's valley, I discovered several pools, both natural and those enhanced with structures designed to capture the water for soaking. I could not resist the temptation to be clean.

The water must have been warm, as steam rose from the surface of the pools once the air cooled in the evening. I could not fathom their interest in the concrete-lined pools, as they were filthy with suspended sediment, hair, and dead skin. However, the natural pools called to me.

I waited patiently into the night until my selected pool was finally abandoned. The last pair of visitors left after they finished a noisy mating session in the grass adjacent to the pool. I thought the lawn seemed an unlikely place to engage in that type of activity, but these creatures had many strange habits.

When alone, I sat on the stone ledge surrounding the pool and submerged my feet and shins. The water felt warm, vastly different than the frigid streams I had experienced on my journeys through the mountains.

Despite the water's questionable hygienic status, I braced my arms on the rim of the pool and lowered myself. Once the water covered my shoulders, I ran hands across my legs and chest, as I hoped to rid my fur of debris and insects. I swayed and felt the familiar sensation of hair swaying in the water. The feeling made me long to be home, where warm life-sustaining pools were plentiful.

There was considerable risk in lingering too long, but I leaned back to dip my head part way. I wanted to submerge, but covering my ears would be reckless. Visitors might return.

I heard a faint sound and straightened. The noises were distant and subtle. I relaxed and decided they were probably voices inside the cloth-covered tents.

In one swift movement, I placed both hands on the stone border and hoisted out of the pool. I waited until well beyond the perimeter of the woods before shaking myself dry. The action made me grimace in disgust. I had seen dogs perform this maneuver after they swam in mountain streams. The similarity had made me question, *how low had I fallen?*

I abandoned my recollections of summer when I reached the summit of Church Mountain. The top seemed sufficiently devoid of trees, but giant skyward-pointing disks and metal spikes dotted the ridge.

I speculated whether the devices would complicate my plans. They seemed harmless, but how could I know their purpose? With no time to scout a different peak, I decided the mountain would suffice.

Chapter 50

DYLAN COX

Dylan returned to the cabin in mid-afternoon. Despite the low-level sun, the day turned out to be remarkably warm. He smiled as he thought about Tom's recent report of Chicago's gray, wet days.

With a lack of wind, the air felt comfortably balmy as Dylan stepped to the porch and opened the front door. The cabin felt like a meat locker.

Must be well insulated. Dylan laid a palm against a chilly, stacked-log wall bordering the river-rock fireplace. Dylan's nose tingled from the residual scent of the wood fire. He took a long look at the hearth, mantel, and stacked stones leading to the ceiling. Had Jen kept up with a chimney maintenance program? He decided to mention it to Kate. She could choose whether to have it done before she put it up for sale.

Before Dylan headed outside to wait for Kalev, he made up another batch of hummingbird nectar. With most of the pre-measured packets gone, he should have stopped to pick up more while in town. Perhaps Kalev would be thirsty when he returned from a visit to his people. Dylan scoffed as he questioned his use of *people*.

What does one call a group of Sasquatches? He wanted to avoid cheesy alliteration, such as a swarm, school, or syndicate of Sasquatches. So Dylan decided to borrow from other animal groups.

Monkeys belonged to troops or tribes, but that didn't seem quite right. Packs referred to canines and mules. While ants, beavers, and weasels bore little physical likeness to Kalev, they were highly intelligent and industrious. So Dylan settled on a *colony* of Sasquatches.

Dylan relaxed on the porch. He straightened when Kalev approached with the confidence of a returning comrade.

When Kalev noticed the full jug of nectar, he grinned and gave Dylan a nod. Dylan felt pleased with the silent but visible sign of appreciation. Kalev pulled his chair close to Dylan's and sat.

Kalev tapped Dylan's arm and gave the signal for an intended transmission. Dylan turned toward the giant and waited with anticipation and open eyes. Soon, he envisioned a farm with barns and rows of recently plowed fields. Tiny shoots of new crops lined the crown of each row.

While the sky was fully dark, Dylan could see the landscape with ease, another example of Kalev's extraordinary night vision. The brilliance of color faded, but details and shapes remained clear. Dylan heard an occasional vehicle passing on the road adjacent to the farm and the sounds of animals in the barn.

The landscape moved, as Kalev must have turned away from the farm and looked into the forest. His view bumped upward, and Dylan assumed Kalev had jumped over something to enter the woods. Perhaps a boulder or a fence?

The vision grew dim and then re-focused elsewhere. The new scene emerged deep in a forest with thick trees and the ground littered with broken boughs. Dylan saw a shredded tent and the carnage of an animal attack. This place seemed familiar. It might be the spot where Dylan and Jen came across a dismembered hiker. Animals had killed the guy while he slept in his tent. Dylan considered whether Kalev had also seen this horrific site.

As the vision faded, Kalev's face came into view. His eyes were full of sorrow and grief. Dylan responded without pause as he placed both hands on Kalev's forearm.

He thought about his discovery of the body. Dylan imagined the hiker's helplessness at being attacked in a tent that should have provided protection but was woefully inadequate against the threat of predators.

Dylan recalled his encounter with the bear and mountain lion on the night when Kalev had saved him. He assumed Kalev's sadness expressed regret that he could not save the hiker. "If only you'd arrived a few hours earlier."

Dylan sent a transmission with his view of the night he had met Kalev. He envisioned the bear and cat as they approached and then retreated without attacking. The predators had crossed into the forest only feet away from Kalev, who watched them disappear into the woods. After he sent the message, Dylan held both hands open and shrugged. He tried to ask whether Kalev understood why the animals had left.

Kalev nodded. He stood and stepped off the porch. Once he settled on the ground beyond the deck, he laid a hand on the ground with the palm facing upward. Within moments, a squirrel scampered down from a tree and nestled into Kalev's hand. Without hesitation or cautious sniffing, it had responded as if summoned.

Kalev gazed from the squirrel to Dylan and back. The Sasquatch gave no physical signals, such as a head nod or hand movement, and the squirrel stared at him. When Kalev nodded at the animal, it jumped to its feet and scampered up a tree. Once back in its domain, Dylan could hear the squirrel's reprimanding chatter from branches. With one glance, Kalev silenced the animal.

Dylan's perplexed look must have convinced Kalev that Dylan needed further proof. He continued the lesson by calling a large black raven to sit on the porch railing. The bird beat its wings and flew at the window to peck the glass with one sharp movement before it flew away.

Startled, Dylan asked, "Did you send the bird to fly into the window when I was here a week ago? I thought it was odd for a bird to be out at that time of night. They run into mirrored windows or when they think they can fly through to the other side, but not at night." Dylan sent a vision of the startled raven he discovered on the porch. The bird had flown into the window and nearly knocked itself unconscious.

Kalev sheepishly shrugged.

Dylan said, "Well, at least you're honest with me. You could have hurt the bird by commanding it to fly into the window. What were you thinking?"

He responded to Dylan's agitation by holding up a finger. Dylan waited for the next demonstration. Dylan spotted the shadow of a large bird before he saw it. With a whoosh, a hawk landed in front of Kalev. The bird lumbered around the ground and shifted from side to side as if dancing for

Kalev.

While the hawk hopped, Kalev glanced under the porch. Within seconds, a mouse slipped from underneath and crept toward the bird.

Dylan tensed. He figured the outcome would not bode well for the mouse. The mouse skittered directly under Kalev's sizeable thigh, but Kalev lifted his leg and stared at the mouse until it moved toward the hawk. The bird gave full attention to the tiny rodent. Kalev's scrutiny alternated between the two animals.

Dylan held his breath as the mouse approached the hawk and sat before the bird with its nose upturned and tail lacking movements to indicate frustration or anxiety. The hawk flattened, with its head low and tail elevated. Its thickly feathered shoulders moved up and down. Despite his ignorance of bird movements, Dylan felt it was not preparing to attack.

Gently, the hawk spread its wings over the mouse and cupped the ground, as if to protect the tiny creature from the view of other potential threats. They stayed in position until Kalev released his hold. Once liberated, the mouse scurried under the porch, and the hawk took to the sky.

Dylan released his breath and relaxed his shoulders. "Okay, I get it. You're here to protect and not harm."

Chapter 51

KALEV

Loose rock crunched as a car neared the turnoff for the cabin. I leaped to my feet and fled. Now what? Once behind the blowdown pile, I yanked a sapling out by its roots and flung it onto the top of the stack.

I skirted the open yard and stayed behind the boundary trees to keep out of view. When I reached a stout lodgepole pine, I pulled myself midway up the trunk until I could see the front porch, Dylan, and the approaching car.

This was not the vehicle of the previous day's female visitor, but I recognized the white car with blue and gold stripes and letters. This was the same car that came after the bear and mountain lion made short work of Dylan's mate last summer and the past week's snooping male. At that time, the vehicle's lights flashed from the front, but I saw none on this approach. Once the car parked, I watched an athletic male, dressed in clothes the color of the night sky, cross the yard toward Dylan.

The male wore a firearm strapped to his waist. The great leveler between Dylan's kind and beasts, I had watched others put these devices to work to threaten other beings or kill animals.

Once, I saw a female pull her gun and shoot a rattlesnake barring access to a family's home. The inhabitants did not understand the snake made *its* home under the wooden steps connected to their house. After she missed the animal with her first two shots, the angry snake had snapped forward and struck the empty air. The third bullet had hit the mark, and the snake collapsed into a trembling pile.

I studied the male visitor as he walked to the porch. He walked with assurance but lacked the determination of hunters whom I had observed. Was he planning to harm me with his firearm?

Dylan extended a hand. While they shook, the male grasped Dylan's shoulder. The action seemed friendly, but I speculated whether he meant to hurt Dylan. I tensed, ready for action. Dylan responded with a smile. He did not jerk away or seem intimidated. My racing heart slowed.

Dylan knew this male. Maybe he prearranged for him to come. Were they conspiring to capture me? I was only hours away from completing my mission. I had no intention to fail at this point.

I scrutinized the pair and searched for any clue that Dylan planned to divulge my hiding place. He did not nod toward the woods. No sign of deceit glimmered in his eyes.

Dylan motioned for the visitor to take a seat on the chair I had recently vacated. As the pair engaged in conversation, I strained to understand. None of the words sounded familiar, and I cursed myself for delaying more lessons to learn their language. Neither seemed animated or stressed, but I suspected the stranger's motives. Why was he here?

The male picked up the half-empty nectar container and shot Dylan a quizzical look. Dylan laughed and waved a dismissive hand toward the jug. After an exchange of words, the male smiled and set the container back on the porch.

As they continued their primitive oral exchange, I inched down the tree. I would not let the intruder interfere after my hard work to strengthen a relationship with Dylan.

With only a single tree between me and the porch, I drew a breath and eased toward the parked vehicle. I knelt beside the car and planned my next move. I could reach the porch and subdue the visitor until the cat and bear arrived, but Dylan might realize they had killed for me several times before.

The appropriate course of action was to be calm and stay hidden. I tried to suppress my insecurities and fear of Dylan's disloyalty. Unless he called attention to me, I would remain patient. Given time, the visitor certainly would leave without mishap.

Their voices remained calm, and I heard no sounds to signify they planned to cross the yard. But the niggling feeling remained. What if they intended to trap me? I seethed at Dylan's deception.

At that point, I was still undetected and crept from the car door to the front fender. I held my breath and peeked.

Chapter 52

DYLAN COX

Dylan spotted Kalev's furry forehead as it rose above the car hood. He saw raw anger in Kalev's face. Dylan's white-knuckled hands gripped the chair.

I need to deescalate this situation, or we'll both be in trouble. Dylan manufactured a broad smile and touched the Sheriff's arm. "Sorry I didn't stop at the station right after I got back to town."

Sheriff Austin extended his legs and crossed one calfskin boot over the other. "Not a problem. I only wanted to come by to thank you for connecting with Destiny in Oregon. As you can imagine, I didn't want to fess up about knowing she and Trip were out there. Your acting as a go-between worked out well. You could give her the message about Nate's death and keep our records clean."

Dylan leaned toward the officer to seemingly give full attention while Austin continued. "Officially, Nate told us Destiny took her life. Therefore, she wasn't a suspect in Trip's disappearance. When she called to report that Nate had deceived us about her death and she took the boy to keep him safe, she became a whistle-blower rather than a kidnapper."

The Sheriff's spin sounded well-reasoned and plausible. He continued. "Our permanent record of the events supports her lenient penalty. She wasted resources but did not obstruct the investigation."

"I'm glad for my role in moving the case to a conclusion." Dylan lowered his head and added, "While Nate and I had our moments, I'm sad he and Trip didn't have a chance to resolve their issues before the attack."

"That's a tough one for Trip, but Destiny's a good mom. She'll help the boy through his grief and regrets." Austin placed a hand on the arm of Dylan's chair. "Be mindful of your emotions, too. While you and Nate were on the outs, he was still family. You may have a tougher time with his death than you imagine right now."

Dylan felt only relief. Nate had taunted him for nearly thirty years. Yet he hoped Nate did not suffer at the end. The teamed-up mountain lion and bear were likely swift to kill. Nate's death was another case where Kalev showed up too late to stop their attack.

The Sheriff interrupted Dylan's thoughts. "Any idea what Nate was doing at the cabin?"

"He had no reason to be here. Do you have a guess?" Through his peripheral vision, Dylan watched the Sasquatch glare at the Sheriff.

"Jen knew Trip was with Destiny. Do you think Nate might've suspected she had information about the boy's whereabouts?"

"It's possible, but Nate didn't know about Jen's involvement. Anyway, if he suspected she'd left clues to Trip's location at the cabin, it would be the first sleuthing he did on his own to find Trip."

Austin sighed and slowly nodded. "While he grandstanded about being a victim, he never offered to help with the investigation."

"I think he preferred to have others work on Trip's disappearance and retain the role of an aggrieved father." As Austin spoke, Dylan spied Kalev as he slunk back into the woods. Hopefully, the Sasquatch had concluded the Sheriff did not pose a risk to Dylan or Kalev.

Austin hooked his thumbs into his front pockets. "You're probably right about that." He nodded his head toward the boarded-up window. "We did the best we could to sweep up the broken glass and cover the window. I let Kate know she ought to have someone fix the pane before it snows. Not all handymen have four-wheel drives to get up this road in winter. Anyway, snow will blow through the cracks if it's not fixed properly."

"Kate will know people who can fix it for Augie."

The Sheriff shifted in his chair. "We found a shovel near the door. It seems like Nate might've been digging around the foundation."

"Before I left town, I talked with Nate at his gallery. He asked about

Jen's father possibly hiding valuables on the property. Maybe he came out here to hunt for treasure."

"I knew Jen's dad. He served at a base in California, probably the Marines, but it could have been the Navy. Once his tour finished, he didn't have much time for the government. Thought people's lives would be better with less interference. I can't imagine he'd hide anything without telling Jen how to find it."

The Sheriff pulled a parcel from the breast pocket of his uniform shirt and handed it to Dylan. "Speaking of valuables, these were found in the pocket of Nate's slacks when we recovered the body."

Dylan accepted the tissue-wrapped bundle and opened it on his knee. He picked up a vintage gold class ring inset with a pale purple amethyst stone. "Why would Nate have a Salida High School ring?"

"That's what we wondered. There's a wedding band with an inscription of 'To RR with love.' Plus, an I.D. bracelet."

Dylan lifted a heavy steel-linked chain from the bundle. The name *Bobby* was engraved in double block letters across the front. "I'm assuming Bobby and RR were Robert Rickard—Jen's father?"

"I thought so, too. The class ring's year is consistent with when her dad graduated from high school."

Dylan slumped. "Nate took these things from the cabin?"

"Looks like it. We believe he was up here searching for valuables."

"Do me a favor and don't mention any of this to his parents. Despite his failings, they held their only son in high regard. They'd be devastated to learn he was a petty thief. Nobody's around to press charges, so I hope you can let this slide."

Austin nodded in agreement as Dylan rewrapped the jewelry and passed it to the Sheriff. He continued, "Since these things were at the cabin, they belong to Augie, right?"

"After I confirm with Destiny that they did not belong to Nate, I'll take them over to Augie and see what he wants to do with them."

"Strange to think about how much sentimental value we place on small objects. Memorabilia goes from precious to worthless as the last heartbeat of a family line fades away."

"Whatever Nate's motives were to poke around out here ended up killing him." The Sheriff returned the package to his pocket and buttoned the flap. "Are you concerned about staying alone at Augie's cabin?"

"I'll be fine. This place doesn't spook me. I have a guardian angel."

Austin grunted and stood. "I hope so. There've been no sightings of bear or cat in the county since Nate's attack. Hopefully, they've moved on." He extended a hand to Dylan. "Well, I'm headed back to town. Call me if you hear anything out of the ordinary."

"I certainly will." Relieved the visit was ending, Dylan stood and shook Austin's hand.

As they walked to the patrol car, Dylan draped an arm across the Sheriff's shoulder and steered him to the car.

Dylan watched him drive away. But before he could turn back toward the cabin, Kalev shot from the woods to grab him. Kalev seized Dylan's biceps with massive force.

"What the fuck?" Dylan yelled and tried to wriggle away.

Kalev shook with fury. He released an arm and clutched Dylan's chin between a thumb and forefinger. As Kalev forced back Dylan's head, the Sasquatch stared into his eyes. Dylan tried to pull free.

"I didn't invite him. Let me go!"

Kalev loosened his grip, and Dylan stepped back. He struggled to gain composure. Dylan placed both hands high on Kalev's chest. As he studied the Sasquatch's face, Dylan said, "You can't know what I'm saying, but you *must* trust me."

Kalev's head tilted, and eyes squinted. Dylan took one of the Sasquatch's giant hands and tugged him toward the front porch. Reluctantly, Kalev followed. Dylan shoved him into the chair and sat next to him in a huff.

"Relax," Dylan said. Kalev ignored the directive. His shoulders were military straight. The Sasquatch breathed in and out with the force of a sprinter.

Picking up the jug, Dylan took a sip and offered it to Kalev. The Sasquatch accepted the container. Instead of taking a drink, he lowered it to rest on his knee.

Dylan hoped the creature's anger would diffuse if given time to cool off. With eyes never leaving Dylan's, Kalev leaned forward to place the jug on the porch.

Slowly, methodically, Kalev inched backward until his back rested against the chair. He reached a tentative hand over the gap between the chairs and petted Dylan's leg.

"I'm not sure what I did, but I guess you forgive me," said Dylan.

Lessons continued through the afternoon, with Dylan growing to understand more about what Kalev had seen in his nearby travels. Dylan expanded Kalev's vocabulary with visions of people, places, and actions. Through his thoughts, the Sasquatch repeated concepts by connecting words.

Kalev confirmed that Dylan slept on the loveseat in the cabin and drove into the town to visit friends or buy groceries. He also reaffirmed that Dylan came from a place called Chicago, with steel structures and vastly more people than Salida.

They took a break for Dylan to retrieve the lantern and dinner from the cabin. As they ate in silence, Dylan consumed his tuna sandwich, and Kalev drank nectar. They listened to periodic yips from a coyote and an owl hoot.

Once Dylan swallowed the last bite, he crunched the paper into a wad and set it by his foot. Kalev leaned forward and took both of Dylan's hands in his own. Kalev closed his eyes, then sighed as if nervous about taking a further step.

After he pointed to his furry forehead, Kalev placed a giant palm on Dylan's head. Dylan laughed and imagined his head looked like a basketball in the hand of a professional NBA player.

Kalev lifted a finger to his lips to ask for silence. Dylan complied.

As Kalev closed his eyes in concentration, Dylan sensed a vision like none that came before. Memories flooded into his view, not from Kalev's past but Dylan's.

From early childhood, he watched his parents dress and feed him, trips to Brookfield Zoo and to fish in Minnesota, and a dozen Christmas trees surrounded with packages. Teachers from grade school, high school, and university flew by—some stood in front of chalkboards and others handed back tests. He saw girlfriends from relationships past, boys who rode skateboards with Dylan down Suicide Hill, and Tom as he stood by the dining table and made plans for the business.

The vision sped faster until Dylan could barely discern the people and events. His temples throbbed, not like a stabbing knife but a vice that tightened and loosened. When he felt close to passing out, Dylan pushed Kalev's hand from his head and yelled, "Stop!" The vision abruptly ceased.

Dylan panted with exhaustion and blinked to focus on Kalev. The Sasquatch smiled and cradled the side of Dylan's face in his hand. While no words came from Kalev's lips, Dylan distinctly heard, "Thank you."

"What just happened?" Dylan asked.

Kalev reached and patted Dylan's arm. While the Sasquatch did not speak aloud, Dylan heard, "I needed to understand your language more quickly than our earlier visions allowed. I accessed your memories to learn how you communicate."

Dylan scoffed. "Now you know everything that I know?"

"Enough to understand your primary language."

"Primary?"

"Yes. You know several. The others do not simply convert to your primary one."

"You've got that right. It took me years to master them."

Kalev nodded. "Later, you can assist me in understanding why they are different and why some have many words for the same action or object. But one session cannot transfer all of your knowledge. I need a greater context to see how the words fit into your culture. We are very different."

"To say the least." Dylan marveled at Kalev's voice as it echoed inside Dylan's head. "You have me at a disadvantage. When will you transfer your knowledge to me?"

"It does not work that way. I cannot send it to you. You would need to know how to *take* information from me. I will teach you, but it will take time."

Kalev looked up toward the first sliver of moonbeams as they broke through the trees and cast shadows into the yard. Instead of words, Kalev sent the repeated vision of Sasquatches leaning forward in a circle.

"Why the vision instead of words?" Dylan asked.

"We communicate with rapid-fire images. Taking time to identify each thing and action is cumbersome and inefficient. If you want to learn how we engage, you must make sense of visions as well as using your words."

"First, I want to know if you had a name before I gave you one?"

Kalev laughed. "If a Sasquatch refers to another, the vision of the individual is sufficient. Why would we have names?"

"Good point. But to me, you'll always be Kalev."

"A king from an ancient mythological kingdom in Estonia. Right?"

"I thought it was fitting."

"Someday, you will show me the location of these places."

"You didn't tap into my geography class? We used maps."

"It is not that simple. My view of this world and yours is different."

Dylan nodded and speculated how Sasquatches might perceive the globe without the benefit of seafaring mapmakers and satellite images. Were they Flat-Earthers? He wanted to know more. "When are we going to see your colony?"

"We will leave soon. We must be at the top of the mountain when the moon is fullest."

"Your people certainly have a sense of the dramatic. What mountain are you referring to?"

Dylan followed the direction of Kalev's finger as it pointed to the summit of Church Mountain, barely visible behind the towering pine trees. "Okay. What should I wear? Do I need to bring a gift?"

"Be prepared to hike. The night is cool, and your skin is fragile."

"Hey, just because I don't have a built-in fur coat doesn't mean I can't prepare for this weather. Give me a few minutes, and I'll get ready."

Dylan brought the lantern back into the cabin and borrowed a small backpack from Jen's stash of equipment.

Inside, he stowed a water bottle, rain jacket, and a couple of energy bars. After he put on a heavy fleece jacket and laced his boots, Dylan stepped onto the porch and locked the front door.

He opened the car's trunk and stuffed in his belongings along with the trash bag with food waste—both his and Kalev's.

Consistent with the plan he devised with Tom over the phone, Dylan put the door key on a ledge above the frame and the car keys in the dirt under the front tire. If he never came back, at least Tom would be able to return the rental car.

Pretty dark thoughts, Dylan concluded. More nervous than he expected, Dylan shouldered the pack and followed Kalev into the woods.

Chapter 53

KALEV

The full moon seemed to help Dylan adjust to walking in the darkness of night. As planned, I took a route next to the spring flowing behind the cabin. My long strides followed the thin trickle of water. I balanced on flat rocks and avoided the sporadic tree limbs spanning the creek bed. After only a few minutes, I glanced back and realized Dylan could scarcely maintain my pace.

He slipped on the rocks and stopped to maneuver over each branch crossing and nearly fell each time. Dylan stopped to grope each barrier. First, he would lift one leg and then the other in slow methodic movements. His pace would not suffice.

I waited as he approached. Dylan sputtered and called on me to slow down. As he drew nearer, he said, "Let me show you what I can see, and you'll understand why I'm slow."

I paused to accept his transmission. My vision filled with shadows and no color. I pushed away his thoughts and sent my version of what surrounded us—vastly lighter with every rock and root clearly visible.

"Now do you understand?" Dylan asked.

"Living with artificial lights has made your eyes lazy. We are fortunate to have eyesight perfectly adapted to see both in the night and day."

"Good for you. But if you want to reach the top with me, you'll need to go slower."

He was right. But slowing our pace was not an option. A more accessible route could improve our efficiency. I directed him to an animal track next to the creek bed. As we entered the trail, Dylan tripped on a tree root and fell to his hands.

He called out with pain and jumped to his feet. "Damn cactus!" he cried. I took his hand and spotted a dozen needles sticking from his flesh.

After I grasped the spikes between my teeth, I pulled them out and spat them on the ground. I scrutinized his palm for any stray spines and transmitted, "I have removed them. You will be fine."

I had learned about cactus the previous summer. While removing the needles from the fruit took time, the watery flesh tasted more pleasant than other plants that burned my throat or tongue.

After a short distance on the trail, we merged onto a gravel road. Not my preferred route to the top of the peak, but with Dylan's stunted abilities to travel at night, we would never make the summit by the time the moon peaked.

I speculated whether to carry Dylan and knew our progress would be faster. But I delayed proposing the change until I could gauge our forward progress.

Even though Dylan tripped a couple more times, his pace improved, particularly when the moonlight fully illuminated our route. He slowed when trees bordered the sides or when a switchback sent us into a shadow. When Dylan's breathing became labored, I would stop for him to recover and take a sip of water.

Once, Dylan called for me to wait. His face glistened red as beads of sweat tracked from his brow to drip off his chin. "Give me a minute. I need to take off some clothes."

As he removed his jacket and tucked it into the backpack, he asked, "If we're on such a tight schedule, do you think we should have left earlier?"

"I underestimated your pace," I confessed.

"Maybe we should have taken a practice hike this afternoon."

"I have watched hundreds of hikers with your build and dexterity. My predictions about your abilities are free from miscalculation. However, my observations of hikers walking at night are virtually nonexistent. Your vision, without the benefit of the sun or even moonlight, is far more impaired than I predicted. I accept my error." As he shouldered his pack,

I added, "We will need to persevere and only take short breaks to reach the top in time."

"Let's go then." Dylan motioned forward.

A few cabins dotted the hillsides, but most seemed abandoned. In one occupied domicile, smoke snaked from the chimney, and the windows glowed with the flashing light of a television. I recalled Dylan's memories about satellite television and noticed the disk mounted on the side of the dwelling. These were concepts I would not have understood only hours before, but I still lacked clarity about the purpose of television. Did they need a box to tell them stories? Why not simply listen to each other? Odd creatures.

While we walked uphill, I reviewed Dylan's memories of learning languages. Besides English, a tongue spoken in this geographic region, he knew several others. I did not understand who talked in that way or why Dylan chose to learn them specifically.

After I thought about many of their words, I decided to name a few things on my own. While Dylan called his brethren *humans*, I decided to call the frail beings *halveks*. From now on, their home would be referred to as Porgu and mine as Reval.

When we arrived at the halfway point, I allowed Dylan a short break. He leaned against a smooth rock and dropped his pack between his feet. Dylan pulled out his water bottle and gulped down nearly half of the contents. Once his breath normalized, he gobbled a snack as if he had not eaten in days. Between bites, he said, "Tell me what to expect when I meet the others."

I transferred my response. "They are like me."

"I get that they look like you, but tell me more. Will there be both men and women? Have they been watching me, too? Are you their leader? Why do they want to meet me?"

I considered his questions and measured how much to divulge. Finally, I transmitted, "You will have the privilege to meet both males and females. Some will be my family members."

"Parents? Siblings?"

"You will know more when you meet them."

"Why the secrecy? You've probed my life. You know I have no brothers or sisters, and the people who raised me are not my birth parents."

"If you do not know your birth parents, then how would you know you have no siblings?"

Dylan cocked his head. "You've got me there. I could have a dozen brothers and sisters. But without information about my parents, I will never know. Are family units important in your society?"

Kalev nodded.

"Why can't you tell me more about your family?"

"It is best you experience them without predetermined ideas about who they are and how they live."

Dylan scoffed. "I already have preconceived notions of the Sasquatch. So far, I've learned that most of what I thought I knew is completely wrong."

I smiled. "That is why you should take this meeting without any additional bias. Meet them with an open mind."

Dylan smirked. "Since you've accessed my memories, my mind has already been opened. Please help me to prepare."

I looked down at the tiny being and knew nothing could prepare him for what he would experience. "Trust me. You do not need to know more about them."

After several hours of following the road, we reached the summit of the peak. I watched Dylan gaze out at the lights of Salida on the valley floor. He shivered and dug into his pack to retrieve the stowed jacket. After he zipped the coat up to his chin, Dylan shoved his hands into the pockets. He turned to me and looked expectantly around the summit.

I indicated toward a flat space, sufficiently far from the antennas. My next transmissions would determine my success or failure. I needed to entice Dylan to accompany me. If he did not willingly agree to come along, I would go home in defeat.

I sat on the ground. Telepathically, I said, "Please, join me to sit."

Chapter 54

DYLAN COX

Before he complied with Kalev's request, Dylan scanned the broad treeless ridgeline. It extended down to connect a row of lower peaks. *This place must be either where we'll meet the others or a handy stopping point for a break.*

From this distance, Salida became a cluster of tiny lights contrasting with the black valley floor. Occasional headlights sped down the inky ribbons of highway. Where could they be traveling at this time? Night shift at the hospital? Heading home from the bars? Dylan looked toward the sky. He expected to see a multitude of stars, but the lustrous full moon obscured all but the most brilliant constellations.

Kalev tugged at Dylan's jeans.

"Okay, give me a minute." Dylan sat cross-legged and faced Kalev. Their knees touched. After a slow nod, Kalev sent a curious message with images of naked people. One sunbathed in the nude. Others walked around in groups near outdoor swimming pools. Why would Kalev suggest the rest of the journey should be sans clothes?

Dylan shivered at the thought. "Are you expecting me to take off my clothes?"

"It is necessary," transmitted Kalev.

Dylan tried to think of one good reason why he needed to meet Kalev's colony in the nude. Did Kalev feel clothing would intimidate the others?

Or perhaps this would be a signal to the other Sasquatches that Dylan felt trusting enough to appear vulnerable. Of course, they were always naked. Maybe this was a matter of merely fitting in.

He had come too far to abandon the meeting at this point, and he stood to remove his clothes. "Can you explain why being in the buff on this frigid night is *necessary*?"

"You need to trust me."

Dylan looked around for a protected area to stash his belongings. A few trees bordered the summit. Dylan walked toward them, and Kalev rose to follow.

Before he took off his jeans, Dylan pulled out his cell phone from his back pocket. Kalev immediately pointed to Dylan's backpack lying on the ground.

"Okay. I'll leave it here," Dylan said, but not before he sidled next to the creature and snapped a selfie. Even with Dylan on tiptoe, the photo barely captured the top of Kalev's head and Dylan's chin. Without a flash, the frame mostly outlined two hominids in front of Salida's city lights in the valley below.

Dylan showed the screen to Kalev, who rolled his eyes and snapped a finger toward the pack. Dylan laughed. He typed a caption for the photo and shut it off before he slipped it into a plastic bag inside his backpack.

When he checked his pockets, Dylan found a keyring. "Here are my house keys from Chicago. Probably not going to need them anytime soon. I should have left them in the car."

Dylan stroked the four-inch rope of hair hanging on the ring, a memento of his first hike with Jen. They had trekked to a high alpine lake, the site where a week earlier a predator had slaughtered a herd of mountain goats. He had collected fur from bushes nearby the attack site and woven the strands into a braid.

Dylan looked at Kalev. "I hate to leave this out in the open. The braid means a lot to me. Jen and I thought it was from the goats, but I had the fur analyzed. The results came back *anomalous primate,* which means inconsistent with the commonly known primates such as humans and apes."

Kalev extended a hand, and Dylan passed him the ring before he started to remove his jacket.

The Sasquatch held the braid against the fur along the top of his hip. He lifted a strand to compare.

Dylan slipped his coat back on and bent to examine the braid against Kalev's fur. While tough to be confident in the moonlit darkness, he believed they looked the same. "Have I been carrying around your fur for the past four months?"

Kalev returned Dylan's stare and transmitted, "Seems like you have. Perhaps we were destined to meet."

"Sounds poetic, but that's not the point. Were you there when something slaughtered the goats?"

Kalev stroked the braid. Remorse swept across his face. "I was too late to save them," he transmitted.

Dylan turned to his pack. Kalev could have prevented those tragedies. The Sasquatch's frustration must have been insurmountable. Dylan stepped out of his jeans and slid them inside the pack.

The Sasquatch continued, "The mountain lion and bear acted with merciless instincts. If I came sooner, I could have stopped them."

Dylan ignored the gooseflesh on his bare legs and reached forward to place a hand on Kalev's forearm. "Don't take this on yourself. Wild animals can be unpredictable and vicious."

Kalev nodded as Dylan removed his remaining clothes.

"Geez, it's freezing out here." Dylan rubbed his arms and jogged in place to keep warm. Kalev stepped forward to embrace Dylan and rubbed Dylan's body with his furry arms.

Kalev's hair felt soft and warm. Dylan snickered and imagined the embrace came from a giant animated carpet. Albeit one that desperately needed cleaning.

Suddenly, the Sasquatch stopped moving. Dylan felt the fur on Kalev's broad chest stretch upward, as Kalev tipped his head toward the heavens.

Moments earlier, the sky had been clear. Directly overhead, Dylan saw a massive charcoal black cloud chase across the moon.

Kalev sent a message. "Don't be afraid. This is your destiny and my mission. You must remain calm."

Calm? The past week burst at the seams with everything but tranquility. Besides running into a dead end on an epic quest to discover his birth parents, beasts had attacked and killed Nate, he had two brushes with death, and he befriended a giant Sasquatch.

As Kalev's message faded, Dylan's view went blank. The blackness receded as he saw a human couple walking in the woods. The woman carried a sleeping baby tucked next to her chest in a colorful cloth sling.

The hikers paused, and the man softly stroked the baby's head. Both parents lovingly gazed at the infant as they talked.

"Who are these people?" Dylan asked.

Kalev transmitted a single word. "Watch."

The first vision faded, replaced with two Sasquatches viewed from behind. The shorter one had slight shoulders and chestnut-colored hair, and the taller seemed broad like Kalev but with lighter fur. The pair huddled together, with heads bowed.

As the point of view moved around the couple, Dylan saw they held something. He spotted a tiny hairless baby. It wriggled in their arms, full of giggles and waving arms. The smaller Sasquatch pursed her lips and blew air toward his face. The infant responded with smiles, his pale green eyes wide with delight.

Dylan pondered why Kalev would send messages about couples doting over infants. Perhaps this was Kalev's attempt to comfort him about his lack of knowledge surrounding his lineage. Like a visual greeting card with a tag line of "love makes a family, not biology."

Or maybe Kalev wanted Dylan to feel protected from what would come—like parents sheltering their child. The message felt lost in translation. Dylan still had much to understand about how they communicated.

Dylan heard the thunder rumble, first from far away. Then loud enough to shake the ground. He hugged Kalev tighter. The next crash of thunder came with a simultaneous lightning burst. Dylan saw cascading sparkles of a hundred fireworks. He felt as if he was falling.

Right before he lost consciousness, Dylan heard Kalev transmit the words, "Target neutralized. Mission complete."

October 20

Naked, Tiina sat on the pool's edge. She followed her daily exercise routine and extended her legs to hover above the surface. Seconds ticked away as she pursed her lips and breathed in staccato gasps in an attempt to dispel her anger.

Let him wait, she thought. She needed time to sort out how she felt and decide his fate. She inched her heels downward. Her abs and thighs trembled from the strain. Seconds ticked by, and the pool glimmered in the fading sunlight. Tiina relented to gravity's pull to flutter her feet and form ripples that cascaded to the far end.

Earlier, when she was oblivious to his imminent return, Tiina spent the day with the other Council members as they considered the list of volunteers for transfer to Porgu. They evaluated whether candidates had the skills and temperament to make the arduous journey. As typical, more than a dozen individuals petitioned to go. They were eager and desperately wanted to experience the dangerous and primitive conditions.

While she had never volunteered to make the journey, Tiina served on the selection committee and debriefed returning researchers. Many came back fulfilled, able to contribute to the group's knowledge of Porgu's crude society. Others returned weak and suffered from acute loneliness and malnutrition. All were unequivocally different. Kalev had left months earlier, and she wondered how he had changed.

Exhausted from the day's discussions, she desperately needed this soak. Tiina held fast to the edge and slipped into the pool and submerged to just above her waist. With elbows splayed, she hung like a rings gymnast in support position. Toes pointed, Tiina scissored her legs and admired her long toned thighs and hard belly, still firm as anyone half her age. Despite being nearly a half-century old, she served as the youngest member of the Council. Tiina contributed youth and optimism while the others offered caution and experience.

In the afternoon session, her colleagues had issued final decisions on two petitions. One was approved, and the other denied. As the pair were siblings, Tiina suggested they separately notify the family for each application—perhaps with a day between each announcement. There was no need for the family to struggle between a celebration or acting quietly empathetic.

The pronouncement to reject the brother took extensive deliberation. On the positive side, his mother had transferred with few ill effects and returned with breakthrough data on coastal habitat development. But the Council ruled her son's temperament erratic and his addiction to social engagement too strong. Ultimately, they suggested he could resubmit an application in five years.

If left exclusively up to Tiina, she would have approved his request. His enthusiasm for the trip felt infectious. But more seasoned, skeptical members prevailed. While disappointed for the petitioner, she recognized the value of decisions made by committee. Different views and perspectives kept mishaps to a minimum. Tiina hoped her contributions helped find the best researchers able to endure the rigors of the journey and the hardships of solitude.

Moments before her meeting ended, Kalev's transmission had crept into her thoughts, not a bold trumpeted announcement for all to hear but a niggling whisper meant only for her. He had returned and wanted her to join him. She glanced around and could see that none of her peers were aware of the message. *He's calling only to me.*

Inch by inch, Tiina submerged the rest of her body. She floated on her back and felt her silky hair spread like the tendrils of a plant dispersing their roots. First, one flick of a leg to engage muscles from hip to toe, then the other. She bent her hands at the wrists and waved them to propel herself forward.

Low branches hovered overhead to filter the daylight. Leaves rustled in a faint breeze. She reached the far end and spun to retrace her path. Eyes closed and ears below the surface, silence withheld the outside world. Calm and quiet enveloped, yet she could not suppress her curiosity. Where did he go, and what had he learned?

Like a rock crashing through a window, the second notification blasted into her mind. *He's calling out to someone besides me*, she thought. But who? Was he injured? Why the urgency?

Tiina jammed her feet into the bottom and stood upright as moisture dripped from her hair to splatter the surface like a shower of rain. Perhaps she should disregard the message. Kalev had left suddenly—without warning or permission. Her lips drew into a line, eyes narrowed. Gone for nearly half a year, he had left her to cover his absence with lies.

Torn between anger and curiosity about his journey, she stroked to the pool's edge. In one swift movement, Tiina placed her palms on the rim and lifted her body into a crouch. She straightened, thinking and deciding. With complete disregard for her wet body, Tiina dashed into the forest to meet the returning adventurer.

ACKNOWLEDGMENTS

I must start by thanking my writing partner Susan Bavaria. From reading early drafts to giving me suggestions on character development and scene-setting, she was vital in my journey to complete this book. Two special beta readers, my sister Tina Pickell and brother-in-law Bruce Iannuzzi, provided in-depth comments that resulted in this book's complexity and consistency. David Ditchkus, Sherry Richardson, David Kramer, Laurel McHargue, and other beta readers spent countless hours reviewing drafts and providing helpful comments.

I appreciate members of the Rock Mountain Fiction Writers Speculative Fiction critique group. Their thoughtful comments and suggestions helped to address pacing, word choice, and clarity.

Thank you to my neighbor Jim Finn, a friend and devout Sasquatch believer, for planting the seeds that grew into this series. This project started as a joint effort with my nephew Cody Tracy. Without his infectious passion for writing and confidence that I could complete the book on my own, it would still be an outline of an idea.

While none of the events in this book happened, I thank business owners in Salida for allowing me to use names of their establishments, including Phillip Benningfield fellow-author and owner of Café Dawn and owners of the Palace Hotel.

I give heartfelt thanks to my cousin, Kris Edison, for her advice about licensure for pharmacy professionals.

My final thanks are to my loving husband, David. For all the times we've been hiking, and I've asked you to remove my phone from my pack so I could record an idea and taken hours away from our vacations and at home-time to write and edit—I give you my sincere thanks.

If you are familiar with Salida, Colorado, you will know that some of the places in this book are real. However, none of the places where 'bad things happen' are real. That includes Jen's cabin, Nate's gallery, and a few others. None of the places in Oregon or Utah are real, and all of the tribal stories are fiction. Absolutely all of the people in this book are fictional.

L.V. DITCHKUS is the author of *Crimes of the Sasquatch and Mission of the Sasquatch, Books I and II of the Sasquatch Series*. While writing these and the soon to be released third book, she's led adventure travel trips, hiked and snowshoed hundreds of miles, and volunteered for wilderness advocacy and writing organizations. She and her husband live in a rural mountain community in central Colorado, where she gains inspiration from the five 14,000+ foot tall peaks viewable from her window.

Check out her blog at LVDitchkus.com

www.ingramcontent.com/pod-product-compliance
Lightning Source LLC
Chambersburg PA
CBHW021116110726
47900CB00007B/2208